# THE LIAR

A. RIVERS

*To my husband.*
*No matter how long we're married,*
*there are always new things to learn,*
*and new ways to love each other.*

# PROLOGUE – FOUR MONTHS EARLIER



I hurried across the concrete toward the train, dragging my suitcase behind me. The cold air stung my cheeks and burned in my lungs as I gasped for breath.

I was running late.

I was never late.

But then, I wasn't usually blocked by a truck parked across the road or stopped by security either.

I glanced at the electronic clock above the screen of departure times, and within the two seconds I was distracted, somebody stepped into my path. I bowled into the man head-on. He stumbled backward, his arms windmilling as he tried to catch himself.

My palms landed on his firm, muscular chest, which I might have enjoyed if not for the fact my suitcase hit my calves and I tripped, nearly taking him down with me.

With difficulty, we righted ourselves. I sprang away from him, my cheeks hot.

"I'm so sorry," I said, meeting his sparkling green eyes. "Are you okay?"

One side of his mouth hitched up—and oh, was that a dimple?

"It's all right." His voice was deep but gentle, well-suited to a teacher or a doctor, and his accent gave away the fact he was American like me, rather than Canadian. Another tourist, perhaps. "No harm done."

"Are you sure?" I'd hit him with a lot of force.

His smile widened. "Completely certain."

I released a sigh of relief. "Thank God. Everything is going wrong this morning. I swear I'm not usually such a disaster."

"I'm sorry to hear you've been having bad luck, but my day has definitely taken a turn for the better." He reached behind himself and grabbed the handle of his suitcase. "Are you on the trip through the Rockies?"

"I am." My heart fluttered. Was he flirting with me? It happened so rarely that I couldn't be sure. As a female detective, I was used to most men outside of the police force being intimidated by me, and my colleagues were firmly off-limits.

"Excellent. Me too." He offered his hand. "I'm Westley Gallo, but you can call me West. Can I help you with your things?"

"I'm Joanna." I glanced down at my suitcase. "I'm fine with it."

He winked. "I know you don't need the help. I can tell you're the type of person who's always on top of everything, but maybe, let me pretend for my ego's sake?"

I arched an eyebrow. "Why do I get the feeling your ego is perfectly fine?"

"Because you're an insightful woman."

"Okay, then." I passed him my suitcase. Yes, perhaps chivalry was old-fashioned, and maybe he was laying the charm on a bit thick, but the closet romantic hiding deep inside me thought it might be nice to have someone take care of me for once, even if only for a few minutes.

Side by side, we strode toward the waiting train. Somehow, West's mere presence made me forget why I'd been in such a panic. This train was a luxury experience, one I hadn't paid for since I'd won the trip in a giveaway, but nonetheless, I doubted they'd leave without all their passengers on board.

We reached the door and showed the attendant our tickets. He scanned them, handed them back, and gestured for us to enter. West hefted my suitcase up alongside his without even mentioning the weight. I wasn't a light packer; I liked to be prepared for all situations.

Inside, we were greeted by another attendant in a stylish maroon and gold uniform. They escorted me down the corridor to a room on the left.

"This is where you will sleep, Madam," the attendant said.

My mouth fell open. The cabin was even more gorgeous than I'd imagined, with a bed along the wall nearest to me, a comfortable padded bench seat along the opposite wall beneath the window, and a small, dark wooden desk with an antique chair at the far end.

"It's beautiful," I breathed.

The decor was upscale but not ultramodern and made me feel like I could curl up in the corner with a book and a glass of tea and be right at home.

"I'm glad you like it." The attendant stepped sideways. "Sir, you are in this cabin."

I glanced back to find them gesturing at the room beside mine.

West grinned. "What a happy coincidence." He nodded to the attendant. "Thank you for your assistance."

The attendant bowed and excused themself. West

vanished into his cabin, leaving my suitcase in the corridor outside mine. I pulled it inside and tucked it away beneath the desk.

I released a breath. Finally. I was here, I had everything I could possibly need in my suitcase, and there was no reason to worry. I could let everything go.

"Would you like to get a drink?"

I flinched and spun around. West stood in the doorway, resting one of his hands against the frame. For a big guy, he moved quietly.

"Sorry. Didn't mean to startle you." He flashed that dimple again. "So, a drink?"

I considered his offer. I'd planned to stay in my cabin for a while, but then I hadn't expected to meet a handsome stranger, and my māma had made me promise to relax and go with the flow. She may have also dropped a few hints about finding a nice, rich husband, but that was hardly a surprise. She wanted me settled.

"I'd love to. Hold on a second." The key was on the desk, so I grabbed it and my purse and used the key to lock the cabin behind me. I may be on vacation, but I was still a cop and wary of leaving my things unattended. "Do you know where the bar is?"

"I looked at a map of the train online before we boarded. It's this way." He gestured farther along the corridor.

Be still my heart. Good-looking, polite, and organized. Māma would be beside herself.

"Lead the way." I followed him through two doors, past another series of private cabins, through another two doors, to an elegantly appointed space with half a dozen sofas, several bar tables, and a bar tucked into the corner. Classical music played softly over the speakers.

We approached the bar, and the woman behind it smiled.

"What can I get for you?" she asked.

I bit my lip. Usually, I'd drink something nonalcoholic at this time of day, but I was on vacation. I could afford to be a little naughty. "I'll have a sauvignon blanc, please."

She turned to West. "And you, sir?"

"The same."

"What cabin should I charge them to?"

I started to give my cabin number, but West beat me to it.

"My treat," he murmured as she poured the drinks. "I invited you, after all."

My stomach flipped over. When he looked at me like that, it was easy to forget we weren't alone, and that I hardly knew this man.

He took our drinks. "Would you prefer a sofa or a table?"

"Table." That way, I could gaze into his eyes.

We chose a table beside the window, halfway along the carriage. He set my drink in front of me and raised his glass. I chinked mine against it in a toast, then sipped. I couldn't help but notice the way his lean throat bobbled as he swallowed.

"This may sound silly," he began, placing the glass down and leaning on his forearms, "but I'm really glad you ran into me."

My heart slammed against my ribcage. "Me too." So, my attraction to him might not be one-sided. Aware I knew nothing about him other than his name, I added, "Tell me about yourself."

As we talked, I found myself shifting closer to him, erasing the distance between us until my side was pressed against his. My heart was light, my head somewhere in the clouds.

West told me he was from Chicago, like me, and had recently changed jobs. He worked as a bartender, and he'd also won this trip in a contest. Perhaps that's why our carriages were beside each other.

My insides fluttered with the excitement of a new infatuation; I couldn't stop smiling.

He seemed so perfect. Too good to be true.

As it turned out, that assessment was more accurate than I ever could have imagined.

# 1



*JOANNA*

I checked my phone, but there was still no reply from West. It was unlike him to go so long without responding. Then again, his shift at Henry's, a bar frequented by Chicago's finest, had begun thirty minutes ago, so it was possible he was busy.

"Everything okay?" Hanson asked from behind his computer. Our desks fronted onto each other, but I hadn't realized he'd been paying me any attention.

"Just waiting for a message," I told him, not keen to disclose that I was hoping to hear from my husband.

Hanson and I were too different to be friends, but we'd always treated each other politely. Something in our interactions had changed since I'd married West. It was as if he approved of me finally behaving like a woman "ought to" by getting a husband.

While he meant well, it made me feel a little icky. There was nothing wrong with being a single career woman.

My phone rang, and I answered without looking, hoping it might be West.

"Lee," the voice on the other end said.

I deflated. It was my boss.

"Yes, sir?"

"I want you and Hanson to report to my office immediately."

"We'll be there in a minute, sir." I ended the call and turned to Hanson. "Thackery wants us in his office."

Hanson grunted, and his bulldog-like face scrunched with displeasure. I got it. We were supposed to be half an hour from the end of our shift. Getting called in to talk to the boss now couldn't be good. Unfortunately, that was just how policing rolled. Criminals didn't wait for the most convenient times to commit crimes.

I stood, pocketed my phone and grabbed a notebook. Hanson shot the notebook a glare. He was a decent cop, but he was part of the old guard and believed that the police wasted too much time writing reports and covering our asses when we should have boots on the ground.

He liked to skirt the rules. I was known for being by-the-book. We weren't exactly a partnership made in heaven.

We strode down the corridor that separated the Homicide Department from Missing Persons. The captain's office was halfway along, on the right. The door was ajar, so I knocked and opened it.

"Sir?"

"Come in."

I entered and stepped aside so Hanson could join me. Captain Thackery didn't motion for us to sit. Instead, he tapped a few keys on the computer before raising his gray-flecked head.

"I need you to report to a crime scene near the lakefront. There's been a woman found murdered in her apartment."

I frowned. "You wouldn't rather Neal take the lead?"

Detective Neal, who would be arriving anytime now to start his shift, had made it clear he liked taking on the cases in that area, and he could get nasty if other detectives encroached on his territory.

Thackery shook his head. "Neal won't be in tonight. Bad prawns, apparently."

Hanson and I both grimaced. Even though I didn't like Neal, I wouldn't wish a bout of food poisoning on anyone.

"We'll drive over now," I told him. "Who's already at the scene?"

"The medical examiner is on the way, as are a team of crime scene techs. There's a pair of beat cops keeping lookie-loos away until reinforcements arrive."

Hanson and I took our leave. Hanson muttered under his breath as we packed our bags and hastened to the car.

"Deborah will have my head," he said as he climbed behind the wheel—because God forbid he should allow a woman to drive. "She's been cooking all afternoon. She's testing a new recipe."

"She'll understand." After more than thirty years married to a cop, Deborah Hanson undoubtedly understood the demands of the job more than most.

"I'm sure you had plans with your man too," Hanson said, pulling out of the parking garage and onto the street.

"I'm supposed to bring him dinner at Henry's," I admitted, taking my phone out to send West a quick message explaining that I'd be late.

We didn't speak much as Hanson navigated the city streets. That was all right with me. I wasn't much of a talker. We drove past the apartment building that Thackery had directed us to, but there were no parking spots available, so we had to park a block away and walk back.

As we passed a coffee shop, I glanced inside, and my heart nearly stopped.

I jolted to a halt, nearly tripping over my feet.

No.

No, no, no. It couldn't be.

A chill stole over me and my chest squeezed painfully. Seated in a booth at the coffee shop, holding hands with a beautiful blond woman, was my husband.

My stomach lurched. I shut my eyes and opened them again, praying I'd been mistaken and that the man in the coffee shop only resembled West. But no, it was definitely him.

A wave of nausea washed over me, and I clapped my hand to my mouth, unable to tear my gaze from them. The blonde was leaning toward West, her hair spilling over her shoulders, framing cleavage that a Playboy bunny would be proud of. She was all curves and creamy skin, the complete opposite of me with my slim build, dark hair, and olive complexion.

"Why'd you stop?" Hanson asked, jolting me out of my reverie. He followed my gaze through the window, and his eyebrows inched up his forehead. "That's your man, isn't it?"

"Yes. It is." I jerked into motion, forcing my legs to carry me past the coffee shop, toward the crime scene that awaited us.

I couldn't handle it if West saw me here. I needed time to get my thoughts straight before I faced him. A little quiet, so I could piece together what I'd seen.

"Slow down, Lee," Hanson wheezed, struggling to keep up. "Maybe it wasn't how it looked."

"You're probably right." My voice seemed to come from somewhere outside of myself. I felt like I was hovering above my body, watching everything from a distance.

You're detaching, my brain helpfully supplied. It often happens to victims of crime or—

Nope. Not going there.

Perhaps Hanson was right and there was a reasonable explanation. God, I hoped there was. My throat ached and I blinked back tears as we turned into the apartment building. Hanson pressed the button for the elevator.

Don't fall apart now.

I drew in a shuddering breath. Hanson glanced at me, but I ignored him. I was strong. I was practical. I wouldn't leap to conclusions or let my personal life interfere with the job. Right now, I had to focus. A woman was depending on me to figure out what happened to her. I couldn't afford to break down.

We took the elevator to the third floor. There were four apartments on the floor, and it was immediately obvious which one we were here for because of the young male officer stationed at the door.

He nodded to us deferentially. "Detectives."

"Officer Jackson, what do we have?" I asked.

Hanson always lets me liaise with the younger officers, probably because he never bothered to learn their names.

Jackson cleared his throat. "The victim appears to be a Miss Sasha Sloane. At least, I'm assuming as much because this is Miss Sloane's apartment and the building manager described her as a brunette in her late twenties, which fits with what I've seen of the vic. Dr. Kelly is there now, along with a crime scene team. I'm sure they can tell you more."

"Thank you, Officer Jackson."

"No problem, ma'am." He smiled, his teeth bright against his darker skin. He moved out of the way so we could enter the apartment. Almost immediately, the sickly-sweet scent of death filled my nostrils.

Breathing through my mouth to avoid the worst of it, I looked around. Miss Sloane's apartment had a spacious living area, a kitchen tucked away in the corner, and a view of the water through the window. There was a vase of real flowers on the coffee table and very little in the way of clutter.

The victim, possibly Miss Sloane, lay on her back in front of the windows, as if she'd been gazing out of them when she'd been attacked. Her eyes were wide and as green as West's—nope, not thinking of him. Dark, lush curls fanned over the floor around her head, and her lips were parted, as if in surprise.

A woman in coveralls knelt over the victim, studying the slash across her neck, stretching from ear to ear.

"Cause of death?" I asked.

"Most likely exsanguination caused by sharp force trauma," Dr. Kelly said, straightening and turning toward us. Her expression softened slightly as we made eye contact. Perhaps she was relieved not to have to deal with Detective Neal. The man was a worse misogynist than Hanson and always treated her as if she were incapable.

Hanson snorted. "No surprise there."

She narrowed her eyes at him. "As for time of death, we won't know for sure until I've done the autopsy, but I would estimate it to be between twelve and twenty-four hours because she's in full rigor."

"So, she was probably killed sometime between yesterday evening and this morning," I mused. Perhaps she'd had a fight with a lover. Although the lack of disturbance to her surroundings didn't bear that out. If she'd been in an altercation, I would expect things to be knocked over or broken, but nothing seemed amiss.

"Perhaps a boyfriend or husband did it," Hanson said, his mind traveling down the same road as mine.

Dr. Kelly huffed. "That's for you to determine. I'll be sure to confirm whether she had intercourse prior to her death."

"Of course. Thank you," I said, then scanned the victim again, noting what I hadn't before. She wore a black silk robe that was cinched tightly at her waist. Her makeup was perfectly done, her lips painted red, and she had a fresh manicure. A quick glance at her feet revealed a matching pedicure. "By the looks of it, she indeed might have been meeting a lover."

I'd only dress like this if I wanted to impress someone, but it was possible she'd just wanted to feel nice, and it had nothing to do with romance. Not everyone was as mission-oriented as me.

We spent an hour looking around the apartment but found no obvious leads as to who may have killed her, or why, so we headed back to the station. I should have been mulling over the case, but instead, all I could think about was the way West had held that woman's hand in the coffee shop.

"I can hear your gears grinding," Hanson said reluctantly, as if he'd rather not have this conversation but didn't think he could avoid it.

I looked out the window, so I wouldn't have to see his facial expression. "If I'm to believe that West wasn't doing anything wrong, then what else do you think could have been happening?"

"Maybe she was an old friend, or someone he knows who is having a bad day. Holding someone's hand doesn't always mean you're screwing them," Hanson said.

A puff of breath escaped me. "I know, but it doesn't sit well with me."

West wasn't the type of guy to hide a female friend from me. At least, I hadn't thought he was. But then, I also hadn't thought I'd see him holding some woman's hand in a coffee shop when he was supposed to be at work, so maybe I didn't know my husband as well as I'd thought.

"Talk to him about it before you do something crazy," Hanson grumbled, lacking tact as usual. I was sure that, in his eyes, having any kind of emotional response to a man's bad behavior made a woman "crazy."

Okay, maybe that wasn't fair. He wasn't a bad person, he just had some old-fashioned perspectives.

When I didn't respond, he continued with, "Want me to notify the next of kin?"

I straightened and turned to him. "No, we should do that together."

It wasn't fair of me to dump that job on him just because I was wallowing in hurt and confusion.

He scoffed. "Your heart won't be in it. What kind of message will it send the family if the detectives who deliver the news are distracted?"

I deflated. He had a good point. "Okay. Thank you, Denny."

"You're welcome, kid."

That almost made me smile. We'd been partners for three years and he still called me that. But I suppose when you've been on the force as long as him, anyone younger than forty could be considered a "kid."

My phone vibrated and I checked the screen. Immediately, my gut tightened.

**West:** *Order anything you like. I'm not feeling choosy.*

Hanson glanced at me. "Is that him?"

I swallowed. "Yeah."

"Did he say anything about... you know?"

"No." I pursed my lips. "Nothing."

Somehow, the silence felt significant.

I sent back a message.

**Joanna:** *I'll bring sushi to the bar?*

A reply arrived less than a minute later.

**West:** *Sounds good.*

Huh. So, whatever he'd been up to, he really was at work now.

We arrived at the police station, and I went inside to

finish up a few things, then walked to Henry's, stopping by a sushi place on the way.

When I arrived with a chicken roll for him and an avocado roll for me, West was behind the bar, looking for all the world as if he'd been there for hours. I knew better though.

I sidled up to the end of the bar and waited for him to finish serving a couple of rookie cops. When they had their drinks, he sauntered over, leaned across the bar and kissed me. I turned my face at the last moment, so his lips landed on my cheek rather than my mouth. I just couldn't kiss him when I didn't yet know whether he'd been betraying me.

His eyebrows drew together, but then he smiled so quickly, I might have imagined it. He took the paper bag from me and slid out the chicken roll, knowing it was for him.

"How was your day?" I asked as he opened the container and doused his sushi with soy sauce. "Do anything interesting?"

"Nothing out of the ordinary." He smeared wasabi onto a piece of sushi and raised it to his lips. "How about you?"

"We got a new case," I said. He didn't ask for details. He knew that I wouldn't share them here, where anyone could overhear.

"Open and shut?" He ate the sushi in two bites.

I tore open a soy sauce packet and spread it across my own sushi roll, even though I wasn't really hungry anymore. "I doubt it. So, you spent today at home?"

He shrugged and nodded to a customer to indicate he'd be with them in a moment. "Home, the gym, and here."

Liar.

I watched as he wiped his fingers on a napkin and took the customer's drink order. Another pair of rookie cops formed a line behind them, keeping him busy for several minutes. I ate as much as I could stomach and tucked the rest of my meal inside the paper bag, so West wouldn't notice I had no appetite.

The line for drinks only grew longer.

"I'm going to go home," I called to West. "Want me to put your sushi in the fridge so you can finish it later?"

"Yes, thanks, Jo."

I packed his meal into the small refrigerator in the back room and left through the rear exit so I wouldn't have to see him again. I walked home, grateful for the extra time to work through everything that was going on inside my head. When I arrived at our apartment building, I took the stairs, delaying my arrival for as long as possible.

I needed to clear my mind, but I also didn't want to be alone with my thoughts. It was a bad combination.

I let myself in and locked the door behind me. Once inside, I went to the bathroom, stripped out of my clothes, and showered. I always felt the need to clean myself after attending the scene of a homicide. The stench of death clung to me otherwise.

I dried, dressed in sweatpants and a hoodie, and put on a load of laundry.

Then I paced.

How were you supposed to confirm whether your husband was cheating on you? Some people might recommend asking him to his face, but I didn't want to confront him with any doubts if they were unfounded.

What would I do if this was one of my cases?

I'd search for evidence.

Guilt churning inside me, I padded into our bedroom and halted in front of his nightstand. I reached for the drawer but then stopped. I shouldn't. It would be wrong of me to break West's trust by going through his belongings.

*He lied to you.*

Okay, so that was true. But maybe there was a good reason for it.

Damn it.

I opened the drawer. Nothing looked out of place. I quickly checked through the items inside and then searched the two drawers beneath. Glancing over my shoulder to make sure I was still alone, I went to the dresser and sifted through his clothing. Except for the wad of emergency money I already knew he kept in a sock, everything was in order.

I sat on the bed and wracked my mind. If I were unfaithful, what evidence might I leave behind? The financial trail would be obvious, but we didn't share a bank account. What else? A second phone, perhaps? Had I ever seen him with one? I didn't think so. But perhaps he'd just hidden it well.

I sighed and allowed myself to consider a more important question: What would I do if he had been unfaithful?

Divorce him?

The idea left a sour taste in my mouth, but it was the only option. If he was running around behind my back with another woman, I couldn't get over that. Maybe it wouldn't be a big deal to some people, but I'd been raised on fairy tales and happily-ever-afters. I wouldn't bounce back from a betrayal like that.

But what if Hanson was right and I'd read too much into what I'd seen?

I buried my face in my hands. There was no way around it. If I wanted to keep myself from losing my mind, I'd have to ask him about it.

Decision made, I went to pour myself another glass of wine and settle in to wait for him to return home. His shift ended at midnight, so I put a true crime documentary on the TV and half-watched it while I counted down the minutes.

Finally, a little before one in the morning, a key scraped in the lock and the door swung open. West stepped inside and shut the door behind himself. When he turned and saw me sitting on the couch, his forehead furrowed with concern.

"What's wrong?"

## 2

WEST

Joanna was clearly upset about something. She'd been behaving strangely earlier, and now here she was, waiting for me to get home. I moved toward her, eager to take her into my arms and comfort her, but she held up her hands as if to ward me off.

"Don't," she snapped. "Stay right there."

My heart almost stopped. "What? Why?"

Why wouldn't she let me touch her? I couldn't just stand over here and let her hurt without doing anything about it.

"Just don't." Her shoulders hunched inward, but then she released a shuddering breath and forced them back.

I frowned. What the hell had happened?

I knew she had a new case today. Perhaps it was a particularly gruesome one, or something about it had struck too close to home.

"Talk to me, Joanna," I urged. "Tell me what's going on."

She crossed her legs and raised her chin. "I want to know something."

"What? I'll tell you anything." At least, anything I could.

"Is our marriage exclusive?"

My jaw dropped. "Excuse me?"

She stood, holding herself rigidly. "You heard me."

Yeah, but I didn't understand the question.

"If you're asking me whether I think it's acceptable to see other people while married to each other, then the answer is no." I had no idea why she'd even ask that. I adored her, and as far as I was aware, the feeling was mutual.

Even if I was still just keeping up a ruse and didn't love her, I wouldn't disrespect her by being with another woman, and I hated the very idea that she might want to touch another man.

She was mine.

Her chin jutted out. "I saw you with a blond woman today. Holding hands." She gritted the words through clenched teeth. "You looked... cozy."

Oh, no. Fuck. I was in trouble.

"You didn't mention it earlier, when I asked about your day," she continued. "Why not?"

She prowled toward me, and my eyes wandered to her hip. Thankfully, I couldn't see the outline of her service weapon there. At least she was giving me a chance to come up with a valid explanation rather than shooting first and asking questions later. Considering how fiery she could be, I had to give her credit for that.

"It wasn't what it looked like." I thought quickly. I couldn't tell her the truth. That wasn't an option. But I didn't want her to believe I'd been unfaithful either. That would kill her—and me. Especially when she'd been strong enough to come straight out and ask me for the truth.

She was an incredible woman, and I was a lying sack of shit.

Joanna propped one of her hands on her hip. "What was it, then? Was she an old friend? If so, I'd love to meet her. I've met so few of your friends."

Because the only friends I could introduce her to were part of my cover. Everything about my life was a lie, except for the way I felt about my wife.

"There's no reason for you to meet her," I said firmly. "There's nothing between us. She's someone I used to work with, and she was having a bad day, so I was trying to comfort her."

That wasn't a complete lie. It was about as truthful as I could be.

Unfortunately, Joanna's expression said she didn't believe me.

"She worked in the bar you were at before you started at Henry's?" she asked.

"Yeah." I cupped her face, gazing into her dark eyes, my gut tightening at the fear and hurt shining in them. "I love you, Jo. You're the only woman for me. I would never do anything to betray your trust."

The words tasted like sawdust. I wished they were true, but one day, she'd learn who I really was, and then she'd discover the many ways in which I'd let her down. But none of them were like this. I'd never betray her with another woman.

It did the trick though. Her gaze softened and she turned her face into my palm, brushing a kiss over the sensitive skin.

"I'm sorry for doubting you," she whispered, the last of her suspicions fading away. "I was scared, and I didn't want to get hurt or be made a fool of. My parents and friends have already asked why we got married so quickly. I don't want to prove them right in thinking I'm a naive romantic."

Guilt thickened my tongue, making it impossible to speak. The fact is, I had taken advantage of her romantic nature. I needed access to her colleagues and romancing her was the easiest way to get it. When she realized that, she'd feel like a fool. But there was nothing wrong with her. I was the asshole.

"I love you," I told her again, because that, at least, was true. "You're entitled to feel anything you want, but believe me when I say that you don't have to worry about me cheating on you. I want you and only you."

Whether she'd still want me a few months from now remained to be seen.

I couldn't think of anything else I could say that wouldn't either reveal too much or be a lie, so I stepped closer, trying to bring her into the shelter of my arms, so I could comfort her the only way I knew how: by worshiping her body.

She relaxed into my embrace and rested her head on my shoulder. I was tall, but so was she. For a woman, at least. Tall and lean, with an athletic figure and compact curves. A core of steel with a hint of softness overlaying it.

Absolute perfection.

I lowered my lips to hers, but after the first brush, she buried her face against the side of my neck. I frowned. It was almost as though she didn't want to kiss me.

My chest constricted. Did she still not trust me? Had my reassurances not been enough?

I couldn't lose her. Not just because of my job but because she meant more to me than any woman ever had.

"Jo?" I murmured against her hair.

She released a shuddering breath. "Just... not tonight."

Nausea churned in my gut. The implication was clear. She was holding onto a thread of doubt. Part of her believed I might have been with someone else. A large enough part of her to stop her from making herself vulnerable with me.

My breath caught. I wanted to scream at the unfairness of it. Of all the things she could have accused me of, infidelity was the only sin I hadn't committed. I belonged to Joanna, heart and soul. Perhaps I couldn't explain away what she'd seen as well as I'd have liked to, but it hurt to know she thought me capable of such a betrayal.

"Can I hold you?" I asked quietly.

She nodded.

I took her hand, relieved when she let me clasp it without protest, and led her to the bedroom. With gentle touches and careful movements, I removed her clothes one item at a time. My spirit reveled in every section of skin that appeared, because even if she didn't want to make love, she at least trusted me enough to be naked with me.

Once she stood before me, her arms wrapped around her waist, her dusky nipples peaked from the cool air, I got to work on my own clothes. First, the T-shirt came off, then I unzipped my jeans with clumsy fingers. I pushed them down, stepped out of them, tossed the shirt in the hamper and bent to fold my jeans. They went on top of the dresser.

I kept my underwear on, not wanting to make her uncomfortable. I took off my socks and tossed them in the laundry hamper, then went to my nightstand to switch on the lamp. The top drawer wasn't quite closed all the way. I didn't mention it, but I was almost certain she'd rifled through it when I wasn't home.

Fair enough.

I didn't like it, but if I'd seen her holding hands with another man, I'd have been a whole lot less calm about it than she was. I'd have marched straight in there and demanded to know why the hell he thought he could lay his hands on my wife.

All things considered, she was being quite reasonable. I was grateful for that and hated it at the same time. Grateful, because selfishly I didn't want to lose her. But I hated it because she deserved better. She should rant and shout at me and demand to know the truth.

Once again, she was showing all the ways in which she was too good for me.

"I'll be back in a moment," I said, debating whether I really needed to shower. But at least one patron had spilled some of their drink on me, and I didn't want to join her in bed while sticky and smelling of booze.

"Okay." She didn't tell me not to take too long or to come back to her soon, as she usually would. Nor did she offer to join me. She barely even acknowledged me.

I hurried through the fastest shower of my life, my heart racing. I strained my ears to hear any movement from the bedroom above the rush of the water, half-afraid I'd return to an empty bedroom.

As soon as the soap had been rinsed from my body, I shut off the water and toweled dry. I gave my teeth a cursory brush and opened the door to the bedroom. My shoulders relaxed. Even in the dim light, the lump beneath the blankets was obvious. She was still here.

I switched off the light and made my way carefully across the dark room. I eased under the covers and drew Joanna into my arms.

"I love you." I nuzzled into her hair. "You're the best part of my life."

Her sleepy murmur went straight to my heart. I ran my hand down her side, and she allowed me to snuggle her. I listened as her breathing gradually deepened, until I was almost certain she was asleep.

It would be a long time until I calmed down enough to sleep too. I clutched her more tightly, fear clawing at me, as if I subconsciously believed she would disappear the instant I stopped touching her.

My phone buzzed. Not my day-to-day phone, but the other one.

I gritted my teeth. I didn't want to release her for even a

second, but the message could be urgent. Gently, I disengaged myself from Joanna and reached for it. The display's brightness was turned all the way down, so the light shouldn't disturb her.

   **A:** *How did the meeting with Portia go?*

**3**

The rich scent of coffee greeted me as I opened my eyes, and I smiled instinctively, but my smile vanished as memories from yesterday returned. No matter how sweet West might be to make sure I was caffeinated as soon as I woke, he was keeping secrets from me.

An image flashed into my mind. West's big, strong hand wrapped around the dainty hand of the pretty blonde who'd been at the coffee shop with him. I couldn't help wondering whether, if I'd stayed around longer, I'd have seen him kiss her.

Suddenly, the coffee didn't smell so appealing.

With a sigh, I dragged myself out of bed. I padded across the carpet on soft feet, hoping not to alert West to the fact I was up and about. I chose a pair of long, dark pants from the closet, paired them with a navy blouse and a black blazer and dug out a set of underwear and socks from a drawer.

I shut myself in the attached bathroom and locked the door. When we'd moved in together, we'd asked why anyone would put a lock on a private bathroom, but now I was grateful for it, because it meant West couldn't catch me unawares.

I showered, dressed, and took my time moisturizing my face and applying a little mascara—not something I'd normally do, but it delayed my inevitable encounter with West and had the added benefit of making me feel prettier. Perhaps if I made an effort more often, my husband wouldn't be out holding hands with other women.

I snorted at myself in disgust. As if I could be in any way responsible for his being unfaithful. If another woman had made a comment along those lines to me, I'd have told her the only one to blame for a cheating husband was the cheat himself. Not the other woman. Not the wife. Only him.

Somehow, it was hard to remember that when faced with the reality. But West knew who I was when he married me. He knew I don't wear dresses, do my makeup, or get around in high heels. He'd claimed to love me just the way I am, and until yesterday, I'd had no reason to doubt him.

So why was I doubting him now?

He'd told me there was nothing between him and that other woman. Why was I having such a difficult time believing him? Perhaps because his excuse had been flimsy. I'd been trained to detect lies, and something in his expression, or his tone, had given him away.

I stood in front of the mirror and scanned my reflection as steam billowed around me, my mind once again wandering to the curvaceous blonde. I was as different from her as night and day. My hips were narrow, my breasts barely a B cup, my hair long, straight, and black. I'd always liked it, but many men preferred blondes. Was West one of them?

Or maybe it wasn't my appearance that caused him to stray, but my work hours and obsession with the job.

Between my long shifts and his unusual bartending hours, we didn't see each other as much as I'd like.

No. None of that was a valid excuse for unfaithfulness.

Assuming he'd been unfaithful in the first place.

*Stop jumping to conclusions*, I told myself. It gets you nowhere. *Now, pull yourself together and face him.*

I turned away from the mirror to unlock and open the bathroom door. I grabbed my bag and put my service weapon inside, then carried it out to the living area. West was sitting at the table, eating from a bowl, a cup of coffee to his right. Another bowl and coffee were stationed on the opposite side of the table.

His gaze warmed as it landed on me, and the corners of his eyes crinkled. "Good morning. Sleep well?"

Not at all.

I forced my lips to curve upward, so he wouldn't suspect. "Yes, thank you. Have you been cooking?"

He nodded. "I made fried noodles the way your mama does. Hope you're hungry. I might have overdone it a bit."

I moved closer. "It looks great."

I pulled out the other chair and sat. The noodles honestly did look delicious. West was a great cook. But I still had no appetite.

I sipped the coffee instead, closing my eyes to savor the rich, bitter taste. I'd grown up drinking more tea than coffee, but caffeine quickly became a staple for all detectives.

"You're up early." I looked across at him. There was a note of accusation in my voice, and I hoped he didn't hear it. He usually woke later than me since he worked later into the night. Was this breakfast a peace offering because he had a guilty conscience?

He shrugged. "I woke up around five and couldn't get back to sleep."

I studied him more closely. Shadows darkened the skin

beneath his eyes, so perhaps he was telling the truth. "Sorry. I hope I wasn't snoring or anything."

"No." He gave me a thin-lipped smile. "My mind was busy, and it wouldn't quiet."

I was tempted to ask what had been keeping it busy but decided not to. If I wanted him to think I'd believed him last night, then I couldn't question him too much.

I settled for saying, "If there's anything you need to talk about, I'm here."

"Thanks." His expression said he wouldn't be taking me up on the offer. He gestured toward my bowl of noodles. "Aren't you hungry?"

"Oh." I'd forgotten I was supposed to be eating. I dug my fork in, twirled it, and loaded the noodles into my mouth. The delicious flavors of onion, soy sauce, and sesame hit my tongue. My stomach rumbled in response, apparently deciding I could eat after all. I chewed and swallowed.

"Very tasty, as usual." I helped myself to more, but stopped when it began to feel heavy in my stomach.

"Would you like me to pack leftovers for your lunch?" he asked, setting his fork down and pushing his bowl away from himself.

"I can do it."

He drained his coffee and stood. "Let me."

I narrowed my eyes as he carried his dishes to the kitchen. Was it just me, or was he being a little too solicitous?

He returned with a plastic container full of fried noodles and placed it to the side of me. "Here you go."

"Thanks."

I finished my coffee and stood. "I'd better get going. Hanson and I have a lot to do for our new case."

"Anything you'd like to talk over?" he asked. He often provided a willing set of ears to listen to my theories and for me to bounce ideas off, but for some reason, I didn't feel able to do that right now. Perhaps because letting him in on my cases required a level of trust I was having difficulty maintaining.

"Maybe later."

I packed the noodles into my bag and left, making sure to kiss his cheek on the way out, in an attempt to smooth over any awkwardness from breakfast. We certainly hadn't been as easy with each other as usual, and I wondered whether he knew I still wasn't convinced he'd been truthful with me yesterday.

I drove to work, parked in the basement garage, and took the stairs up to our floor. I stashed my lunch in a refrigerator in the break room and ducked into a private meeting room. I brought up a number on my contacts and hit 'Call' before I had time to change my mind.

"Hey, Jo," Zeke drawled, as laid back as ever. "Why are you gracing me with a phone call so early in the day?"

"You owe me a favor." Blunt. No-nonsense. If I prevaricated, I might lose my nerve.

"Oh?" His tone sharpened. "What do you need?"

I exhaled slowly, grateful he hadn't argued. I'd worked alongside King's Security several times over the past few years, and I'd let them get away with more than I probably should have because I knew they always acted with the greater good in mind.

I lowered myself onto a chair and set my bag on the ground at my feet. "Yesterday, I spotted West in a position with another woman that could be considered... compromising."

He muttered something inaudible, then, "Shit, Jo, I'm sorry. Want me to wreck his credit score? Get him fired? Have him arrested?"

"No." I rubbed my temples, preferring not to think about

how he'd go about doing any of those things. It certainly couldn't be legal. "The thing is, it could have been innocent, but when I asked him about it, I'm fairly certain he lied to me."

"Okay." He sounded intrigued. "Tell me what you saw."

I explained, and when I was finished, he hummed in thought.

"I agree it could be innocent," he said after a while, "but the fact he wasn't honest about it doesn't bode well. What do you want me to do?"

"Dig into his life." The words were simple, but the weight behind them was not. "I want a deep dive into his background. His family, friends, career, financials. If there are skeletons in his closet, I want to know what they are."

"Done. I'll make it a priority."

"Thank you." I wouldn't consider Zeke a friend, but I appreciated that he was someone who understood the importance of maintaining tit-for-tat relationships with people who could be useful.

"If I find out he's been sleeping around, I know people who could make him disappear for you," he said darkly.

I barked out a laugh. "Are you admitting to an officer of the law that you consort with criminals?"

He chuckled. "I'll have the info soon. Don't worry. King, Kade, and I have your back."

My throat tightened and tears prickled my eyes for the second time in as many days. I blinked them back, furious with myself for allowing my emotions to get the better of me.

"Thank you, Zeke."

"No worries." The line went dead.

I placed my phone on the table and released a shaky breath. What had the world come to that I was relying on someone as reckless and morally gray as Ezekiel Watts to be on my side when my own husband wasn't?

I pulled myself together and headed to my desk. Hanson had just arrived, and a take-out cup of coffee sat beside my keyboard. I glanced at it warily. Hanson didn't bring me coffee. We weren't that type of partners. We did our business, tolerated each other, and lived our own lives.

"What's with the drink?" I asked, jerking my chin toward it.

"Green tea with jasmine," he said. "You like that herbal shit, right?"

"I do." I dropped onto my chair and started up my computer without looking at him. "Why?"

Was this some kind of pity gift?

Hanson looked awkward. "Just drink it, Lee. Don't make this weird."

"There's the Hanson I know."

It seemed the old grouch was capable of cheering me up after all.

He cleared his throat. "The Sloane autopsy is scheduled for nine."

"Great." Autopsies were far from my favorite part of the job, but they were an excellent way to get answers.

"Yeah," he scoffed. "Great. I'm gonna need half-a-dozen Tums to get through this."

I turned away so he wouldn't see my smirk. Even though Hanson had been on the force for far longer than me, he still got green at autopsies. He'd tried smearing menthol rub beneath his nose, chewing gum, and even positioning himself so he didn't have a proper view of the body, but nothing seemed to improve his queasiness.

Not even his beloved Tums.

I checked my watch. "I guess we'd better head down."

He groaned but followed as I grabbed a notebook and

strode to the elevator. We took it to the second-lowest floor, where the medical examiner's office was housed. Dr. Kelly was making preparations to begin the autopsy and her assistant, Dr. Leonard, was jotting notes on a tablet.

"Good morning," I said, coming to a halt a respectful few yards from the table.

"Morning, Detectives," Dr. Kelly said. She glanced at Hanson and her lip curled. "How's your stomach today?"

"Fine," he grunted, even though his usually rosy complexion was already paling.

"Of course it is."

Dr. Leonard snickered, then immediately covered his mouth and ducked so he wouldn't have to meet Hanson's eyes.

"We're ready to begin," Dr. Kelly declared, switching on an audio recording device. "The time is 9:02 a.m. This is the autopsy of Miss Sasha Renee Sloane. Present are myself, Dr. Erika Kelly, my assistant Dr. Jeffrey Leonard, and Detectives Joanna Lee and Dennis Hanson of the Homicide Department."

With the introductory spiel done, Dr. Kelly moved on to the more practical aspects of the autopsy. I watched, trying to maintain a clinical detachment. I almost succeeded until Dr. Kelly made a sound of surprise.

"What is it?" I demanded.

She leveled me with a look that said she didn't appreciate my impatience. "Miss Sloane was pregnant."

My heart sank.

"Pregnant?" Hanson was aghast. "Someone murdered a pregnant woman?"

"It would seem so." She sounded grim. "She was in the early stages of pregnancy—perhaps only ten weeks along. It's likely that no one would have known unless she told

33

them—and that's assuming she was even aware of it herself. That early, it's possible she hadn't realized yet."

I turned to Hanson, whose back was toward the body. "Did her family mention a boyfriend when you notified them?"

"No." His voice was tight. "I specifically asked, and her parents said that, as far as they knew, she wasn't seeing anyone."

I considered that. "She could have gotten pregnant from a one-night stand, or even have used a sperm bank, but it seems more likely to me that she just didn't tell her parents about the man in her life. Perhaps they hadn't been seeing each other for long."

"Perhaps," Hanson allowed. "She could also have been… you know."

I swallowed as my throat constricted. "Any sign of sexual violence?"

"No obvious indications," Dr. Kelly replied without looking up. "But if it had occurred six weeks ago, she'd likely have healed by now anyway."

"When we're done here, I'll check the database to see if she ever reported a sexual assault or laid a complaint against a former lover," Hanson said, his knuckles white as he clenched his hands against either nausea or disgust.

"I'll get her phone for someone to go through. Hopefully, they'll be able to find evidence of whether she was dating anyone."

The autopsy concluded without any further surprises. Sasha Sloane had bled out as a result of having her throat cut. No foreign DNA was found on her body, but traces on her hands indicated that they may have been wiped down with a chemical cleaning agent.

Hanson and I ran our respective errands and reported back to our desks.

"Sloane never reported any crimes," Hanson said, his breath gusting from him as he dropped onto his chair. "She had one speeding ticket, a couple of parking fines, but other than that, she hadn't had any interaction with the police as far as I can tell."

"Damn." So that was a dead end. "Tech is working on the phone, but they haven't found anything immediately obvious. Let's eat, then go back to her apartment. Maybe we missed something."

"Eat?" Hanson scowled. "Who the hell could eat after the horror show downstairs?"

I rolled my eyes. "Have a donut. It'll make you less cranky."

"I'll have you know, I'm off donuts." He puffed out his chunky chest, obviously proud of himself. "Debs and I are on a diet."

"Good for you." I had no doubt it was all Deborah's doing. She was trim and fit. Her husband, not so much.

I ate my noodles at my desk while Hanson chowed down on a homemade salad. We cleaned up after ourselves and Hanson drove us to Sloane's apartment in one of the pool cars. As had been the case yesterday, there were no parking spots directly outside the building, so we parked a couple of blocks away and walked.

As we passed the coffee shop, I couldn't help glancing inside. Fortunately, West wasn't among the patrons, nor was the mysterious blonde. Hanson nudged my arm and harrumphed in an unspoken show of support.

We took the elevator to the third floor. There was no one stationed outside today but crime scene tape was wrapped around the door handle and spread across the doorway. I used my pocketknife to slit the tape and inserted a key into the lock.

The apartment was a wreck. It was a good thing the

crime scene technicians would have taken plenty of photographs prior to searching the place because they hadn't left it in the same shape they'd found it. Fingerprint powder coated most surfaces and the drawers and cupboards had been opened, their contents strewn about.

I grimaced. Gathering evidence was a critical part of building a case, making an arrest, and getting a successful prosecution, but it often felt like a second violation of the victim when their personal space was treated so carelessly.

"I'll start in the bedroom," I told Hanson, wanting to preserve what little of Sasha Sloane's privacy I could.

"I'll take the dining area."

I nodded and went through to the bedroom. As with the living area, it was a mess. I went through her dresser, sifting through the contents, taking note of anything interesting, and checking for false bottoms on the drawers and anything out of place.

When I'd finished with her bedroom drawers, I went through the closet, checking the pockets of each item of clothing and feeling along the seams to make sure nothing had been sewn into their lining. I got down on my belly to look under the bed and inspected her blankets the same way I had the clothes.

I grabbed one of her pillows and stilled. Something inside was firmer than it ought to be. I pulled the pillow out of its case and examined the surface, noting a rectangular shape, with a small slit cut into the pillow. Carefully, I slid my hand inside and withdrew a mobile phone.

Since the tech team already had her phone, this must be a second one.

A secret phone.

**4**

———

*WEST*

I lit the three candles in the center of the table, hoping the romantic ambience would soften Joanna. I poured red wine into a pair of glasses, and switched off the lights in the living area, leaving the kitchen lights on to create enough visibility for us to eat. The door opened, signaling Joanna's arrival, and I slid a tray of pizza into the oven.

She stepped inside and paused, no doubt taking in the fancy table setting and the soft Italian music playing in the background. I strode around the kitchen counter and pulled out one of the chairs, then presented it to her with a flourish. She approached hesitantly and dropped her bag on the ground at her feet.

"What is this?" she asked.

I hid my grimace. Part of the reason for this whole setup was to avoid further questions by romancing my wife until she no longer had the wherewithal to be suspicious. We were off to a great start. She used to go along with my romantic plans with a sweet, indulgent smile. Now, she didn't trust me.

"Dinner." I guided her to the chair, and she lowered herself onto the seat, her eyes narrowed. "I've prepared pizza. It's cooking now."

She pursed her lips. "With your mamma's special sauce?"

"What else?" I ignored a twinge of guilt. As far as Joanna knew, my mother had died a couple of years ago. Another lie.

"What's the occasion?"

I sat opposite her, frustrated that we were squaring off against each other yet again when I'd much rather kiss her and whisper sweet nothings. "Do I need an occasion to spoil my wife?"

"I suppose not." She wrapped her fingers around the stem of her wine glass, lowered her nose to the glass, and inhaled deeply. If I'd ever seen her do this before, I might think it was her way of savoring the wine, but I hadn't. She was sniffing the drink because she was suspicious of me. Did she really think I'd lace her wine?

"I wanted to cook, and it's been a while since we had pizza." The explanation was bullshit and she seemed to know it.

"Why aren't you at Henry's?" she asked. "Aren't you scheduled for tonight?"

I flashed her my most charming smile. The one I used on little old ladies and, before I'd met Joanna, on pretty women. "You caught me. I called in a favor so I could have the evening off to romance my beautiful wife the way she deserves."

She inclined her head in acknowledgement. "It smells delicious. Thank you."

"You're very welcome." Even if I was beginning to get the impression that my mission to distract her would be a dismal failure, I'd never been subjected to her detective side before. I'd always known she was tenacious, but perhaps I'd underestimated just how much.

"Consider it an early Valentine's celebration," I added on a stroke of inspiration. Tomorrow was conveniently Valentine's Day, after all. "Since I'm working tomorrow."

Her eyebrows furrowed. "Is Henry expecting many Valentine's Day bookings?"

I chuckled and ran my hand through my hair. "No, but he'd never risk being understaffed."

Most people's idea of a romantic night out didn't include a dusty bar frequented by cops. Still, there were a few couples who both belonged to the department who might go there.

"He does like to be prepared," she agreed.

"So"—I raised my glass to my lips and sipped—"how was your day?"

It was the kind of question I'd asked many times since our whirlwind relationship had begun, but for the first time, her gaze sharpened, and I got the impression she didn't intend to tell me everything.

"We discovered our murder victim was pregnant," she said.

I barely managed to hide my shock. Not at the fact that a pregnant lady had been killed, but if I was correct in thinking that her latest case was the murder of Sasha Sloane —which seemed likely given she'd seen me with Portia— then a pregnancy added a whole new dimension.

"That's terrible." I drank another mouthful to buy some time. "Was she far along?"

"Only a few weeks."

So perhaps no one had known. "That's sad. Have you had any luck hunting down whoever killed her?"

She sipped her own wine, holding it on her tongue for a few moments, although, whether it was to delay her response or because she enjoyed it, I couldn't be sure.

"We have a couple of leads we're following up on," she said vaguely.

I frowned. Usually, she didn't mind talking about the details of her cases in the privacy of our home, even if she kept names and personal details to herself. It was unlike her to be circumspect.

"Anything promising?" I asked.

She shrugged. "We can't be sure yet."

Yeah, she was definitely holding back. But why?

The timer pinged. I got up and checked the pizza. It was perfectly cooked, the cheese golden, the crust thin and soft. I pulled it out, shifted it onto a cutting board and carried it to the table.

I returned to the kitchen to collect the plates and cutlery. I passed Joanna hers, set mine down, and used the pizza cutter to slice the pizza into six pieces. I took a slice, cut a chunk off, and forked it into my mouth.

I often ate pizza with my hands, but that didn't seem appropriate for the vibe of the evening. Or at least, not for the vibe I was trying to achieve.

"Do you remember the first time we shared a pizza?" I asked, hoping to remind her of those wonderful days and nights we'd shared together on a train hurtling through the Canadian mountainside. I'd arrived at the train station thinking of her as nothing more than a job, but by the time we'd reached our destination, I'd realized I was in big trouble.

"That was good." She followed my lead, cutting her pizza and chasing down a bite with wine. "But not as good as yours."

I smirked, and hope unfurled in my gut. If she could compliment me, perhaps all wasn't lost. "You flatterer."

"Mamma Gallo raised her son to know proper Italian cuisine," she reminded me.

My heart sank. Yes, my mamma had taught me to cook, but Joanna didn't know nearly as much about her as she thought she did.

"What is it?" she asked, concerned.

I shook my head. "Nothing. I'm fine."

She didn't look convinced, but she let me get away with the lie. "Did you have a good day?"

"Of course. I cooked one of my favorite foods and now I'm eating dinner with my incredible wife."

She arched an eyebrow. "What did you get up to this morning?"

"I worked out." Truth. "Ran a few errands. I had to pick up some groceries for dinner." Also technically true. It didn't matter that I left out a few of the errands. "And then I made a tiramisu."

"Tiramisu?" She glanced at the pizza. "I'd better be careful not to eat too much of this. I have no doubt that if your mamma taught you the recipe, it will be the best I've ever tasted."

I laughed. "That's a lot to live up to."

She looked at me from beneath her eyelashes. "I know you're good for it."

Damn. Did she know what that did to me? She was pushing all my buttons, and part of me enjoyed that, but the rest knew how much it would hurt when she decided she was done with me. I supposed the pain was what I got for falling for the woman I set out to target.

If that wasn't karma, I didn't know what was.

The conversation lulled as we ate our meal and emptied

our wine glasses. I refilled them but made a mental note not to serve myself anymore. If I drank too much, I risked giving away more than I wanted to Joanna.

In the entirety of our relationship, she'd never seen me drunk. Only acting. I'd considered telling her I was a sober alcoholic, so I'd have an excuse to avoid alcohol completely, but that would make her ask questions about my past, and it was more important to keep her from prying into my history than to avoid sharing an occasional drink.

When we'd eaten as much pizza as we could, I packed away the leftovers and presented Joanna with a piece of tiramisu.

She groaned. "It looks amazing. You've got to stop feeding me like this or I won't fit into my work clothes anymore."

"Uh-huh." I rolled my eyes at the absurdity of her statement. Not only did she have an incredible metabolism, but she exercised regularly and sparred with some of her colleagues every week. She was far from at risk of gaining weight. Not that I'd care if she did. Joanna would be incredible no matter what shape she was in.

I passed her a spoon and reached for the tiramisu between us. She snatched the plate away and glared at me.

"Get your own," she grumbled. "This is mine."

Shaking my head, I returned to the kitchen and served myself a separate piece.

"Good?" I asked.

"The best." She spoke around a mouthful of cake and cream. "I'm going to need this for my birthday."

"Anything for you."

Well, almost anything. I still couldn't tell her the truth.

We polished off our plates and set our cutlery down. She wiped the corners of her mouth on a napkin.

"I know what you're doing," she said conversationally.

I stiffened.

"You're trying to distract me from thinking about the woman you were with yesterday." Her lips pressed into a thin line. "While I appreciate the delicious meal, you should know that all you've succeeded in doing is making me wonder if there really was something to it."

I tried to take her hand across the table, but she withdrew it out of reach. Suddenly, all of the rich food settled in my gut like a hunk of lead.

"There is no other woman for me." I met her eyes, silently pleading with her to believe me. "You are the only one I want. The only one I will ever want. Now that I have you, do you really think I'd do anything to jeopardize our relationship?"

Her shoulders slumped. "I don't know what to think. When it comes down to it, we don't actually know each other very well. How can we? We've only known each other for four months. We got married after dating for two."

I grimaced. I should have known that would bite me in the ass. I needed to move quickly for the sake of my job, but the quick progression of our relationship had definitely raised a few eyebrows.

Joanna hadn't questioned it at the time. At her core, she was a romantic, and she'd been swept away by the romance of it. But she was also pragmatic, and that part of her had finally come to the fore.

"Maybe we don't know everything there is to know about each other, but we know who we are deep down." If I sounded desperate, that's because I was. Even I wasn't that good of an actor.

"Do we?" She laughed bitterly. "Our work schedules aren't compatible, so we don't spend a lot of time together. Even couples who've been married for years still learn new things about each other, so it stands to reason that a couple like us could hide much bigger secrets."

I caught my breath. Was she suggesting there might also be things I didn't know about her? Surely not. Between the deep dive my handler did and everything I'd discovered about her along the way, I was confident I knew everything there was to know about Joanna Lee.

"You know me better than anyone." My fingers curled into a fist. I wished she'd let me hold her hand. I needed the contact to ground me.

She stacked her plate on top of mine and laid our cutlery across the top. "I'm not sure I do."

"But you do! I—"

"Everything went so fast, we never stopped to think," she interrupted, not giving me the chance to finish my sentence. "We were swept away from the moment we met at the train station."

"You liked it," I accused.

"Maybe." Her expression became wistful. "But perhaps we shouldn't have been so thoughtless."

Ouch. Was she calling our feelings for each other "thoughtless"?

"Do you..." I trailed off, summoned my courage, and tried again. "Do you think our marriage was a mistake?"

My heart was in my throat, and it hurt to look at her, but I didn't allow myself to lower my gaze.

She bit her lip. "I don't know what to think."

I stared at her, her words ricocheting around my mind. I felt like I couldn't breathe. How could she experience the love between us and not believe it was real?

"Have you always been honest with me?" she asked, propping her chin on her palm.

I hesitated for the briefest of seconds, but it was immediately clear that miniscule hesitation had been enough to destroy her faith in me. She drew back slightly, her expression shuttering.

"Of course I have." The lie burst from me, painfully loud in the quiet room.

But from the twist of her lips, I knew: I'd been too late.

**5**

———

*JOANNA*

My phone rang as I was going through interview notes related to the Sasha Sloane case the following afternoon. I checked the caller ID, saw that it was Zeke, and excused myself to a private room, eager to learn what he'd discovered. I closed the door and shut myself inside the depressing space with its yellowing walls and gray carpet.

"Detective Lee," I said briskly.

"Hey, Jo." Zeke's tone had an excitable quality that led me to think he'd discovered something interesting.

"What did you find?" I asked.

He huffed. "Seriously? No 'how's it going, old friend?' What about 'you're a ray of sunshine in a drab world?'"

I didn't respond, knowing that he'd get to the point more quickly if I refused to play along.

"Right." He dropped the act. "There's something about your husband that you should know."

My stomach lurched. "What?"

"Are you sitting down?"

I sat on the uncomfortable plastic chair. "I am now."

But being seated didn't stop the nausea rolling through

me. Zeke wasn't one to pull punches. If he'd told me to sit, then whatever information he'd come upon must be bad.

"Okay." He sighed. "I'll cut to the chase. Until six months ago, Westley Gallo didn't exist."

My mind stuttered. "What?"

I'd expected him to tell me about a girlfriend he was seeing on the side, or perhaps a gambling debt or sex addiction. Not... this.

"What do you mean?" I demanded.

Zeke waited so long to speak again that I checked to make sure the call was still connected.

"I'm sorry, Jo, but Westley Gallo is an alias."

I shook my head. "Why? What could someone gain by pretending to be a bartender?"

"Your trust," Zeke shot back, having clearly already thought this through.

"How do you know it's an alias? Are you sure?" I closed my eyes and imagined West's bright smile that lit him up from the inside, and those adorable dimples that appeared in his cheeks when he was about to laugh. How could that man—the man I loved—be a pretender?

"I'm certain." Zeke's tone was firm. "Whoever created the alias did a decent job, but not good enough to fool my team. Westley Gallo has a birth certificate, schooling records, and even an employment history, but if you dig beneath the surface, it all begins to crumble. If there's one thing I can tell you for certain, it's that the man you married is not Westley Gallo."

My heart started to race. If I hadn't married Westley Gallo, the charming bartender from Chicago, then who the hell had I married?

"Do you think this is some kind of long con?" I asked, although I couldn't imagine why a con man would target me. I wasn't rich. I didn't have family money. I was comfortable, but I still needed regular paychecks to get by.

What kind of imposter had I invited into my life—into my bed?

"I don't believe so." Zeke sounded sympathetic. "I know you're probably doing some mental gymnastics right now, but bear with me."

I drew in a deep breath and exhaled slowly. "Go on."

"Westley Gallo may not have existed six months ago, but Weston Conti did. Then, six months ago, he left his apartment and never returned."

"But what—" I cut myself off. Zeke would get to the point if I gave him the chance.

"Weston Conti is a federal agent who specializes in undercover operations."

My jaw dropped. "You're saying this man Conti is an undercover agent, and... what? You think he's my husband?"

My phone vibrated against my cheek.

"I just sent you Agent Conti's headshot," Zeke explained. "Look familiar?"

With shaking hands, I switched the phone to speaker and opened the photograph. Staring back at me was a pair of familiar green eyes set in a handsome, square-jawed face.

"Holy shit."

"I've only met West a couple of times, but that's him, isn't it?"

"Yes," I whispered, unable to take my eyes off the image.

The stranger who wasn't a stranger. A man I thought I'd known until two days ago.

I'd realized he might be keeping secrets, but I had no idea it would be something as monumental as his entire identity. Even his name was a fabrication.

Hell, I'd been calling myself Joanna Gallo outside of work for weeks now. I'd kept my maiden name professionally because it was easier. But West had stood by and let me call myself by a false name.

I'd been a fool. An utter fool.

"Why would he go undercover to marry me?" My voice shook and I wasn't sure I really wanted to know the answer. "I'm not involved in anything illegal. The worst thing I've ever done was park a police car in a no parking zone with the lights on when I was running late."

Zeke made a sound of amusement. "I forget how strait-laced you are sometimes."

"I'm a cop. It's literally my job to abide by the law and to enforce it when others don't."

"Apparently, it's your husband's job too."

I shuddered. "Can we not call him that?"

"What? Your husband?" He tutted. "You did marry the man, Jo. And you didn't even run a background check on him."

"I didn't think there was any reason to," I gritted out.

Of course, Zeke would think I ought to have been more suspicious of him. Zeke verged on paranoid. It was a miracle he hadn't driven his girlfriend, Fiona, crazy.

"You can't think the best of everyone." He cleared his throat, as if sensing I was about to lose my cool. "Getting back to the point, Agent Conti is currently involved in a classified investigation. I did a little snooping and I think I know why he pursued you."

"Was this snooping legal?"

He ignored the question. "His team is investigating a ring of dirty cops who are on the payroll of Carlos Ortez."

My breath hitched. "Of the Ortez organized crime syndicate?"

"Bingo. The feds suspect the reason he's been so slippery is because he's paying off a bunch of local police officers.

We're talking double digits here, not just one or two bad seeds."

"What the hell?" How could my fellow officers stomach taking payoffs from a worm like him? Ortez was a blight on the city, spreading pain and misery everywhere he went.

"I know. It's bad," Zeke agreed. "I need you to think. Has West ever mentioned him?"

I wracked my mind, trying to recall whether we'd ever discussed the Ortez family, or anything to do with organized crime, but I came up blank. "I can't remember. You think he believes I'm involved? Is that what this is about?"

"My guess would be the opposite," Zeke replied.

I tapped my foot impatiently. "Explain."

"As you've said, you have an impeccable record. You're one of the few detectives who would be above suspicion. My guess is that they knew other cops might have reason to be wary of someone new in their life, but you didn't, so you'd be more open to manipulation."

"Great."

"Not to mention that being with you would give Conti a level of access to your colleagues that goes beyond what a usual bartender would have," he continued, ignoring my exclamation. "Even one at a cop bar."

I slumped against the back of the chair and pushed a loose strand of hair off my face. "So, you're saying that West dated me in order to get close to my colleagues because I was the easiest way in?"

How insulting was that?

He'd targeted me because I was a good cop, single, and had no other romantic prospects. I wondered whether he and his team had discussed the female detectives in the department before selecting me and had ultimately decided I'd be desperate enough for love to overlook any red flags.

Zeke sighed. "Yes, I'd say it's likely that you were chosen

because you're a single female detective with a reputation for being by-the-book."

I felt sick as I considered the ramifications. Not only had I been manipulated, but I'd been taken advantage of by someone who'd vowed to love me. I'd fallen for his act completely.

No wonder West was an undercover specialist. He'd convinced me that he was my happily-ever-after.

I'd never had a shred of doubt.

"Do you think our entire relationship is just an angle he was working?" I asked, hating that I could cling to hope even in the face of this evidence. "Is anything about our marriage real?"

Did he feel anything for me at all?

"Technically, you aren't married." Zeke's tone was achingly gentle. "I've checked the paperwork. He filed it using his alias, which isn't who he legally is. Ergo, you aren't legally married."

My hand flew to my mouth, and I forgot how to breathe. Somehow, it was this fact that brought home the magnitude of West's deception. I'd willingly tied myself to a man who didn't exist. I'd eloped at West's suggestion, thinking it so romantic that he didn't want to wait when, in reality, our farce of a marriage was just a necessary step in his charade.

At least I hadn't dropped a lot of money on a fancy reception or a honeymoon. The only thing I'd splurged on was my dress. We'd agreed to honeymoon for our one-year anniversary instead of immediately after the wedding since everything had happened so quickly.

Exactly the way he'd intended it to.

My chest constricted, and I struggled to draw in a breath.

"Are you okay?" Zeke asked.

"I can't... I c-can't..."

I couldn't even string two words together, let alone enough to explain the complicated tangle of emotion and panic winding tighter in my chest.

"Joanna," he said sharply. "Close your eyes. Now breathe with me. In-two-three-four. Out-two-three-four. In-two-three-four. Out-two-three-four."

My lungs screamed as I did my best to follow his instructions. After a minute or so, some of the pressure eased.

"Thank you," I murmured, embarrassed by how overwrought I'd become.

"Do you need me to call someone to be with you?" he asked.

"No." The last thing I wanted was for anyone to see me like this.

He didn't speak for a long moment, but then said, "Okay. There's something else. Do you think you can handle it?"

"Yes." I'd always been a person to tear off a Band-Aid quickly.

"You never won that trip to Canada. It was a setup from the beginning. Conti's boss bought two tickets and arranged for you to be declared the winner of a false contest that never existed."

A bitter sob escaped me. "He staged our meet cute."

Of course. Because not even that could be legitimate.

"At least you got a free trip out of it," Zeke offered, but I wasn't in the mood to look on the bright side.

"Is that all?" I asked.

"For now." He hesitated. "Are you sure there's no one I can get to sit with you?"

"I'll be fine. Thank you. I appreciate everything you've done."

He snorted. "All I've done is—"

I ended the call. I couldn't maintain a conversation with him right now. He'd understand.

I stood up, walked to the corner and lowered myself to the floor, drawing my knees up to my chest. I buried my face and struggled to draw in long, even breaths.

I wanted to cry.

But I was at work. Surrounded by detectives who'd notice my red-rimmed eyes immediately. I couldn't risk it.

I allowed myself a few minutes to silently fall apart, and then I scrambled to my feet, straightened my clothes, and headed to Captain Thackery's office. I knocked and waited for him to invite me in before opening the door.

"Captain, I'm not feeling well. I'm going home early."

His eyes widened. "What about the Sloane case?"

"Hanson has it under control."

"But—"

"Sir, I will be of absolutely no use to you if I stay here." I rubbed my temples, which were already throbbing.

"Fine." He obviously didn't like it, but I rarely took time off, so he had no legitimate reason to argue. "I'll see you tomorrow."

"Yes, sir."

I left his office before he could change his mind. I stopped at my desk to let Hanson know I was leaving and then packed my bag and drove home.

When I arrived, I half-expected to find the blond woman on the sofa, but the living room was empty. I frowned. With everything Zeke had told me, the blonde had slipped my mind earlier. Now, I wondered whether she was a colleague of West's, meeting under the guise of a date, or perhaps his real girlfriend.

Did he have one of those? I should have asked Zeke. I hated to imagine it, but it was possible there was a wife or girlfriend waiting for him.

I dropped my bag on the living room floor and went to the spare bedroom, where we kept our home gym equipment. West was running on the treadmill, his feet hitting the machine in a rapid rhythm. He was facing away from me, so I took a moment to appreciate his muscular back.

My fake husband was fit as hell.

*Of course he is. He's a goddamn undercover agent.*

Yeah, that would take some getting used to.

I must have made a sound because he glanced over his shoulder at me, then paused the treadmill. He jumped off and grinned as he came in for a cheek kiss. I dodged him and crossed my arms defensively.

"Hi, Westley." I raised my chin. "Or should I say, it's nice to meet you, Weston Conti?"

His face fell and he backed up a step. "How did you find out?"

My heart cracked. He wasn't even going to deny it. Not that I wanted him to lie to me any more than he already had, but for some reason, it would have soothed me.

"You admit you lied?" I wasn't about to tell him where my information had come from. He'd probably figure it out soon enough.

His jaw firmed. He moved forward again, reaching for me. I darted away. I couldn't stand to have him touch me.

His hand fell to his side. "I did. I'm sorry."

I huffed in disbelief. "You think saying sorry is enough to fix this?"

"No." His hand twitched, as if he might reach for me again, but he curled it into a fist at his side instead. "I never wanted to hurt you, sweetheart. It kills me that you had to be part of this."

"I didn't have to be part of this." My nostrils flared as my temper rose, and I did my best to squelch it, so he wouldn't see just how upset I was. "You chose to involve me."

He hesitated for a moment, then nodded. "You're right.

We did. But I didn't know at the time that I'd fall in love with you."

I scoffed. "As if I believe that."

"It's true." He stalked toward me, and I backed up until I was pressed against the wall. "You were supposed to be a job. And yeah, perhaps it's crappy to use someone that way, but it's literally what I was trained to do. From the instant I met you, I knew you'd be different."

"I'm no one's exception." I whispered the words, scarcely daring to breathe in case my chest brushed against his.

His nostrils flared. "You're mine. I love you, Joanna. Whether my name is Westley Gallo or Weston Conti—I love you."

I ached to believe him. I wanted to so badly. But I'd already been fooled once. I couldn't allow it to happen again. He didn't love me, he just didn't want me to mess with his assignment. Perhaps he thought that if he seduced me, I'd go along with him.

I ducked around him and backed into the hall. "I don't believe you. I want you to pack your bags and leave my apartment."

I needed him gone, for my own peace of mind. Presumably, Weston Conti had his own home somewhere. He didn't have to share mine. In fact, the sooner he got the hell out of here, the better.

Jo," he growled, a warning in his voice. "If you force me to leave, you'll be jeopardizing a long-term investigation into one of the worst crime families in Chicago. Do you really want to do that?"

# 6



I stared at West, a stranger wearing my husband's skin. How dare he have the audacity to use me, hurt me, and then dump the responsibility for the success of his undercover operation on my shoulders?

Yes, Ortez was bad news and I wanted him dealt with, but why did that have to come at the price of my peace of mind?

West gazed back at me with flinty eyes. His expression never wavered. This, then, was who he truly was. He'd never been the charming, sweet man I met in Canada. The one who liked mountain biking, cooking, and brain teasers. The real West was sharp, hard, and distant. Did I even know him at all?

My throat tightened, but once again, I managed not to cry.

"That sounds like blackmail," I choked out.

"Not blackmail," he countered, something flickering through his eyes that could be guilt. "Just the truth."

I straightened my shoulders. "If you want to talk about 'truth,' why don't we start with the fact that I'm a detective and you must have known there was a chance I'd catch on to you? I'm sure you have a contingency plan that doesn't rely on me keeping your secret. You'd be a fool not to."

Liar or not, I didn't think West was a fool.

"Any change of plan at this point would waste time and resources." He shifted his weight and his muscles rippled. I forced myself not to react. "I know you. You value justice. Are you willing to take the chance that over a dozen dirty cops could go free just because your ego is bruised?"

There was a very real possibility I was going to throw up. He knew exactly what buttons to push. "You manipulative asshole. This isn't on me. Don't you dare try to blame me for finally waking up and doing what I need to protect myself."

He flinched. It was barely perceptible, but I was completely focused on him, so I noticed.

"You're a good person." His tone suggested he was being reasonable. "Your goodness is one of the things I love most about you."

"Stop saying you love me!" I spat. "It isn't fair."

"I know." He didn't look sorry for it. "Sometimes, life isn't fair. We both know that. Right now, you're angry, but when your head is clear, you'll be upset with yourself if you ruin our operation. Take some time to think about it before you throw everything we've worked for away."

The thing was... he spoke sense. I would be mad at myself for jeopardizing an operation that could end with Ortez behind bars. But somehow, in the moment, that just made me madder.

Fury burned inside me, and I clung to it like a life raft because, if I let go, I might be forced to experience the other emotions crowding around me—like sadness, grief, and loss.

I blinked rapidly and blew out a breath, angling my face away from him, so he wouldn't see the tears in my eyes. "You bastard. You know what all my vulnerabilities are, but I have no idea what yours are. I don't even know who you really are."

A sound in the back of his throat made me glance up. His mouth was pinched at the corners, his eyes filled with hurt.

"You do know who I am." He didn't move toward me, thank God. I was in no state to fend him off. "I'm the same person I always was. Even if things you thought you knew about my past aren't accurate, they're not what makes me who I am. Inside, where it counts, I'm still the same guy you fell in love with."

I snorted humorlessly. "All I have is your word for that, and sorry, but your word doesn't carry much weight right now."

"I'm still me." This time, he did reach for me.

I yanked away from him. "I need space."

I started to turn, desperate to leave the apartment, but he grabbed my shoulder.

"You can't go."

"I won't ruin your precious investigation," I snapped, tearing away from him. "Not yet, at least. I need time and space to think, and I can't do that around you."

"Oh."

Was it just me, or was there a note of regret in his voice?

Keeping my back to him, I spoke again. "I may come across as practical, but I have a soft heart, and you took advantage of that."

"I'm sorry." To his credit, he sounded it.

"Yeah, well, sorry doesn't count for much."

I managed to hold it together while I packed a bag and slung it over my shoulder.

"Where are you going?" he asked quietly as I headed for the door.

"To Hallie's."

"Drive safely."

I didn't answer. I gritted my teeth to keep from saying anything—or losing it—hurried to my car and drove on autopilot to my best friend's apartment building. I parked in a guest space and took an elevator to her floor. I knocked on the door and, as soon as she opened it, the tears that had been building inside me burst free.

"Jo?"

I fell into Hallie's arms, crying. She hugged me tight, stretching onto tiptoes to comfort me properly. She was much shorter than me, and I buried my face in the crook of her neck, my back heaving as I sobbed.

"There there," she murmured, stroking my hair. "Come in and tell me what's wrong."

She guided me inside, closed the door behind us, and slid all three locks into place. She wrapped her arm around my waist and led me to the sofa. I flopped onto one end, and when she lowered herself down beside me, I rested my head on her shoulder.

Now that I'd started crying, I didn't seem able to stop.

"Wanna talk about it?" she asked.

I sniffed miserably. Where was I supposed to start?

The man I'd loved didn't exist.

I'd been manipulated into believing pretty lies by a flinty-eyed liar with deceptively sweet dimples.

I wasn't even legally married.

Not to mention the fact that, apparently, a good number of my colleagues were crooked.

But deeper than that, beyond the loss of what I'd thought was my happily-ever-after, was the fact that I'd always held a fundamental belief in the power of love. I thought I'd know my soulmate when I met them, and I'd been wrong. West was absolutely not that person. If I'd been mistaken about that, then what else had I been wrong about?"

"Jojo. Talk to me. I can't help if I don't know what's wrong. Do you want me to call West?"

"No." I bolted upright. "Don't call West."

Her eyebrows flew up. "Oookay." She nibbled her lower lip. "Did West... do something? Are you fighting? Did he hurt you?"

I almost snorted at the absurdity of it. I was a trained fighter. Yet, she wasn't wrong. West had hurt me. Just not in the way she meant.

"Everything between us has been a lie," I whispered.

Somehow, whispering felt easier than speaking aloud.

Hallie frowned and swiped a strand of her dark hair aside when it fell across her face. "Why do you say that?"

I looked her in the eye. "His name isn't Westley Gallo. It's Weston Conti. I just found out."

Her mouth formed an O. "Why would he lie about that?"

I looked down at my hands, the fingertips cold despite the warmth of her apartment. "Because he's a federal agent on an undercover assignment. I'm part of his cover—only I didn't know it."

"What?" She looked as stunned as I'd been by the revelation. "Explain."

So, I told her about how I'd seen him with the blonde and asked Zeke to find answers. Then, how everything had turned upside down.

"You can't tell anyone any of this," I reminded her, drying my damp cheeks on my sleeve. "I'm sure it's classified, and I promised not to mess up his assignment."

Hallie smirked. "You do remember that I've worked on classified assignments before too? At King's Security, they train us to keep our mouths shut. Your secrets are safe with me."

"Thanks."

She shrugged. "We're friends. That's what we do. Now, let me get us a drink and we can talk about your options. Would you prefer beer, wine, liquor, or tea?"

"No coffee?" I asked.

"Not in your state. You need soothing, not amping up"

I felt a flash of amusement. "Have you been spending time around Sage?"

Sage was Hallie's boss, Kade's, fiancée—a quirky, homeopathic-remedy-loving yoga instructor.

"A little. So, what'll it be?"

"Tea, please."

I could really go for a drink. Perhaps a strong wine or a gin and tonic, but if Hallie and I were going to discuss options, I'd need a clear mind. Hence, tea.

Hallie stood. "Put your bag away. I'll make the tea."

I hauled myself upright, wincing at how much effort it took, and carried my duffel bag to the spare bedroom. It was simple with a double bed, white walls, dark gray carpet, and a matching wooden dresser and nightstand.

I placed my bag on the bed, unzipped it and rifled through to find the pajamas I'd need for tonight and an outfit for tomorrow. I hung my pants, shirt, and blazer from the door handle and plugged in my phone charger beside the nightstand. I glanced at my phone, half-expecting to see missed calls and messages from West, but there was nothing.

I donned the pajamas, returned to the sofa and tucked my legs beneath myself on one end. Hallie carried over two steaming mugs of tea, placing them on the coffee table.

"Have you thought about what you might do?" she asked.

I grabbed my mug and raised it to my nose, breathing in a faintly herbal smell. "Is this chamomile?"

"Yes, with a few other things in the mix. It should help settle your nerves."

My lips twisted wryly. "You've definitely been listening to Sage." I blew across the surface of the tea to cool it. "The way I see it, I have three options: One, I demand a separation. He deceived me and betrayed me, and there's no reason I should have to tolerate his presence in my life."

Hallie intertwined her fingers and rested them on her knee. "But that might unravel whatever he's managed to achieve so far. Do you know what, exactly, he's been up to?"

"No," I admitted. "So I can't predict what will be inconvenient versus completely screwing up his operation beyond repair, and I don't want Ortez to go free if there's a chance to lock him away."

She pressed her lips together. "We might need to learn how high the stakes currently are. What's option two?"

"Option two is that I pretend nothing is amiss and continue acting like I'm happily married for however long it takes him to complete his assignment."

"Which could be months or years."

An unpleasant prospect. I also wasn't sure I was a good enough actor to convince people that nothing had changed. My more casual acquaintances, sure, but my closer friends and family would notice something amiss.

"Option three is a combination of the two," I continued, flattening my palms against the sides of the mug to warm them. "I let people believe we're together but one of us secretly moves out. There's another apartment available for rent in our building. Perhaps he could move in there and no one would notice."

"Other than your family," she pointed out.

"Yeah." I sighed. "There's no getting around that."

Hallie hummed in thought and sipped her tea. "From what I know of you, option two isn't really an option. Whatever his reasons, West hurt you." Her eyes flashed in a rare show of temper. "He married you under false pretenses. No matter how you rationalize it, I doubt you could actually go through with pretending everything is fine."

She was right, of course. I was rational enough to understand why he did what he did, but I also knew myself well enough to realize that trying to live with him and keep up appearances would be like allowing a wound to fester.

"Option one would be satisfying." I was willing to admit —even if only to my best friend—that I could be petty when provoked. I wanted more than anything to be able to tell West to get the hell out of my apartment and never return. It would be best for my mental health to rip off the Band-Aid. Get it over with quickly and begin healing.

"Only temporarily," Hallie replied. "As soon as he was gone, you'd start stewing over all of the terrible things that might happen if Ortez remains at large because you were too selfish to set aside your pride."

When I narrowed my eyes at her, she continued quickly.

"Not that you are selfish. Far from it. But that's what you'd tell yourself."

I groaned, placed the mug back on the ground, and buried my face in my hands. "How do you know me so well?"

She laughed. "Years of friendship and a psychology degree."

I raised my head. "Touché. What about option three? Surely there's a way we could make it work."

Her forehead furrowed as she thought. "How often do you see your parents?"

"We have a monthly dinner, and other than that, it's pretty sporadic." I didn't see them as much as I'd like to. Work kept me too busy. But that wasn't a proper excuse. I should do better.

Hallie drank more of her tea, not even seeming to notice that it was still steaming. "So you put on a good face for your family dinners, and beyond that, you don't really need to worry. But I do think that having him move out could draw too much attention. If anyone is watching him, they'll notice if he moves his stuff and find it suspicious."

"True." I hadn't considered that. My heart sank. "He's going to have to stay."

Hallie's expression was sympathetic. "Unless you decide you don't care about getting dirty cops off the street, then probably. But you could move him into the spare room. Surely he won't argue. He should just be grateful you aren't kicking him to the curb."

"Ugh." I reached for my tea and gulped, ignoring the slight burn as the hot liquid slid over my tongue and down my throat. "I won't do it forever though."

Having him there would only be a reminder of what I'd lost... and how stupid I'd been.

She cocked her head. "So give him a timeframe. Say he has X amount of time to break the case or you're no longer willing to play along."

"How long do you think he needs?" It would be easier to guess if I knew exactly who he was investigating and how he was going about it.

"He's had four months," she pointed out. "The first month might not have been useful, but surely, he's had enough time to get a foothold."

"So, I'll give him another two." Eight weeks. I could do that. Any longer and I might forget why I couldn't allow myself to feel all the soft emotions he'd stirred in me in the past.

"Good girl." She drained her mug. "So, that's the plan?"

I nodded firmly. "Yes."

"Great." She pushed to her feet. "Then it's time for wine."

I chuckled despite myself. "You couldn't be more right."

I followed her to the kitchen and emptied my mostly full mug of tea down the sink. It had been a nice idea, but now that I didn't have to worry about muddying my thoughts, I really would prefer something to take the edge off.

Hallie popped the cork out of a bottle of white wine and filled two glasses. I took one and we chinked them against each other.

"Cheers to a miserable Valentine's Day," I said.

She tipped back her glass. "I'll drink to that."

We returned to the sofa, and I checked my phone again. Now, there were several messages from West.

"I've got one too," Hallie said. "He wants to know if you're all right."

I huffed. "Just leave it. I told him where I was going, and he knows I can take care of myself. I don't owe him anything more than that." Not after what he did. I angled myself toward her and leaned against the arm of the sofa. "So, are there any dating prospects on the horizon for you?"

Hallie rolled her eyes. "Believe it or not, guys aren't lining up to date a female bodyguard. If the irregular work hours don't put them off, then the fact I could put them on the ground in under thirty seconds usually does the trick. For some reason, men seem to find that threatening to their masculinity."

My lip curled. "Men are ridiculous. They should be glad their partner is capable of defending themselves, not put off because their fragile ego makes them want to be the most physically powerful person in a room."

Hallie sighed wistfully. "Maybe one day I'll find a guy who doesn't mind that I can bench press as much as them, but that day hasn't come yet."

I patted her leg. "You'll get there."

She deserved love. Hallie might be strong, with the kind of muscles obtained from years of martial arts training, but she was also sweet, kind, and completely loyal. She was a closet romantic, just like me. Or rather, like I'd been. I suspected I wouldn't be quite so naively optimistic about love in the future.

"Want to watch a movie?" I asked. "Maybe a comedy?"

She perked up. "Absolutely."

She grabbed the remote so we could choose one, and within a few minutes, we were snug on her sofa, sniggering at a movie with an outrageous premise.

When the movie ended, we cleaned up, brushed our teeth, and said our good-nights. I plugged my phone in to charge. The screen lit up, displaying the collection of messages from West. With a sigh, I opened them and looked at the most recent.

**West:** *Please just let me know you're okay and when I can expect you home. I'm worried.*

A tendril of emotion curled in my chest. It wasn't fair that he could affect me so much when he'd lied about everything.

**Joanna:** *I'm fine. I won't be back tonight. Not sure when I will.*

He replied almost immediately.

**West:** *I love you. Sleep well.*

I scoffed as I placed the phone face down on the nightstand.

He loved me. Yeah, right.

As I closed my eyes, an image of the blond woman from the coffee shop flashed into my mind once again. He still hadn't explained who she really was to him.

Was she his actual wife, waiting patiently for him to come home?

## 7

*WEST*

Finally, a little after dawn the next morning, my phone rang. I snatched it up, already dressed and sweaty from pounding out my frustration on the treadmill. A hollow pit formed inside me when I saw the number was private rather than Joanna's.

"Hello?" I answered, raising it to my ear.

"Conti, what the hell is so urgent that you were blowing up my phone all night? I was overseeing an op, damn it."

I grimaced. "Adam."

My handler was good at his job but shit with people. I supposed that was why he usually had a supervisory role rather than being hands-on, trying to build relationships in the field.

"Joanna knows the truth."

He fell silent. "How much of it?"

His tone had taken on a dangerous edge.

"Enough to be furious. She knows my real name. She knows about our undercover operation—at least in part. I don't know whether she has specific details, but I doubt it."

He groaned. "For God's sake, Conti. I ordered you not to

tell her anything. I know you think she's beyond reproach, but it's too high of a risk to read her in."

"I... didn't."

I winced as Adam released a string of curses.

"Then how does she know?" he demanded. "The last time I saw her, she was completely smitten with you. She'd have believed anything you said."

I felt a pang of guilt at his words. I hated that he viewed her the way everyone else on the team did: as a tool to use rather than the woman I loved. Joanna may have been smitten with me when Adam last saw her, but I was equally smitten. It was a shame she'd never believe me now that she'd discovered my true identity.

"She saw me with Portia at the coffee shop near Sasha Sloane's apartment building. I didn't realize they'd be the ones called to the scene. Neal almost always takes the cases in that area, but he called in sick."

Adam muttered under his breath. "So, what? She saw you with Portia and immediately went, 'This man is clearly an undercover agent using me to infiltrate the Chicago PD and rid it of any cops who accept mob payouts'?"

I strode to the window and mopped my hair off my sweaty forehead. "No, but it made her suspicious. I was supposed to be at work. My best guess is that she used one of her contacts at King's Security to dig into my background. They employ several former hackers who could have found my real employment records."

"Fuck. It gets worse." Adam was beginning to sound pissed. "We have no idea how many people know about the op now. We can assume at least two. Joanna and whomever she spoke to at King's Security. It's possible there were more, if her contact pawned the job off onto someone else or needed help getting past our firewalls."

I didn't add the fact that I had no doubt Joanna had

confessed everything to Hallie. Joanna would have asked her to keep her mouth shut, and she'd do it. That is if Hallie wasn't the one who'd gotten the intel in the first place.

"Okay." Adam exhaled roughly. "Damage control. First, we need to find out exactly who she talked to about your real identity. Then, we need to track them down and make sure they don't talk to anyone else. We can't have wagging tongues or else months of work will go up in flames."

"I'll make a few calls." First, I'd try Joanna, and then Hallie, but there was every chance that both women would ignore me as they had last night. If that failed, I'd have to cast a wider net and hope I didn't add more complications rather than resolving existing ones.

"Do that as soon as you get off this call. I want answers by noon. Got it?"

"Yes, sir." Prick. He was acting like I'd done this intentionally.

Adam was quiet for so long, I began to wonder if he'd hung up, but then he asked, "Just how angry do you think she is? You know what they say about a woman scorned. Do I need to pull you off this operation?"

I pinched the bridge of my nose. "No. There's no need for that. I doubt she'll blow my cover. Her sense of justice outweighs everything else. She'll see that it's for the greater good to go along with us."

But fuck, I hated relying on that. She shouldn't have to face me when she was obviously hurting. She should be allowed to do what it took to protect herself, and the thought that being forced to deal with me might cause her pain made me want to stab something.

Still, a selfish part of me was grateful for it too. Because of her over-inflated sense of right and wrong, she'd be stuck with me for long enough that, perhaps, I'd be able to persuade her to give me a second chance.

"It's a good thing we're certain she's clean," Adam mused. "Do you think she still cares for you now that she knows you've been using her?"

I flinched. I wanted to protest his phrasing, but I couldn't. I had been using her, even if it was for a worthwhile cause.

*Is anything worth bruising her sensitive heart?*

"I hope so." I didn't deserve it, but I wanted her forgiveness so badly.

"Conti..."

"What?" I snapped.

"You haven't gone and caught real feelings for this woman, have you?" He asked the question with more tact than I'd have expected.

"I couldn't help it," I admitted.

"Fuck me." He muttered something again. "Keeping an emotional distance is the first rule of undercover work."

I rolled my eyes, annoyed by his self-righteousness. "Yeah, well, you try resisting a beautiful woman with a heart of fucking gold and a moral compass that always points due north."

Adam sighed. "You know, that really isn't my type. I prefer the crazy ones who aren't afraid to break a few rules. That said, do you think it would help win her over if you tell her about your father? Maybe you'll get sympathy points?"

"Maybe."

I didn't want sympathy points. Nor did I want to manipulate Joanna any more than I already had. I recognized that I might have to though. I'd never hesitated to do my job before, whatever it took, but I'd never met anyone like Joanna Lee either.

"If you need to, you have my permission. Do you know where she is now?" Adam asked.

"Her friend's place. Don't worry. The friend won't be an issue."

"She'd better not. But if the worst comes to the worst and your pretend wife blows your cover, we'd better decide what we're going to do."

"I really don't think she will." Joanna might not want to see me or speak to me again—and I wanted to scream even considering that possibility—but she wouldn't do something so pointless and petty.

"If she does, you need to get out of there," Adam said. "Take the identifying documents for one of your older aliases and pass over the border into Canada. We have a safe house in Toronto you can use to lie low until we're sure you're safe to return. The dirty cops will be after blood if they find out about you."

I nodded. I already had the GPS coordinates for the safe house programmed into my phone—the untraceable one. "What about if she kicks me out but doesn't blow the case?"

Adam was quiet for a moment. "We can probably salvage that, but we'll have to take another angle. We can play the spurned ex card. Haven't you told me there are plenty of cops who aren't fond of her? Perhaps you could use the supposed separation as fuel to bond with them."

My stomach soured. The cops who didn't like Joanna were, for the most part, bigoted and misogynistic assholes who were threatened by a biracial female detective who refused to tolerate being called "sweetheart" and asked to fetch coffee.

"I will if it comes to it." The last thing I wanted to do was compound my betrayal of her by befriending those that were stains on the police force, but Adam was right that I had to make the best of the situation.

"Good. I'm going to make some calls. Let me know as soon as you hear from her."

"I will."

Adam hung up.

I tossed the phone aside and headed for the shower. When I was finished, I sat on the sofa with my laptop on my lap and opened the tab showing Joanna's call history. I'd had a tap on her phone since we'd first met, and it would be useful now to narrow down who had blabbed to her about my true identity.

I scrolled through the call log, pausing when I got to a number she didn't call often. The number would display as private during a call, but thanks to my tracking technology, I could see exactly who it belonged to.

Goddamn Ezekiel Watts.

According to the call log, Zeke and Joanna had spoken for several minutes, and it hadn't been long afterward that she'd arrived home and confronted me. So, yeah. I think it was safe to say that Zeke was the reason I'd woken without my wife in my arms.

But what had made him decide to investigate me? Had it been a whim, or had Joanna reached out to him after she'd seen me with Portia because she thought I was cheating on her?

I scrolled farther back in the call log, grimacing when I saw that Joanna had called him first. She must have asked for help. At least the fact she'd gone to him directly meant I might only have to warn one person off, and Zeke understood the importance of secrets. I just had to cross my fingers he'd done the investigative work himself.

I grabbed my cover phone and dialed Zeke's number. It rang out. The second time I called, he answered just as I was about to give up.

"What do you want?" he demanded.

Great. He sounded about as thrilled to speak to me as I was to speak to him.

"Can we meet?" I asked. "There's something we need to discuss."

"Be at the lakefront in an hour." He didn't waste time asking questions. "I'll find you there."

I ended the call.

An hour later, I was standing on the Lakefront Trail when Zeke sauntered toward me, clad in a leather jacket and black jeans, heavy rings adorning his fingers. I nodded to him in greeting. He didn't respond. When he was only a few feet away from me, he drew his fist back and struck out at me so quickly, I didn't have a chance to shield myself.

His knuckles smashed into my cheekbone, and I reeled backward, the metallic tang of blood in my mouth. I must have bitten my tongue. I raised my hand to my cheek, feeling a split where one of his rings had cut the skin, and I stared at him, hardly able to believe what he'd done.

"What the fuck?" I breathed, my cheek throbbing. My eyelid was already becoming puffy. I brushed my fingers over it. I had no doubt it would be swollen shut before long —nor that I'd be rocking a killer black eye.

So much for staying under the radar.

Zeke wiped his knuckles on his shirt and glanced around, probably to check whether we'd garnered any attention. We hadn't. It was cold enough that few people were out, and those that were, weren't lingering for long enough to notice our altercation.

"That's for breaking Jo's heart," he growled, adjusting his stance so he'd be ready to take me on if I fought back. "Usually, my revenge would be more subtle. I'd tamper with your credit score or fake a BOLO. But considering that you're deep undercover and I don't want to mess with that, I have to settle for a punch."

His words hurt more than the punch ever could have.

"I broke her heart?" I knew she'd been upset. No doubt

she felt foolish and betrayed, but the thought of breaking her that way... I could hardly stomach it.

Zeke's lip curled and he looked at me as if I was stupid. "You pretended to be someone you weren't in order to make her fall in love with you. What the hell did you expect to happen?"

I didn't have an answer for that.

Zeke lifted his hand to ward off anything I might say. "If you're here in a mistaken attempt to intimidate me into keeping silent, there's no need. I've been undercover before. I know the drill."

Relief filtered through me. "Thank you. Does anyone else know?"

"From me?" He shook his head. "Only Jo."

The relief deepened.

"You should be ashamed of yourself," he added, obviously on a roll. "Taking advantage of someone as idealistic as her. Low move."

I hung my head. "Trust me, I know. It was our best path to getting in with someone relatively senior on the force though."

"And now?" His tone was taut. "Do you regret it?"

I considered my words carefully. "I deeply regret that she was hurt. But if I could go back in time, I'd do it all over again. Because Joanna wasn't the only one to fall in love."

Zeke snorted. "Good luck convincing her of that."

## 8

---

*JOANNA*

I stayed at Hallie's place for two nights before I capitulated and called West. I was curled on the sofa, my feet beneath me and the phone pressed to my ear. Hallie stayed close for moral support.

"Joanna. Thank God," he said when he answered.

I told myself it wasn't relief in his voice. He didn't actually care about me, right?

"How are you?" he asked.

I didn't dignify that with a response. Surely, he knew I wasn't doing well. It would be ridiculous of him to think otherwise.

"We should meet," I told him, drawing my knees to my chest and wrapping my free arm around them. "There are things we need to discuss."

"Yes, of course." He sounded eager. Way too eager. But then, I supposed his entire operation might hinge on what I did or said next. "Just say when."

I hesitated, reluctant to concede anything, but Hallie and I had already agreed that having the necessary conversation at our apartment would probably be the safest option, since I had no doubt he'd made sure it was clean of listening devices.

"How about at the apartment after your shift ends?" I'd rather see him somewhere neutral, where we didn't share so many memories, but privacy mattered more than my own desires at this point.

"Perfect. I should be home a little after midnight. I..." He paused. "I look forward to seeing you."

I ended the call and glared at the screen, internally torn between cursing him out and melting a little. Why did he have to sound so sincere? He was an excellent actor.

I turned to Hallie. "It's done."

"Good job, Jo. You were so strong."

I sighed. "I don't feel it. It's going to be so difficult being alone in the place where we've lived together. We had so many good times. How am I supposed to remember they're all fake?"

She smiled sympathetically. "Maybe not all of them were fake. Could he have meant it when he said he had real feelings for you?"

I rested my head against the sofa cushion. "I don't see how. You don't lie to and manipulate the people you love."

"He could have been backed into a corner," she offered.

I shook my head. "I can't allow myself to consider any shades of gray. If I do, I'll start hoping, and that's a surefire way to get hurt."

Hallie nodded as if she understood. Really, I doubted most people could, but I appreciated the effort.

"You do what you need to," she said.

I huffed. "What I need to do is pack my bag."

She winced. "Just remember that you're always welcome here. If you go back and it hurts too much, then my spare bed is waiting for you whenever you want."

I forced a smile. "Thanks, Hallie."

"We're friends. Friends take care of each other. Especially when they're in male-dominated careers, surrounded by stupid men all day, every day." She pursed her lips. "Not that I'm bitter or anything. It's just easy to get frustrated sometimes."

"Trust me, I know." There were days when I'd love to see how Hanson would deal with the crap I've had to put up with.

I went to the spare bedroom, packed my belongings into my duffel bag, and carried it out to the living area.

"Got everything you need?" Hallie asked.

"Except for a hug."

She laughed. "We can't have that."

She gave me a quick hug and I squeezed her back tightly, absorbing all the strength that I could from the embrace. When we separated, she touched my arm.

"Don't forget: you can come straight back if you want to."

"I know."

I left and drove home, the vehicle crawling down familiar streets more slowly than needed as I delayed the inevitable. Fortunately, West's shift wouldn't be over for hours, so the apartment was empty when I finally arrived.

I dropped my bag on the living room floor and wandered into the bedroom. I considered packing his clothes into a suitcase and shifting them into the spare room, but as I gazed at the massive bed, memories of all the times he'd made love to me there paraded through my mind.

No, it would be better if I were the one to change rooms. At least then, I wouldn't have to fight off the ghosts of the past while I tried to snatch a few hours of sleep.

Decision made, I spent the next half hour moving my clothes from our shared closet to the spare bedroom. I removed all my toiletries from the attached bathroom and placed them in the near-empty cabinet in the main bathroom. I moved the little jewelry I did have, the book on my nightstand, and then the whole damn nightstand itself.

When I'd moved everything I thought I might possibly want, I lugged the free weights through to the bedroom that was now West's. I didn't want to give him any reason to venture into my personal space.

I dragged the other small pieces of gym equipment through to his room, and then battled to maneuver the treadmill through the doorway and across the hall. We'd put the machine together in the room, so we'd never have to move it, but I wasn't about to take it apart, because there was every chance I wouldn't remember how to put it back together.

Kind of like our marriage, in a way.

West had broken it, and I was doing my best to reshape it into something that would work for us for as long as we were stuck together.

I collapsed on the single bed in the spare room and tried to read a women's adventure novel. My stomach rumbled, alerting me that lunch had been hours ago, but I couldn't seem to find the will to make anything for dinner. West was the cook in our relationship. At least that was still true. He couldn't fake being a good cook.

But where had he learned to cook? From his mamma, as he'd always claimed, or from someone else? How would I know? I couldn't be sure of anything he'd told me. Was he actually an orphaned only child? I supposed it would be easy enough to find out, but that was one reality I wasn't ready to face yet.

By the time I heard the door open, and West enter, I was still sifting through facts I thought I'd known about him and attempting to determine fact from fiction. It was a losing game, but at least it had reminded me of why I had to remain aloof around my not-husband.

With a deep breath, I gathered myself and strode out to meet him. I stopped abruptly in the living room doorway when the scent of fried chicken met my nose. I narrowed my eyes at West's tall, strong silhouette. He must have stopped by the twenty-four-hour take-out place a couple of blocks from our apartment.

"You can't bribe me with spicy fried chicken," I told him, embarrassed by my petulant tone.

He moved into the light, the easy smile on his lips a massive contrast to the blue and purple bruise surrounding his left eye and the cut on his cheekbone. "I'm not trying to, but there's no reason we can't share a nice meal."

"What happened to you?" My mind zipped to worst case scenarios. Had one of the dirty cops found out about the investigation and attacked him? Was he hurt elsewhere too? And why on earth did I care?

He shrugged one shoulder. "Zeke."

"Ah." I turned away so he wouldn't see me smirk. I didn't want him to suffer, not really, but I couldn't deny being a little pleased that Zeke had defended my honor, however misguided the attempt might have been.

"He's protective of you." He held up the box. "Let's eat."

I turned up my nose. "I'm not hungry."

My stomach growled, and I silently dared him to comment on it, but he didn't.

"I'll just serve this up then." He took the box to the kitchen and emptied it onto a plate. "You're welcome to join me at the table or you can watch from the sofa if you'd prefer."

I contemplated sitting on the sofa just to spite him, but my stomach grumbled again, eager to be filled with one of its favorite foods. Traitor.

He placed the chicken in the center of the table and sat on one side. I took the other.

"Can I get you a drink?" he asked, all politeness. "Wine? Beer? Soda?"

"No, thank you." I'd get myself a glass of water if I was thirsty.

"Suit yourself." He grabbed a piece of chicken and bit into it. I resisted reaching for one of my own, at least for a minute or so.

"I've been thinking." I steepled my fingers and did my best to keep my voice even.

He arched his uninjured right eyebrow. "And what have you decided?"

I blew out a stream of air, struggling to remain calm. I'd decided this was the best course of action; I couldn't change my mind now just because it was uncomfortable.

"I'll help with your case." I held up my hand, urging him to remain silent. "If there's a ring of dirty cops inside Chicago PD who are working for Carlos Ortez, then I agree that they need to be stopped."

Some of the tension bled from his shoulders. "Thank you."

I nodded in acknowledgement. "I'm willing to play along for two months. If it isn't resolved within that time, we can discuss the matter further. But once your operation is complete, I don't want to see you again."

"No!" The protest burst from him unbidden.

My jaw tightened. "Excuse me?"

"I love you," he said, the words running together as he raced to get them out. "You can't ask me to just walk away. I love you so much. I won't lose you."

I gazed into his eyes, the green irises almost black in this light. It was impossible to tell whether this was part of his game, but the desperation in his tone and the twinge of something unpleasant deep within me made me wonder.

"I'm sorry." To my surprise, I meant it. If this was causing him distress for whatever reason, I took no joy in that. "It's too hard."

"But—"

"That's my condition." I said it firmly, so he'd know it wasn't up for debate. "I help you, and then you leave me alone. If you won't agree, then tell me now, because we'll have to figure out something else."

He stared at me for a long time, a combination of pain and calculation in his expression. Finally, he nodded. "Okay."

Thank God. If he'd argued, and tried to insist once again that he loved me, I don't know what I would have done. We ate our chicken in silence for a minute or so, gathering our thoughts.

"I have some rules." I'd need them to get through this with my heart intact.

He frowned. "I thought that's what your condition was about?"

"Not exactly. I needed that so I could agree to work with you. These rules will govern how we work together."

"Go ahead, then. Tell me what they are." He looked resigned, and I had to hope that meant he wouldn't argue.

I put down a chicken bone. "First, we don't share a bedroom anymore."

He opened his mouth as if to speak but then shut it again and nodded.

"Two, you don't lie to me again. I'm going along with this because I know how important your investigation is, but if I catch you keeping me in the dark about something, you won't get another chance."

He picked up another piece of chicken. "That's fair. What else?"

I held up a finger. "Just one last thing. There's no unnecessary affection when we're alone or with people who know the truth of our relationship."

I couldn't handle it if he continued to hug me, kiss me, and promise me love. It would be too confusing, not to mention needlessly cruel.

"Fine." He didn't seem happy about it. "I agree to your rules, but for the record, I do love you, and I'm going to prove it."

Emotion clogged my throat. "Please don't."

If I wasn't so proud, I'd get down on my knees and beg him not to make this harder than it had to be.

He studied me, his eyes darker than usual in the dim light. "I'll do what I can not to make you uncomfortable, but one of your rules is no lying, so I won't pretend not to feel anything for you."

I wiped my fingers on a napkin so I wouldn't have to look at him. "Tell me about your assignment."

He hesitated for a long moment, as if weighing whether he ought to push, but then allowed me to move the conversation on.

"Last year, a detective was shot while off-duty. He was investigating Carlos Ortez in relation to a drug bust made at a warehouse in the industrial district."

I nodded, grateful to discuss a case rather than our sham of a marriage. "How did that lead you to investigate dirty cops?"

"Because we found far less product at the warehouse than we expected." He pushed the chicken toward me, his lip curled as if in disgust. "According to our intelligence, we should have confiscated almost ten times as much, and have arrested at least five of Ortez's employees. Instead, we got one low level dealer and hardly enough coke to put him away."

"So, you think someone warned him about the raid?" I asked, following his train of thought.

"The raid was organized quickly, based on a last-minute tip, and only a small number of officers knew about it. There's no reason word should have gotten back to Ortez so quickly." He stacked his hands one on top of the other. "Yeah, we think a cop alerted him before we arrived, so he had time to clear out almost everything."

I considered this. It would certainly be the simplest explanation, even if it wasn't the one people would prefer to believe. "Any idea who?"

His lips tugged down at the corners. "Pretty sure we know, but we can't make an arrest yet. When we started asking questions, it became clear that this guy isn't the only one on Ortez's payroll. There's a reason nothing ever gets pinned on him. We're holding off on any arrests until we can take down the whole lot at once. Otherwise, we risk some of them getting skittish and running."

"Names?" I asked.

"This wasn't in your precinct," he told me. "It was in the fourth district."

"So, I likely wouldn't know them." I frowned. "Why infiltrate my precinct then?"

He shrugged. "We've tried to get an undercover officer into every district. I'm only a small part of the overall investigation."

"So, if I were to out you, it could risk not just your specific investigation, but also the others connected to it." It wasn't a question. I just needed to understand the stakes and voicing it out loud helped.

"Yes. I can't share any details from those connected

investigations though, and I can't give you the names of anyone involved without clearing it with my handler."

I supposed that meant that if the blond woman was part of the investigation, I wouldn't get to learn her identity. But if she wasn't...

"The blonde I saw you with, is she part of the operation?"

He met my gaze levelly. "Yes. She's a professional contact and nothing more."

"But you can't tell me how." Again, a statement not a question.

"Not yet."

I appreciated that he hadn't ruled it out completely. "Is there anything else I should know?"

He grimaced. "Too much. But nothing urgent. Why don't we discuss details as the need arises?"

"Fine." I stood. "I've eaten enough."

His eyebrows drew together. "You've hardly touched your food."

"I'm not really hungry." Despite the earlier growling of my stomach, it was churning uncomfortably, and I suspected that eating more would only make me queasy. "Are you done?"

He glanced at the barely touched chicken. "Yeah."

"I'll clean up then." We both reached for the plate at the same time. Our gazes met across the table. His was soft, with a hint of pleading in it. I released the plate immediately and stepped backward. "Or you can."

I strode out of the living area toward the room I'd claimed as my own. I shut the door behind myself, lay on the bed and curled up on my side, drawing my knees to my chest. I breathed in the hint of mint that always seemed to follow West around and groaned.

How was it that his scent clung to the pillow and sheets when he hadn't slept in this bed recently?

I screwed my eyes shut and let tears spring up behind my eyelids. Why couldn't I escape the damn man?

I tried to draw in another breath, but my chest constricted so much it was almost painful. Somehow, the thought of getting away from West hurt as much as being constantly reminded of him. It wasn't fair. He'd lied to me. I shouldn't be hung up on him like this. After all, what did I really know about him?

He'd pretended to be a bartender. A romantic. He'd claimed to enjoy Chinese martial arts movies and sudoku, but could that also have been a fabrication to get close to me?

I had no idea.

He knocked on the door, and I bolted upright and swiped at my eyes, determined not to let him see me like this.

"Joanna?" He didn't come in.

"What?" I winced at how abrupt I sounded.

He paused. "Would you like to watch a movie?"

"No, thanks. It's late, and I need to answer some emails before bed." And just not be around him.

"You can do that while we watch," he replied seamlessly.

"I have to work tomorrow, and I can't be overly tired."

He sighed. "Don't you think we should talk more?"

It seemed there was nothing for it but the truth. "I really don't. And right now, I want to be alone."

9

JOANNA

I snuck out of the apartment before West woke up. Shame churned in my gut as I packed my gear, quietly closed the apartment door and took the stairs down to the parking garage. But I'd rather live with the shame than face my not-husband after chickening out of watching a movie with him last night.

I drove to the police station, parked, and made myself a cup of black coffee in the break room. I gulped it down en route to the in-house gym, where I discarded the cup just inside the entrance and made a mental note to pick it up later.

I ran three miles as a warm-up, then went through the familiar routine of setting up a squat bar and taking its weight onto my shoulders.

As I counted out my first set of reps, I scanned the other cops making use of the gym. A couple of older men were on the cycles. A female beat cop was doing pull-ups on a bar. Two guys from the narcotics division were sparring on the mats. How many of them were crooked? One? Two? All of them?

My legs burned as I straightened from the final squat of the set and positioned the bar back on the rack. When I joined the police, I never thought I'd have to question the loyalty of my fellow officers. I'd been terribly naive.

Determined not to dwell on such a dark subject, I turned my mind to the investigation of Sasha Sloane's murder as I completed another two sets of squats, followed by three sets of dead lifts and another three sets of calf raises. I stretched my leg muscles to loosen any tightness, showered, and changed into slacks and a blazer.

I took my empty coffee cup back to the break room, then headed for the Homicide Department. When I reached my desk, I found Hanson engaged in a heated conversation with Detective Neal, whose darkly good-looking face was twisted with frustration.

"What's going on?" I asked, dropping my bag and kicking it beneath the desk.

Neal scowled at me. "I want my case back."

I arched a brow, no idea what he was talking about. "Your case?"

He rolled his eyes. "The murder at the lakefront. Female vic. Twenties. Cut throat."

"Ah." Now it made sense. This was more of his territorial bullshit. Too bad I wasn't in the mood for it. "You weren't here. We've done too much work at this point to hand it over without a good reason."

A sneer curled his mouth. "Here's your reason: It's my area. You were only covering for me. I'm ready to take it back."

"Uh-huh." I sat back against my chair and crossed my arms. "What does the Captain say?"

Neal narrowed his eyes. "You're so far up management's ass that—"

"Shut it, Clancy," Hanson snapped. "All I'm hearing is

that you already tried to pull this crap with Thackery, and he told you the Sloane investigation is ours."

Neal grimaced. "He wouldn't have if Deputy Chief Dominguez hadn't been there. But you girls all look out for each other, don't you?"

My nostrils flared, irritation flashing through me. Sometimes, I wished I could smack Neal across his smarmy face. He'd been disrespectful toward Dominguez ever since she'd been promoted to Deputy Chief.

In his mind, a woman of color couldn't possibly have earned the role. It must be a token gesture to prove the police department isn't sexist or racist.

Dominguez was a damn good cop. Better than he'd ever be.

"Neal, we have a fatal stabbing to attend."

We all turned at the voice. Detective Sewell, Neal's beleaguered partner, smiled at us wearily. The bags below his eyes were shadowed, and he obviously hadn't shaved in a while.

"But the Sloane investigation—"

"Isn't ours," Sewell interrupted. He stepped toward Neal, the contrast between them becoming more obvious as he moved closer. Where Neal was tall and good-looking, Sewell was almost petite for a man, and had the kind of face that people forgot as soon as he left a room. "This stabbing happened only minutes ago. Get a move on."

Neal grumbled but shot us a final glare and stalked away. Sewell mouthed an apology behind his back.

"Asshole," Hanson muttered as they exited the room. Thankfully, they must have been out of earshot, because I had no doubt Neal would have called him out on the insult if he'd overheard it.

I sat, suddenly wishing I'd made myself a second coffee. I'd hardly slept last night, and more caffeine would help get my brain firing on all cylinders. Especially since it was warm and stuffy in here, making it difficult to concentrate.

"So..." Hanson let the word drag out. "How are things with the husband?"

I forced myself not to react. "It turns out that I misunderstood what I saw. We're sorting things out, but I think we'll be fine."

He nodded, obviously relieved. "Good, good. I'm happy for you."

And for himself, probably. My being married gave him a way to connect with me. If I was single again, we'd have nothing in common, and he'd have to return to being completely awkward around me instead of just a little awkward.

I withdrew my notebook from my front pocket, grabbed a pen off the desk and wheeled my chair around to join him. "So, what did you find after I left on Friday?"

He opened a tab on his screen, bringing up what appeared to be a series of text messages. "The tech team discovered a string of deleted messages to Sloane's second phone, all from the same number. It's set to private and was never added to her contacts, so unfortunately, we can't trace it."

I rolled my chair closer so I could read the messages. "Was there any identifying information within the chat itself?"

"Nothing obvious. No names or addresses. Mostly, the messages were times and places to meet."

"Hmm." I scanned the messages. They were all brief and to the point. From what I could tell, Sloane never replied, or if she did, she'd deleted her responses more effectively than the person she was messaging. "Do you think it could be the baby's father?"

Hanson sighed. "I don't know. None of these scream romance to me. What do you think?"

I pursed my lips and cocked my head, considering carefully before I answered. "Not blatantly, but if she were seeing someone who didn't want anyone to know about it, then perhaps. Could be an affair with a married man."

"Or she could be a drug dealer and the meetups are to exchange drugs and cash," Hanson mused.

"Could be. It's too soon to know." I straightened and turned to him. "What else do we have?"

He looked uncomfortable. "I have a lead on what she did for work."

"Oh?" Why would he be squirrely about that?

A blush stole across his cheeks. "She was an exotic dancer at a high-end strip club. Ever heard of the Red Letter?"

I shook my head.

"It's one of the classier strip joints in town. And"—he leaned closer and lowered his voice—"it's been suspected for quite some time that the Ortez family runs a prostitution ring out of it."

I blinked, stunned. "Do you think she might have been one of their girls?"

He rested his hands on his paunch. "She was certainly pretty enough."

I stayed quiet, processing. West was investigating the Ortez family. A woman who may have been a working girl under Ortez's protection had been murdered. Could the two be related? The Ortez syndicate was heavily involved in drugs and prostitution. It could be a coincidence that one of their dancers had turned up dead.

"We'll need to ask around," I said, considering the ramifications. "Is the club owned by a member of the Ortez family?"

Hanson pulled a face. "Nah. It's owned by a shell corporation. Tech are still trying to find where it traces back to."

"It could be the Ortez's or one of their allies. That would make sense if they allegedly run a prostitution ring out of the place."

"There's nothing we can do on that front at the moment." Hanson reached for a take-out cup of coffee and sipped, then licked foam off his lips. "Want to talk to some dancers?"

I glanced at my watch. "Surely it's too early for them to be there yet." It was my understanding that strip clubs were open until early in the morning. "Let's give it another couple of hours."

"All right."

I returned to my desk and worked methodically through the most urgent emails in my inbox before checking the file we'd been sent with background information on Sasha Sloane's family. According to our research, both of her parents were still alive, and she had an older sister who was a dental technician not far from here.

I opened another file, entitled Red Letter. Inside was a copy of Sloane's employment contract, a headshot, and several photographs of her scantily clad, spinning on a pole. My eyes nearly bugged out when one of the images showed her holding herself upside down using only her legs. She must have been a strong woman.

Yet she hadn't fought back against her attacker. Had she been caught by surprise? Or had it been someone she trusted?

I hated it when people betrayed their loved ones' trust. And no, that wasn't only because it was too close for comfort after my recent discovery of who West really was.

Forcing myself to focus on the final sheet in the file, I skimmed the relevant information. Over twenty women danced at the Red Letter, but Sasha Sloane was a regular. She performed under the stage name Diamond and usually worked Friday and Saturday nights.

"Lee, you reckon there'll be staff at the strip club by now?" Hanson called over the divider.

I glanced at my watch. It was late morning. "Worth a shot."

I closed the files, returned my notepad to my pocket, and packed everything I might need into my jacket. There was no point in lugging my duffel bag across town.

"I'll drive," Hanson said, coming around the end of my desk, a set of keys already in his grasp.

"Let's go then."

We took a squad vehicle to the strip club and parked outside. The club had a surprisingly low-key exterior, with only a small, red neon sign above the door. Hanson tried the handle and the door swung inward, revealing a set of stairs that climbed into darkness. Dance music played from somewhere beyond.

Hanson and I exchanged a glance.

"Ladies first," he said.

I smirked. "Age before beauty."

He scowled, and I relented, and strode up the stairs ahead of him. Whatever we were about to walk into, I doubted it would be dangerous.

At the top of the stairs, the space opened out into a large, shadowed room. I hadn't expected it to be quite so dark, but I supposed the black paper across the windows kept the sun out. The only light came from directly above the stage, where a pair of women were practicing their routine while a chubby white man and several other women watched from the floor.

Hanson puffed up the stairs behind me and stopped

with his hands on his hips, probably hoping I wouldn't notice his need to catch his breath.

I approached the people clustered around the stage and drew my badge from my pocket, holding it up for them to see as they turned to face me. "Detective Lee, CPD. My partner and I have a few questions."

The chubby guy frowned and gestured for the dancers to continue.

"What's the problem here, detective?" he asked in an oily tone that sent a creeping sense of unease down my spine. The way his eyes roved over me left me in no doubt that he was imagining me with my clothes off.

Rat.

"We're here about Sasha Sloane," I said, refusing to allow my disgust with him to creep into my voice. "I understand she worked here."

"Ah, yes." He adopted a hangdog expression that didn't have an ounce of sincerity to it. "I'm Ed Keenan. We were all so sorry to hear about what happened to poor Sasha."

"So, she was one of your dancers?" Hanson clarified, still wheezing.

I couldn't help but wonder how he continued to pass the department's fitness tests. Perhaps they cut him some slack for being a well-respected veteran officer.

"Of course." Keenan's lips curved slyly. "She danced every Friday and Saturday, and occasionally for special events."

"Such as?" I asked.

He shrugged. "Stag parties, usually. Often, they'd have specific ideas about the type of dancers they wanted. Some like blondes, others prefer brunettes. Sasha had this Snow White thing going on that men loved."

"Did she ever do any private performances?" Hanson

asked, having finally got his breathing under control. "For particular customers?"

"No." Keenan's lips pinched together. "Sasha didn't do that. She danced in public, or for small groups, but nothing more. If she saw any customers outside of the Red Letter, I don't know about it."

Hmm. He seemed awfully defensive. But then, we could hardly expect him to admit to facilitating anything too hands on, could we?

"Can we speak to the other dancers?" I'd trust their take on things more than this weasel's.

Keenan frowned and tilted his head, as if considering whether to refuse, but then relented. "Not for long. They have to get ready for a private show tonight."

"We'll be as fast as we can." Hanson was more placating than me. I'd have preferred to point out that this was a murder investigation, and we'd take as long as we needed.

I stopped Keenan with one hand. "I'm sure you're busy, but before you go, when was the last time you saw Sasha?"

"Tuesday evening." He'd clearly given this some thought, since he had the answer ready. "She wasn't scheduled that night, but she came to talk to one of the other girls. I'd guess she left around eight or nine."

I nodded. "Thank you."

So, Sasha had left here at, say, 8:30 p.m. Dr. Kelly estimated the time of death to be between 11 p.m. and 1 a.m. What had happened in the two-and-a-half to four-and-a-half hours after she'd left the Red Letter?

"Which girl did she talk to?" Hanson asked, just as Keenan was turning away.

A flicker of calculation passed through his eyes, as if he was once again debating how much to say. "Portia. But she's not here today. If you want to speak to her, you'll have to come back tomorrow."

He presented us with his back, summarily dismissing us.

"Let me take the lead on these interviews," I murmured to Hanson. The last thing I needed was him putting his foot in it and either saying something inappropriate or showing any kind of disdain for women who stripped for a living. I might not be warm and fuzzy, but I did my best to be respectful.

He agreed without protest, which surprised me, but perhaps he was simply glad for the opportunity to sit back and relax.

I circled around to the nearest dancer, a stunning Black woman in a hot pink tracksuit. "Excuse me, do you have a moment to answer a few questions about Sasha Sloane?"

Her gaze flicked over me, and I got the feeling I'd been assessed by someone far more astute than I might have expected. But then she put her hand on her hip and grinned.

"Sure thing, honey. What do you need to know?"

An hour later, we'd spoken to all the dancers present—although many of them hadn't wanted to give us the time of day. Perhaps they'd had bad experiences with the police in the past, in which case, I understood their need to be wary.

We'd managed to ascertain a few facts. According to a particularly chatty dancer named Ruby, Sasha didn't do any "touchy stuff," which supported what Keenan had said. Sasha was—as far as anyone knew—strictly a performer.

When I'd asked if Sasha had ever been tempted to break that rule, perhaps for any rich clients, we'd been told her boyfriend wouldn't let her do that. He was protective. Maybe even dangerously so. They all spoke about him in hushed tones, but when pressed, none of them had met the man. They didn't even know his name.

Sasha Sloane's boyfriend was a ghost.

As we trudged back down the stairs, dispirited by the lack of leads for us to follow, a pair of heels clacked on the vinyl behind us.

"Detectives," a female voice hissed. "Wait up."

I stopped and glanced over my shoulder. It was Sapphire, the first dancer I'd spoken to. She hunched down and looked around, as if to make sure no one could see her talking to us.

"What is it?" I asked, closing the distance between us.

"I remembered something. I don't know if it's helpful or not, but I thought it was worth mentioning."

"What is it?" If she'd chased after us in order to share the details, I was willing to bet it had been playing on her mind more than she might want to admit.

Sapphire bit her lower lip. "I've seen Sasha with a man a couple of times. She never danced for him. At least, not as far as I could tell, but they talked."

I perked up. "Her boyfriend?"

But she shook her head. "I asked and she said no. He was just some guy who liked to talk to her. Some customers are like that. They just want us to listen to them."

Interesting. I guess exotic dancers might be like bartenders, in a sense.

"Do you remember what he looked like?" I asked.

"He had dark hair and light eyes. I couldn't tell what color they were, but either blue or green, I think. Maybe gray. He was nicely built." Her expression grew salacious. "Muscular. And he had one of those strong, square jaws like you expect to see in guys from the military or the police."

"How old?"

Her face scrunched in thought. "Maybe in his thirties. I didn't pay a heap of attention. I only noticed him because it was unusual that Sasha wasn't dancing, and also... I wouldn't have minded taking a bite out of him."

Hanson made a sound of disapproval.

Sapphire rolled her eyes. "Anyway, hope that helps. I'd better get back."

"It does," I assured her. "Thanks for telling us."

She bobbed her head and jogged back up the stairs. Hanson and I took the stairs to the bottom and exited onto the streetside.

"At least we know she had a boyfriend now," Hanson said as we headed for the squad car.

"Someone who was the jealous type," I added. "We can assume the baby was probably his, although whether he knew about it is another matter entirely. What do you make of the other guy Sapphire mentioned?"

Hanson shrugged. "It's something to go off. I doubt it's enough for us to get a warrant for the club's cameras so we can identify him though, and there's no way Keenan is letting us see the recordings without a warrant. Not if the rumors are true."

"Mm."

"Maybe she was dating a mobster." Hanson pushed a button on the key fob to unlock the car. "Since they supposedly run this club and all."

Mobster.

I gasped as an image flashed into my mind.

A handsome dark haired, green eyed, square jawed man in his thirties. One who fit Sapphire's description perfectly.

My not-husband.

Hanson was staring at me, concern scrawled across his brow. "You okay?"

"I need to check something," I breathed. "Wait here."

I rushed back into the club, up the stairs, and over to Sapphire. Her eyes widened, but she didn't run. I stopped in front of her, opened my phone and sifted through photographs until I found what I was looking for.

I showed it to her. "Is this the guy you saw talking to Sasha?"

She leaned over to get a better look. "I couldn't say for sure, but I think so. Who is he?"

I ignored her question. "Thank you. You've been very helpful."

I walked away, my mind reeling. Our dead woman had been chatting with West.

Why?

I stumbled down the stairs on autopilot, searching through a mental Rolodex of reasons why they might have any cause to know each other. If he'd been investigating the mob and she worked at a mob business, then perhaps he thought she could help him.

I wasn't even going to think about the fact my so-called husband had been at a strip club frequently enough that one of the dancers was able to describe him well enough for me to identify him.

"What's wrong?" Hanson asked as I opened the passenger door and slumped inside. "You're white as a sheet."

I grimaced. "I needed to use the bathroom. Must have eaten something off."

He cringed but didn't ask anything further. Just as well. I wasn't sure how to explain the fact that my husband had just become a person of interest in our homicide investigation.

**10**

———

*WEST*

I was out behind Henry's, chatting with one of the delivery drivers, when my phone rang. I excused myself and returned inside, checking the screen as I did. My heart lifted. It was Joanna. I accepted the call.

"Hey." I sounded as breathless as I felt.

"Hi. Are you alone?" Her tone was brisk and businesslike.

I looked around. "Yeah. I just popped into the bar to help with a couple of things, but I was about to leave."

"Good." She hesitated for a moment. "Can you meet me at Grant Park?"

My eyebrows flew up. I couldn't imagine why she might ask me to meet her there rather than at our apartment or even Henry's.

"Sure." I checked that the back door was locked and headed out through the fire exit, which automatically locked behind me. "I'll be there in half an hour."

My car—a small sedan with several hidden compartments, which actually belonged to the bureau rather than me—was parked to the rear of the building. I unlocked it manually, checked that the trunk was empty, because in my line of work it paid to be suspicious, and dropped into the driver's seat. I cranked up the heater and drove toward Grant Park.

When I arrived, I walked to meet Joanna, who was standing near the entrance. The park was almost deserted, no doubt thanks to the chilly temperatures and gray skies. My wife—I refused to think of her as anything else—stood silhouetted against the clouds, beautiful, but something about her seemed terribly distant too.

Sad. Alone.

My heart ached for her. I wished I could take her into my arms and comfort her. But I couldn't do that. There was every chance I'd spend the rest of my life desperate for Joanna's affection but never able to have it. I'd just have to hope that, one day, she'd be able to forgive me. Or at the very least, let me make it up to her.

I didn't speak until I drew closer to her. "I was surprised you called."

Although "surprised" didn't really cover it. "Shocked" would be more accurate.

She raised her chin, unsmiling. "I need to ask you something."

"Okay." I stopped moving and slid my hands inside my pockets. "Hit me with it."

She took her phone out and tapped on the screen, then turned it toward me. I leaned close, barely managing not to flinch at the sight that greeted me. It was so far from anything I might have expected that I was caught off guard. Not that I'd really known what to expect at all.

Sasha Sloane's blank eyes gazed out at me. Based on the splash of crimson on her chin and the position of her head, I'd hazard a guess this photograph had been taken at the crime scene.

"Do you know her?" Joanna asked, her voice deceptively even.

She was anxious. Perhaps most people wouldn't be able to tell, but I could. It was in the way her pointer finger tapped against the side of the phone and the subtle shifting of her weight from one foot to the other while she waited for a response. She already suspected the answer. But how had she connected Sasha to me?

Perhaps I shouldn't be surprised. I'd always been told that Joanna was a hell of an investigator.

"Her name is Sasha Sloane," I said, knowing that if I denied an acquaintance, I'd only be digging a deeper hole in which to bury the remains of our marriage.

Joanna nodded. "That's right. She's the subject of the murder investigation I'm currently working on. What I want to know is what she has to do with you."

I rolled my head from side to side, debating how much to tell her. On the one hand, she'd clearly already put some of the pieces together, but I didn't have direct approval from Adam to share any of the details of our operation with her—except for a blanket permission to discuss my father, and this wasn't the time for that.

I sighed. I should have had a drink before leaving the bar. "She was Carlos Ortez's mistress."

A quick intake of breath. 'We knew she had a boyfriend, and that he might be in the mob, but the boss himself?"

I inclined my head, confirming it.

"Is that why you were seen talking to her at the Red Letter strip club?" She folded her arms across her chest and narrowed her eyes.

I winced, feeling both sheepish and guilty. It was one thing for her to know I was undercover, but I hated her being aware that I visited places like the Red Letter. It cheapened our relationship, even if I'd never gone there for pleasure.

"Yes," I admitted. "I cultivated a relationship with Sasha's best friend, another dancer, and eventually, she introduced us."

Her jaw ticked. "A relationship."

I held up my hands, my palms out, placating. "Purely business."

"Of course." She rolled her eyes. "I have absolutely no reason to doubt a thing you say."

"It wasn't like that." It sounded weak, and we both knew it.

"So, what was it like?" she asked. "Tell me."

"Sasha was feeding me information to implicate Ortez's wife in criminal dealings."

A light went off in her head. "She wanted the wife out of the way."

"Exactly." I almost grinned. This was beginning to feel less like an interrogation and more like a pair of colleagues sharing intel. I could work with that. "I promised to pass the evidence along if she gave me enough for a conviction, and meanwhile, I was triple checking everything she sent through, hoping it would give me something on Ortez himself, or the men who work for him."

"Including the dirty cops?"

"Yes. She was an incredible source of information." I wouldn't say I'd liked Sasha, but I'd respected her for knowing what she wanted and going after it ruthlessly. It was a shame it had ended badly for her. I wasn't sure who had wielded the knife, but I had no doubt it was someone from Ortez's shadowy world.

"Do you have any idea who might have killed her?" Joanna asked, as if she'd somehow read my train of thought.

"No." I pursed my lips. "Helena Ortez had plenty of

reason to want her out of the picture, but Sasha was a weak link in their organization as a whole. It could have been any number of people."

Joanna tossed her hair over her shoulder and gazed out over the gardens. "Will her best friend know?"

"She doesn't." I must have spoken too quickly because Joanna's eyes narrowed.

"You've been in touch with her since the body was found?" she demanded.

I braced myself. There was no easy way to say this. "Portia is the woman you saw me with in that coffee shop."

She reeled back, as if I'd hit her, but then her gaze cleared. "You were holding her hand because she'd just found her best friend's dead body?"

"That's right." I was relieved she'd jumped to the right conclusion this time.

"The call that reported Sloane's body was from a male." She tapped her chin. "Portia called you, and you informed the police."

"Right again. Portia doesn't trust the police. Especially not officers in uniform." I didn't blame her. Portia was an escort as well as a dancer, and she'd experienced how badly some cops treated sex workers firsthand.

"Why did you stay in the area?" she asked, but then nodded as if she'd answered her own question. "Because you thought Neal would pick up the case, not me."

I chuckled. "Do you need me here at all? It seems like you've got this figured out."

I regretted the quip the instant her cool gaze landed on me. Usually, she didn't mind my teasing, but I guess that was a perk of being the man she loved. Now, I got to find out how it felt to be the recipient of her scorn.

"Tell me more about Portia," she said, her eyes darting around, scanning the area.

We were alone.

I drew in a deep breath. Adam was going to be furious with me for sharing so much information, but I was trusting my judgment when it came to Joanna and hoping like hell she wouldn't prove me wrong.

"I made contact with her initially, when she was brought in on solicitation charges. She works at a brothel owned by the Ortez family and one of her regular clients is the man we believe leaked information to them about the raid on their warehouse. I got the charges against her dropped and, in return, she's been supplying me with any tidbits she learns from him."

Joanna crossed her arms. "And has she been useful?"

"Yes, in a broad sense. She hasn't given us anything definitive, but enough to implicate several other officers." Now that we knew to watch them, it was only a matter of waiting for them to slip up.

Joanna took this in silently, then asked, "Was she able to tell you much about Sasha Sloane's death?"

"Not beyond the fact she suspects Helena Ortez is responsible. She was reluctant to say much when we spoke. She'd only just found the body and was struggling to hold it together. She might be able to offer more insight now." I debated whether to continue but decided I had little to lose. "She may be more comfortable speaking to a woman."

Joanna scoffed. "Me?"

I shrugged. "Who better? It's your case, and it would be better if this could stay off the official record, so it doesn't interfere with our operation."

Her nostrils flared. "Let me get this straight. You want me to interview the woman who inadvertently broke our sham of a marriage and then ignore protocol to protect my lying fake husband while I'm at it?"

"Um..." There was definitely a right and wrong answer

here, but unfortunately, it wasn't one of the times I could afford to soothe her pride. "Yes. Pretty much."

Her laser-focused glare could slice through steel like butter. She didn't want to, that much was clear. I yearned to take her hand, but I couldn't be sure whether she'd accept the offer or punch me for it.

"There's never been anything sexual or romantic between Portia and me," I assured her. "I'm a physical person, you know that. Holding her hand was about supporting her while she went through something traumatic. Nothing more."

She deflated. "It's just hard to get that image out of my mind."

"I know, and I'm sorry for that, but I've only had eyes for you since the day we met." Goddamn her stubbornness—even if I understood the reason for it. I wanted to gather her against my chest so badly it almost hurt, and whether she'd admit it or not, she could use the comfort too. "No one else can rival your quick wit, or the softness you hide from everyone other than me."

Her jaw firmed, and she swallowed. "Fine. If you're willing to introduce us, then I'll talk to her, but I can't promise it will achieve anything. You've taken the time to earn her trust. I don't know why she'd share something with me but not you."

The pressure in my chest eased. "Thank you."

She squared her shoulders and straightened her back, as if preparing to walk into battle. "Let's do it, then."

I hadn't expected that. "Now?"

She met my eye. "No reason to delay, right?"

**11**

---

I followed West to his car, a yawning pit of dread in my gut. Regardless of what he'd said about not being involved with Portia, I couldn't help remembering how beautiful the other woman was, and how gently West had clasped her hand. I did my best not to let my unease show on my face, although I was certain West sensed it.

He knew me too well.

It wasn't fair, when I hardly knew him at all.

West popped the locks on his car, and I got in the passenger side. As usual, the interior of the vehicle was impeccably clean. For the first time, I wondered whether that was because he didn't want to risk me coming upon any of his work stuff rather than out of a personal preference for tidiness.

He stood outside and made a call. I didn't eavesdrop. When he got in, he turned to me.

"She's free now. She'll meet us at a coffee shop near her apartment."

I intertwined my fingers on my lap. "Thanks for setting that up."

"No problem." He slotted the key in the ignition, turned it, and reversed out of the parking space.

"How long has Portia been one of your informants?" I asked as he drove.

"A little over five months," he replied, glancing across at me before focusing on the road.

Huh. So she'd known my not-husband for longer than I had.

"You said she and Sasha Sloane were best friends. Did they meet at the Red Letter?"

His fingers tightened on the wheel as he veered around a corner. "My understanding is that they auditioned there together. They were friends from high school, although both dropped out before their senior year."

I hummed thoughtfully. "And yet Sasha became the mistress of a mob boss, with an expensive apartment and nice things, while Portia has to work at a brothel to make ends meet. I wonder if that caused any resentment."

"Possibly." He was matter-of-fact about it. "But Portia adored Sasha, even if she was jealous of her. At the end of the day, they were both paid companions of a sort."

"True." One of them likely made out better than the other though. But I supposed a lot depended on whether Sasha had genuinely cared for Carlos Ortez or merely endured his attention. If she had feelings for him—was attracted to him—the situations were definitely not equal.

"Does Portia have much of an arrest record?" I asked.

"Beyond the time we intervened, she had one prior conviction for solicitation and another for shoplifting."

So, not squeaky clean, but no major felonies either.

"Does she do drugs?" If she did, it could impact her reliability as a witness.

"Not that I'm aware of. I've never seen track marks on her arms or irritation around her nose."

Another positive.

"How... willing... was she to help you?" Reluctant informants weren't always to be trusted.

West waggled his hand in a so-so gesture. "She appreciated us getting her out of a jam. I don't think she'd have any problem with it except she's worried her boss will find out."

"Yeah, I'd be worried about that too." I didn't imagine Carlos Ortez was the type to give second chances.

I looked out the windshield. We were entering a more rundown part of town, and several of the buildings we passed were boarded up. The streets were less busy than in the city center, and groups of teenagers stood on the sidewalk, smoking or vaping and staring at us with a combination of hostility and curiosity.

When we reached a small group of businesses, including a hair salon, a vape shop, and a coffee shop, West pulled into the parking area and parked near the rear. I got out and waited for West to lock the doors, then we walked to the coffee shop's back entrance together.

West held the door open for me and I slipped inside, past the bathrooms and into the main part of the shop. Tables were packed in and almost every one of them was occupied. A lively buzz of conversation filled the air. I quickly spotted Portia in the rear corner, walls behind her on two sides.

West nodded to her and guided me to the counter with a hand on my hip. I stepped away, not wanting to encourage any kind of touching.

I ordered an americano and West asked for a cappuccino. The cashier gave us a number and waved us off. West led the way to Portia's corner table. He pulled out a chair and gestured for me to take it. Not wanting to appear rude in front of the woman watching us, I did. He positioned the other chair so that we were at angles to each other.

"Hi Portia." West offered the blonde a smile. "This is my wife, Detective Joanna Lee."

I jolted, surprised by his introduction. I wasn't sure how I'd expected him to introduce me, but certainly not as his wife. It wasn't true and there was no reason to lie to someone who already knew at least a little about his investigation. West's assessing glance told me he'd noticed my discomfort.

"It's nice to meet you," I said politely. Up close, I could see that the whites of Portia's baby blue eyes were tinged with red, and lines of strain bracketed her painted pink lips.

Portia sniffed. "You too. What's this about? West said you wanted to talk to me."

I barely resisted the urge to withdraw my notepad from my pocket to take notes. I got the feeling that doing so may limit any rapport I'd be able to build with Portia.

"Jo is investigating Sasha's death," West said gently.

I eyeballed his hand. If he went for hers again, with me sitting right here, I couldn't be held responsible if I stuck a fork through it. No jury would convict, right?

"Oh." Portia's teeth scraped through the lipstick on her lower lip, and I chastened myself. This woman was anxious. She'd had bad experiences with the police, and she'd recently lost her best friend. I needed to stop being so selfish and help her find the person responsible. "Well, I guess if West loves you then you must be all right."

I glanced at West, curious whether her statement would make him squirm, but he was gazing back at me with an intensity that made me shiver.

"I'll do everything I can to bring Sasha's killer to justice," I told Portia with complete honesty. It was no less than I'd do for any murder victim, although some of them definitely deserved justice more than others.

"Good." Portia's eyes flashed with something dangerous. "Her boyfriend—you know who she was seeing?"

I nodded.

"Anyway, her boyfriend has the resources to cover it up. He has cops in his pocket and I'm sure he's counting on them to make certain no one ever knows what really happened to Sasha." She wrinkled her nose, the expression making her seem much younger. "In fact, I'm surprised his pet police haven't already been assigned the case."

So, she really did know something about corruption in the police force. How much would she be willing to share?

"My partner and I were the only ones available when West made his anonymous call about the discovery of Sasha's body." I placed my hands on the table, hoping it would set her more at ease if she could see that I wasn't doing anything beneath. "Do you know which of my colleagues he has on his payroll?"

Portia wrapped her hands around a half empty cup of coffee. "In the murder department? No." She was quiet for a moment, then added, "One of the other girls spent some time with one of them though."

I forced myself not to give away how desperate I was to know more. "Did she happen to catch his name?"

She pursed her lips. "Sorry, no. She said he was an older guy though. A little overweight. That's all I remember. She only mentioned him because he kept going on about his wife afterward and how she'd leave him if she ever found out."

My heart squeezed, and I schooled my features. So what if her physical description matched Detective Hanson? He wasn't the only detective in homicide who could be described as an overweight, married older guy. And I had no way to be certain the person she'd heard about was even from our precinct.

I leaned toward her across the table and lowered my voice. "Is there anything else you can think of about any police who could be involved? If you want to see Sasha's killer locked away, then I need to make sure the wrong people don't interfere. You understand?"

She sighed, and there was a world of weariness in the sound. "I get it. And I hope you slap cuffs on the bitch responsible and never take them off, but I know how the world works. Even if you and your partner are clean, your boss—or their boss—might not be. I doubt this will ever get to trial."

Determination to prove her wrong flowed through me. Okay, perhaps she had a reason to be jaded about the justice system, but I wouldn't let that happen. Not on my case.

"I'll do everything I can to make sure it does." I held her gaze, allowing her to search my eyes, and eventually, she nodded. "Now, do you have any idea who might have done it?"

She didn't hesitate for a second. "That bastard's psycho wife."

A server appeared at our table and set down a tray. They passed the americano to me and a smaller cup with a foamy top to West. I waited until they'd left before I spoke.

"What makes you say that?"

Portia rolled her eyes. "Sasha wanted to oust the bitch. She was smart. Much more than me. She was learning everything she could about their business. Who was important, who she needed on her side, how they did what they did... She was fucking obsessed with knowing everything, so she could replace his wife when the time came."

I raised my coffee to my lips as I considered this. I sipped but the liquid was still too hot. "How much do you think she knew?"

"Much more than she ever said to me." Portia tipped her

cup back, even though the coffee looked cold at this point. She grimaced at the taste. "It took her ages to piece things together from bits of pillow talk and overheard phone calls, but she could be very determined when she wanted something."

"Sounds like it."

Sasha Sloane may have been a formidable woman, in her own right. It would be easy to dismiss her as Carlos Ortez's stripper mistress, but if Portia's assessment of her was correct, Sasha was seemingly far more cunning than most people had given her credit for.

Sasha was a climber, and those were dangerous.

"Do you know if her boyfriend knew that she wanted to replace his wife?" I asked, since West remained silent.

Portia shrugged. "Beats me. I'd guess that she hinted at it, but if he didn't take her seriously, then she wouldn't have pushed. She is—was—more devious than that." Tears sprang to her eyes, and she touched the tips of her fingers to her lips. "Fuck, I loved that sneaky girl. I can't believe she's gone."

West glanced at me, obviously uncertain about whether to try to comfort her while I was present. I reached across the table and laid my hand on her arm, patting her awkwardly. I wasn't exactly the soft and cuddly type, but maybe it would help.

"Thanks." She sniffled and blinked rapidly. "Um, yeah. So, my money is on the wife."

I squeezed her arm gently. "Thank you for talking with me, Portia. I know it must have been hard for you, but I promise I'll do whatever I can to find Sasha's killer, and you've really helped today."

She visibly pulled herself together, and carefully removed my hand from her arm. I grabbed my coffee and sipped it again. It was still hot, but bearable.

"I'm going to grab a glass of water," West said, pushing his chair back. "I'll just be a minute."

He left, and Portia wrapped her hands around her empty cup again, as if she needed to keep them occupied.

"You're nicer than any of the other cops I've dealt with," she said.

I let out a huff of amusement. "Not many people would say that."

"West would." Her lips curved slightly. "He's crazy about you, but there's something going on between you. Some kind of tension. What's with that?"

I took a mouthful of hot coffee to delay responding for a few seconds. While I'd be within my rights not to answer, something inside me wanted to.

"He's been lying to me," I admitted, trying to keep my face blank. "About something massive. I'm not sure whether I can trust him anymore."

Her expression turned sympathetic. "Men can be the worst. He's one of the best though. He's never made a move on me or been even slightly inappropriate, and the way he talks about you, it's obvious you mean a lot to him. Whatever he did, I'm sure he wasn't trying to upset you."

My lips twitched. I couldn't believe I was having this conversation with the woman I'd thought my husband might be cheating with. At this point, I'd accepted that nothing had happened between them. She seemed sincere, and I got the feeling she wasn't the type of person to sugar coat things.

"Maybe not, but it's still hard to be comfortable with someone when they've broken your trust before." I sipped my drink, which was now just pleasantly warm.

"Yeah." Her shoulders slumped. "Just don't give up on him. Guys like West keep me hoping that I might meet someone decent one day, so if his marriage is on the rocks, then I'm doomed."

There was movement behind me, and West returned to his seat, a half-empty glass of water in hand.

"Would you mind giving me your number so I can call if I have more questions?" I asked Portia, moving on from our discussion of my love life.

"Sorry, but no." She pulled a face. "If anyone finds out I've talked to you, then I'm dead. My life might not be great, but I don't want to lose it. We've probably been here together for too long as it is."

I guessed that was our cue to leave. I stood, and West did too. I thanked Portia for her time and headed to the back exit, leaving West alone with her for a few seconds in case he needed an update on anything related to his operation.

When he joined me, he gestured for me to open the door. I did, and we left the building together. The cold wind nipped at the apples of my cheeks, and I instinctively huddled into my blazer.

"That was helpful," I said as we walked to the car. "Thank you."

He flashed a quick smile. "I hope it set your mind at ease about other things too."

"Yes." That's all I was giving him. Perhaps the right thing to do would be to apologize for accusing him of infidelity, but considering the enormity of the lies he had told, I wasn't inclined to do so.

He unlocked the car, and we got in. As he pulled away, he turned to me. "Have you found anything linking Ortez's wife to the crime scene?"

"Not that I'm aware of." To be honest, that part of what Portia had said wasn't the part that most interested me. "She mentioned a homicide cop who worked for Ortez. Older.

Overweight. Married. You don't think it could be Hanson, do you? Is he one of the people you're investigating?"

I hated to even ask. It felt like I was betraying my partner. But if Hanson was somehow involved, I'd have to tread very carefully. I needed to know if it was a possibility.

"It could be." At least he hadn't immediately claimed Hanson was dirty. "He's not one of the guys we've already got our eyes on, but I wouldn't rule it out."

Great. How was I supposed to solve a murder if my partner—the man I'd trusted to have my back despite our differences—was trying to cover it up?

**12**

———

*WEST*

I closed the tap and thunked a full pint glass down in front of Clancy Neal just as the pub door swung open and Joanna strode in, followed quickly by her partner, Hanson.

"That'll be five," I told Neal.

He passed me a five dollar note. No tip because he was a miserable bastard. Ridiculous considering I was reasonably sure he earned far more money than he declared in his annual taxes.

I added it to the cash register and glanced back over at Joanna. She looked beautiful, with her hair in a ponytail down her back, her blazer switched out for a leather jacket that I knew had a cozy fleece interior. A week ago, she'd have come straight over to give me a kiss, but now she delayed, speaking to a pair of missing persons detectives.

Neal, who was seated at the bar, to the left of the cash register, followed my gaze and sneered. "Ah yes, your lovely wife."

Somehow, he made it sound like an insult.

I wanted to needle him with a quip about how well her investigation into Sasha Sloane's death was going, but my cover required me to get close to Neal. Alienating him wouldn't help me achieve that.

"She is lovely, isn't she?" I murmured, pretending not to notice his sarcasm.

I was surprised to see Joanna here. We'd already spent more time together today than she was probably comfortable with, and she wasn't the type of person to come to the bar after her shift ended unless it was to visit me.

Henry's was currently packed with police officers, detectives, and managers whose shifts had recently ended. Joanna glanced up and caught my eye. Her gaze darted to Neal briefly, and she nudged Hanson's elbow and made her way through the crowd to the bar.

"I'm buying," she called over the hum of conversation. "Two of whatever beer is on tap."

She swiped her card to pay, and I poured the drinks and pushed them across the bar. To my surprise, she leaned over, her lips brushing my cheek. A sizzle of lust shot straight to my groin, but I positioned myself so she wouldn't see the slight plumping of my cock behind the fly of my jeans.

"I thought you might be able to test the waters with Hanson," she whispered, the tickle of her breath sending electricity along the nerves of my face and neck. Every part of me was aware of her. "I haven't had any luck figuring out if he's the detective your friend mentioned."

"I'll try," I replied quietly.

She drew back, smiling, but it didn't reach her eyes. "Thanks."

She took the drinks and shifted along the bar. She left Hanson's beer close enough to me that he and I would be able to chat when I wasn't serving people. Leaning against the counter, she gazed at the bottles behind the bar as if enthralled, probably assuming that Hanson would talk to me while she was distracted.

"Hey, Denny." I greeted her partner with a nod.

I understood why she wanted me to take a shot at him. While he'd been a dependable partner for Joanna, he had a few old school beliefs and might be more inclined to share with another man than with her.

"West." He eyed me warily. Interesting. I wondered what had brought that on.

"How's your day been?" I asked, glad when Dean, the other bartender scheduled tonight, passed behind me and began serving the line forming at the bar.

Hanson grunted. By now, I was adept at interpreting his non-vocal noises, and this wasn't a happy one.

"Any interesting cases?" I persisted.

Hanson gave me a look. "Not that I can tell you about."

"What about me?" Neal called from the other side of the line. "I'd like to know how the Sloane investigation is going."

Hanson leaned forward to look around someone and glared at Neal. "You know I can't share details."

"Not with people outside the department," Neal agreed, standing and shuffling through the queue to get to Hanson. "But surely, we can talk privately. Brainstorm. Share ideas. Maybe I'll be able to help since she lived in my usual patch."

"Piss off," Hanson snapped.

I raised my eyebrow, surprised. Hanson could be a grump, but he wasn't usually so blatantly rude. I glanced between the men, my internal antennae pinging at the hostility that vibrated between them.

A light touch brushed over the back of my hand, and I jolted, spinning to find Joanna beside me. She blinked up at me with her gorgeous, dark eyes, a hint of a smile on her lips.

"I'm going to play pool with Matthews," she said.

I kissed her cheek the same way she had mine earlier, taking advantage of the opportunity to breathe her in. She smelled faintly of coffee. Perhaps she'd spilled some on herself earlier, or maybe she'd just drunk a lot of it today.

"Have fun."

I watched as she sauntered around the bar and joined Officer Matthews at the pool table in front of the window. No matter how long I lived, I'd never get tired of looking at her.

Hanson snorted. "Pick up your jaw or you'll let the bugs in."

I closed my mouth and glanced at him. "You don't ogle your wife?"

One corner of his mouth tipped up slyly. "Every chance I get." Immediately, any sign of his smile vanished, and his expression became oddly intent. He leaned closer, beckoning for me to do the same. "I don't know what you have going on with that blonde, but Joanna is a damn fine woman, and you'd better not do anything to upset her again."

I swallowed around a lump in my throat, taken aback by the warning. I forced myself to laugh. "I didn't know you cared."

His eyes narrowed. "I may not go in for all the feeling crap, but the day I don't care about my partner is the day I ought to turn in my badge. Just know that I'm watching you."

I crossed my arms. "Don't worry. I don't have anything going on with anyone other than Jo."

"Uh-huh." He looked like he believed me about as much as I believed that Batman was real. "People make mistakes. It happens. But it better not happen twice."

"It won't." Obviously, the only way through this conversation was by being firm and redirecting. "Since we're having a heart to heart, what's up with you and Neal? You got something against him?"

Hanson grunted again. "Nothing like that. He just sticks his nose into places it has no right to be."

I cocked my head. "You don't like nosiness?"

"There's never a good reason for it." He looked left and right, then dropped his voice until it was barely audible. "I'm not stupid, Gallo. I know you're somehow involved in Sasha Sloane's death. Perhaps I wouldn't have put two and two together otherwise, but your wife isn't as sneaky as she thinks."

My stomach clenched, but I refused to let him see that he'd gotten to me. "I don't know what you mean."

"Don't try to play me, kid. I've been bullshitting since before you were born. Lee needed a private word with one of our witnesses, who described a man friend of Sloane's who looked a lot like you. Next thing I know, she's taking off, and when she comes back, it's with the news that our vic was a mob boss's girlfriend. I'm willing to bet you told her that."

I opened my mouth to scoff and make a joke about how he was pulling a bunch of random things together to make an image that didn't fit, but he cut me off.

"If you're going to spout more crap, then don't say anything. I'm letting you know where things stand. Somehow, you knew our victim. A beautiful exotic dancer. I don't know how, and I don't want to, but if there's anything you know that might help our investigation—things you aren't willing to share with your wife—you have my number."

"I got it." Even if I was a bit confused. First, he'd warned me not to upset Joanna, and now, I got the feeling he thought I was seeing strippers behind her back, but he was willing to hide it from her for the good of the investigation. What was I supposed to make of that?

"West, I need help," Dean called.

"Be there in a sec." I nodded to Hanson, who drained half his beer in one go. "We'll talk later."

I reported to Dean for instructions and poured drinks while he took orders and payment. As I worked, I mulled over Joanna's decision to tell Hanson about Sasha's relationship with Ortez. It was interesting that she'd shared that information with him but hadn't said where she'd learned it from, even if he'd put two and two together.

Did that mean she didn't trust Hanson? Or was she just trying to protect me as best she could without putting the investigation on hold?

When business died down, I looked around for Hanson, but he'd gone.

"What were you and Hanson talking about?" Neal asked. He'd resumed his position near the cash register and had been steadily downing beers. "He looked even angrier than usual."

"I think that's your effect on him," I teased, deflecting the question. "He didn't get all surly until after you started asking about his case."

Neal sneered. "It should be *my* case. It's my area."

I shrugged, hoping to make my interest seem casual. "Why do you care? Isn't it one less thing for you to do?"

"Because it's my patch," he growled, slurring slightly. "People know that I work the area. They expect to see me, and they know I like things done a certain way. Hanson and Lee will barge in and change things up, and then I'll have to train everyone to do it right all over again. No offense," he added, as if recalling at the last minute that Joanna was my wife.

I rested my elbows on the bar. "If you tell them your usual protocol, perhaps they'll follow it, and you can avoid the hassle."

I didn't believe his claims about why he was unhappy with losing the Sloane investigation, but I was curious to find out how committed he was to the lie.

"Nah." He shook his head. "Hanson is set in his ways, and can you really tell me you think Lee would be open to changing anything just because of my preferences?"

"She might surprise you."

He swirled the beer in his pint glass. "Is she always so straitlaced?"

I stiffened. "What do you mean?"

His face twisted into one of those expressions that said, "Come on, tell me everything. We're all boys here."

"I mean, someone that repressed, she must be kinky as hell in the sack, right?"

Fury knifed through me. If not for the fact that his tongue had tripped over itself so much he was clearly drunk, I might've hit him.

"I think you've had enough." I took his drink off him, my hands trembling with rage. I ached to wipe the smirk off his smarmy face.

*You can't beat up the people you're trying to get close to,* I told myself. *No matter what kind of dirtbag they are.*

"Maybe we're about to find out," Neal muttered.

"What?" My attention snapped to Joanna. Last I'd seen, she'd been playing pool with Matthews, a female officer she got along well with.

Now, she and Matthews were no longer alone. Detective Zachary De Luca was hovering behind Joanna as she bent over the table, his hungry stare locked on her ass. As I watched, he adjusted the position of her arm. His touch lingered for a little too long.

"Fucking De Luca." I pushed away from the bar and strode around it, my long legs eating up the space between me and Joanna. The bar's patrons wisely got out of my way when they saw me coming.

Joanna took her shot, knocking a purple ball into the pocket. She stepped back to study the table and determine her next shot. De Luca's lips moved, as if he were making a suggestion, and she nodded. She bent and hit the ball again, this time without him laying his hands on her. She missed.

"Your turn," she told Matthews.

I wrapped my arm around Joanna's waist, drawing her close, and glared at De Luca. "Thanks for keeping my wife company while I was busy, but I can take over now."

De Luca's grin was far too cocky as he backed away. I kept my gaze on him until he'd returned to his table, and then I grabbed Joanna's hand and tugged her toward the bar.

"I'm halfway through a game," she protested.

"We'll be back in a minute, Matthews," I called to her friend.

Matthews quirked an eyebrow. "I can't promise not to cheat while you're gone."

Joanna grumbled as I led her behind the bar and through the door to the Staff Only area. As soon as the door shut behind us, she snatched her hand away from me.

"What was that about?" I demanded, jerking my chin toward the bar.

She put her hands on her hips. "I could ask you the same thing. That was quite a temper tantrum."

"That was nothing," I bit out, seething inside at the memory of the casual way De Luca had touched her. Had he done so before? He flirted with her often enough, but she always shot him down. What was different now?

Was allowing the flirtation her way of getting back at me for lying to her? If so, it was damned effective. I wanted to tear the asshole's hand off if he ever laid it on her again. I

couldn't tell her that though. She was already having a difficult time reconciling my real identity with who she thought
I was. If I came on too strong, I'd scare her away.

"We need to be seen to be happy." I inhaled slowly to
steady my breathing. "That means no flirting with anyone
else."

Joanna raised her chin, uncowed. "I wasn't flirting."

"Maybe not," I allowed. "But De Luca was."

She marched closer to me and jabbed me in the chest
with her pointer finger. "You don't get to be upset about that.
You and I aren't even married."

**13**

—————

*JOANNA*

I glared at West, my finger pressed against the firm muscle of his chest, as I waited to see how he'd respond.

He held my gaze. "Not for a lack of wanting on my part."

My jaw dropped. "Excuse me?"

He pinched my finger between two of his and lowered it, then wrapped his hand around mine. I was so shocked, I didn't have the wherewithal to resist. "It's always killed me that I wasn't able to give you my real surname. There's nothing I want more than for you to be Joanna Conti."

I had no idea what to say to that.

"Besides." He clutched my hand more tightly. "If we were legally married, you wouldn't be able to get rid of me so easily. I'm obviously eager to wrap up this operation, but I also dread the day we do, because I know you'll walk out on me without looking back."

"What else am I supposed to do?" I asked softly, my insides tightening. I should snatch my hand away, but I couldn't bring myself to.

"Stay with me." His tone was pleading. "Let me prove to you how good we could be."

125

My eyebrows drew together. "How can I trust you when I'll always know that you only pursued me because of a job? We'd never have met if you hadn't set out to target me."

He looked pained. "Things changed, baby."

"Maybe so," I allowed. "But I'll always question the authenticity of every interaction we've had and wonder whether it was real or manufactured for the sake of your operation."

He tried to cup my face, but I scuttled back. His face fell, and I felt a twinge of guilt over my reaction.

"I've never lied about the way I feel about you." His hand inched toward me of its own volition, but then he noticed and dropped it to his side. "Perhaps our first meeting wasn't random, and we moved more quickly than we otherwise might, but our love is real."

Was, I wanted to say. It was real. Past tense.

But even I couldn't be that petty when he was already upset. I could, however, make it clear exactly what he was up against if he wanted to continue to insist that he loved me.

"Do you know how it feels that your team chose to target me for this op because I was easy pickings? A single, biracial female detective with an innocent belief in fairy-tale love?" Even if I was ever able to accept his claims of love at face value, that would always sting. "Don't worry. I'm not so naive anymore."

He winced. "I love your romantic heart, Jo. And I'm sorry. So sorry. I wish I could take everything back, but I can't. All I can do is keep telling you that I love you. Maybe I lied about my name and occupation, but you know who I am at my core."

I shook my head. "The man I thought I knew was kind. He'd never hurt anyone like this." My voice wavered. "Especially not me."

He exhaled sharply as the barb hit. "You're right. He wouldn't. There's no excuse for what I did. But perhaps… perhaps you'd be willing to listen to the reason why I've crossed so many lines for this investigation?"

I didn't really want to, but when he seemed so torn up about it, I couldn't say no.

"Fine. But not here."

He nodded and opened the door to Henry's office. I'd noticed Henry wasn't in the bar, and the office was empty, so he must not be working tonight. West closed the door. I waited for him to drag Henry's chair around the desk and sit before I sat too. Somehow, being seated while he was standing would feel too vulnerable.

He was quiet for a moment while he searched for words. "Do you remember when I said the investigation started because an off-duty cop who'd been working on the failed warehouse bust was shot?"

"Yes." I'd committed everything he'd told me to memory. I was too wary of the information falling into the wrong hands to write it down.

He leaned forward, resting his forearms on his thighs. "That cop was my father."

Sympathy lanced through me. "I'm so sorry."

If he'd lost his dad because of Ortez, it certainly explained why he would be so committed to this operation.

His lips pressed together, as if he were trying to get control of his emotions. "I was with him when it happened. He was shot by a sniper. I tried to save him, but it was a perfect shot to the center of his forehead. There was nothing I could do."

I scooted my chair closer and took his hand, my throat tight, my chest aching. "That must have been awful. I'm sorry you went through that."

He stared down at our joined hands, not speaking. I

didn't blame him. I couldn't imagine how I'd react if one of my parents was shot dead in front of me. I'd be distraught. The image of their cold, lifeless eyes would never leave my mind. It was a miracle that West could sleep at night.

His hand rested limply in mine. "Mamma was a mess. She was so grief-stricken, I doubt she would have gotten out of bed if not for me those first couple of weeks."

My tongue was thick in my mouth. Poor West. Not only devastated himself, but he'd had to be present enough to support his mother too.

None of this justified the way he'd used me, but as he'd said, it did go a long way toward explaining his actions.

"How is your mamma now?" I asked.

He'd told me both of his parents were dead. That was obviously only half true. He still had a mom out there some-where, and who knew when the last time they'd been in touch was?

"My handler tells me she's all right," West said reluc-tantly. "I've only spoken to her a couple of times since I went undercover."

My heart hurt for her. She lost her husband, and in a sense, she'd lost her son too, even though his undercover assignment was only temporary. Not to mention that she must fear he might meet the same end as his father, consid-ering he was investigating his father's killer.

Assuming she even knew. Perhaps he hadn't told her what his operation was.

"I wish I could meet her." I knew it was impossible. At least for now. If anyone suspected West of not being who he claimed to be, then I'd be leading them straight to his real identity the minute I got in touch with Mrs. Conti.

He smiled, although it was a little sad. "She'd like you."

I barely managed not to scoff. "Yeah, because a workaholic cop is exactly what every mom wants for their little boy."

His smile faded. "I'm serious. Mamma is big on loyalty and people who care. You've always been loyal and, no matter what you might think, you have a big heart."

I tore my eyes from his. I didn't know how to feel about any of this. It had been so much easier when I could hate him without knowing what was driving him. Now, being confronted with the fact he'd lost his father in one of the worst ways possible, it was difficult to maintain an emotional distance.

"Stop being so nice," I muttered. "You don't have to pretend your mamma would like me, or that you love me. It's not part of your job anymore, and it's confusing me."

He raised our hands and dropped a kiss on the inside of my wrist, butterfly soft. "You're right. It's not part of my job anymore. That's why you know I mean it when I say I love you. I'm going to keep saying it until you realize that."

"Please—"

I cut him off when he pressed another kiss to my wrist. The pulse there fluttered wildly.

"I love you." His lips moved against my skin, and he held my gaze, his green eyes searing into me with a silent promise. "I want you. And if De Luca flirts with you again, I'll bury him."

I lurched forward, closing the distance between us. Somehow, I ended up in his lap, and then we were kissing.

This was wrong. He was a professional liar. But his whispered promises didn't sound like lies. They didn't feel fake. Nor did the warning in his tone when he'd mentioned De Luca. And damn, it shouldn't turn me on when he threatened someone, but it did.

I was messed up. But only when it came to him.

His lips touched mine, confident but gentle, as if he were

giving me plenty of time to change my mind. I didn't want to. He tasted so good and felt so familiar against me, but if I let myself go on pretending, I'd only regret it later, and that would hurt us both. Much as I was angry at West, he'd lost enough.

I reluctantly extricated myself from him and stood back, panting. "I should go home."

His eyes flashed. "Do you have to?"

I met his gaze. "It's for the best."

One side of his mouth hitched up. "Damn, I hate that you're right."

His phone buzzed. He reached into his pocket and grabbed a phone—not the phone I'd always seen him with but a different one. Sleek, black, and obviously high tech. I raised an eyebrow. It seemed Sasha wasn't the only person who had two phones.

"Hello?" he answered, holding it beside his ear.

I started to move, but he gestured for me to stop.

"Hold on a minute." He lowered the phone and pushed the speaker button.

"I thought of something," a female voice said. It only took me a few seconds to place it. Portia.

"What is it?" West asked.

I kept my mouth shut. He hadn't told her he'd put the phone on speaker, and I'd rather not make her uncomfortable.

"Was a diary found in Sasha's apartment?"

West glanced at me, and I nodded.

"Yes, it was," he said.

"Well, I was thinking." Portia talked rapidly, her tone on the verge of frantic. "I write down notes about my clients every time I see someone, and I know Sasha did the same. It helps us to remember what they like and dislike, and to make their time with us more personal."

"But... Sasha wasn't an escort," West said.

"No, I know." Portia sounded impatient. "She did the same for repeat big spenders at the strip club, and it crossed my mind that she might keep notes every time she saw—you know, her big secret boyfriend."

I pointed to my lips and then the phone, and West nodded, giving me permission to speak. "Portia, this is Joanna. We haven't had a good look at the diary we found yet because it seemed very mundane. Perhaps she coded it somehow? Would you be able to come into the police station? With your help, we might be able to decode it."

"No." The reply was quick and firm. "I'll meet you tomorrow to have a look at it, but not there, and not if I have to talk to anyone other than you and West."

"Okay," I agreed. "Just us. I'll have to check the diary out of evidence first. What time suits you?"

"I'll send West the when and where."

The call cut off.

**14**

———

*JOANNA*

"Are you sure this isn't a setup?" I asked West as we walked to yet another coffee shop, this one in a marginally nicer area of town. Portia seemed to have a thing for holding clandestine meetings in coffee shops, and from what West had said, she didn't like to use the same one twice.

He scanned the area. "We can't be certain, but she's given me good information before, and I trust her as much as I would any other proven informant."

My lips twitched. "Which is to say, not with your life."

He chuckled. "Certainly not with yours."

I touched the gun inside my jacket. Setup or not, I'd come armed. To be fair, I very rarely went anywhere without a concealed weapon.

"What information has she given you in the past?" While he'd shared the broad brushstrokes of their investigation with me, I knew very few of the details.

West glanced at me. "Because of her, we've been able to conclusively connect two dirty cops to Ortez, and there are several more we suspect. We're just waiting for them to slip up."

"Who?" I didn't really expect him to tell me, but it would be nice to know that he trusted me.

He gave me a look. "You know I can't say."

My heart sank. I thought I'd resigned myself to the knowledge that West didn't fully trust me, but it would seem I'd been holding onto a thread of hope after all.

It was ridiculous. He was just being professional and doing things by the book. Hell, he'd already bent the rules by sharing what he had. In his shoes, I wasn't sure how much I'd be willing to blur the lines, so it wasn't fair of me to expect any different from him.

That didn't stop me from being disappointed.

I pushed the door to the coffee shop open and an electronic chime sounded. I scanned the interior, noting that Portia was once again in the farthest back corner. I wondered if she realized that choosing that position effectively trapped her. She probably felt safe, having her back to two walls, but if she needed to run, there was nowhere to go.

"I'll order coffee," West said. "You sit with her. She looks like she might try to bolt."

"Thanks." I made my way to her, taking in the rigid set of her muscles and the rapid tapping of her foot against the floor. She really was giving the impression she didn't want to be here. As I drew nearer, I noticed her eyes were even more red than yesterday. Had she slept at all?

"Were you followed?" she asked, her eyes darting toward the entrance.

"Not that I know of." I could usually pick out a tail, and I suspected West's radar for that kind of thing was even better than mine. "Are you okay?"

Portia huffed. Her hair hung around her shoulders, lank and greasy, as if she hadn't showered since she'd discovered her friend's body. That couldn't be good in her line of work.

"I'll be better when the bitch who killed Sasha is behind bars," she muttered.

I felt a pang of sympathy for her. I'd be a mess if anything happened to Hallie. It was no surprise she wasn't doing well. "Hopefully, you can help us make that happen."

West took the third chair and placed two cups of coffee on the table.

I reached into my bag and withdrew the sealed plastic evidence baggy that contained a photocopy of the most recent of Sasha Sloane's diaries. Portia stretched out her hand toward it, but I motioned for her to stop.

"Be careful not to lose any of it," I told her. "It wasn't easy to get my hands on a copy without leaving a trail."

Portia pulled a face, but nodded. She opened the baggy, withdrew the papers and started reading the one on top. "This is going to take forever."

West and I exchanged a glance.

"That's police work," I said. "Hardly anything happens as quickly as they make it seem on TV."

Portia leaned across the table and studied the words scrawled across the page. I'd flipped through the diary myself at the crime scene, and while we'd decided it was worth collecting as evidence in case it became useful later, I hadn't observed anything that stirred my interest. All she wrote about was what she wore, who she saw, and what she ate.

"So"—Portia picked at the edge of her cuticle but didn't take her eyes off the diary—"Sasha was crazy obsessive about recordkeeping, but she was also paranoid about people getting into her business. Although, with what happened to her, I guess she was right to be. But I'd forgotten until you mentioned it on the phone last night that she used a code."

"She did?" I'd known it was a possibility, but anyone

who read the utterly banal things Sasha had written would consider it unlikely. Perhaps that was the point.

"Yes." Portia nodded vigorously. "Certain foods were code names for people. Makeup items were codes for other objects. Like, lipsticks refer to drugs, and the different colors are different types."

"The places?" I asked.

She raised one shoulder and dropped it. "I'm not completely sure, but I think she did this thing where she'd name a place a block away from wherever she was actually talking about, or something like that. I can't remember all the details off the top of my head, but if we look through this together, I'm sure we can figure it out."

"Huh. That's quite clever."

She smirked. "I told you. Sasha was scary bright. The problem is, she wasn't quite as smart as she thought she was. Obviously. Or else she'd have known someone was going to come after her."

She looked despondent, so I opened my bag and grabbed a notebook and several pens. I couldn't get her friend back, but I could provide a distraction.

"Come on, then. Let's solve this puzzle."

We pored over the diary page by page, and after a while, patterns began to emerge. We went back to the first few pages and started to interpret Sasha's notes.

At first, it was relatively vague. References to drugs and people within Ortez's organization, although they were always referred to by foods, so we had no way to connect them to their real names. Later, the notes became more detailed.

I'd like to think that even without Portia here to assist, I'd have known something was off about the later pages in the book. The code was simple, but she seemed to have given up on trying to use it in a way that looked innocuous to anyone who didn't know what it meant.

"Look at this," I murmured, tracing my fingertip over the plastic-covered page. "I think she's outlining the method Ortez uses to get law enforcement personnel on his payroll."

West turned the book toward himself. "Let's see." He scanned the text, his eyebrow climbing his forehead. "If I'm reading this right, there's a cop who's paid to recruit others. This here is a reference to the Red Door. I think he takes them there."

Portia jabbed the page. "This is the brothel I work out of."

"Huh." I angled my head so I could read it too. "So, this cop took his colleagues to a strip club. If they passed whatever test he had for them, he took them to the brothel."

"And then they're told they can either use the brothel whenever they like and get payouts for brushing things under the carpet for Ortez, or they can lose their career—and potentially their marriage—if anyone sends in evidence that they've solicited sex from a prostitute," West finished excitedly. "Portia, are there cameras in the brothel?"

She shrugged. "Yeah. We're told they're for security, but come on. Who cares about the safety of a few sex workers? You're right. It's probably a blackmail thing."

I frowned. "We care about your safety." I reached into my pocket, withdrew one of my business cards and passed it to her. "If you ever get into trouble, call me. I know you probably won't, but just take it. Then you at least have the option."

To my surprise, she accepted the card and tucked it inside her shirt. "Thanks."

I returned my attention to the photocopied diary and flipped another page. If I focused on Portia, I'd make her uncomfortable. I was scanning the text when something leapt off the page at me.

I gasped. "Look! This is a name! An actual name, not a coded word."

West's eyes widened, and he leaned over to see what I was pointing out. "I know that guy." He glanced around. "Now that we can make progress ourselves, perhaps we should take this back to the police station. We don't want anyone to overhear us."

"You're right." I slid the papers into my bag. "Portia, just so you know, this could be what leads us to Sasha's killer."

Portia pursed her lips. "I hope so."

We left the coffee shop. West offered Portia a ride, but as I expected, she declined. She didn't want to risk anyone seeing her with us.

West and I got into the car, and I drove us toward the police station.

"Where do you want me to drop you off?" I asked.

"Uh..." He sounded confused. "I thought we could finish looking through her diary together."

"At the station?" I let incredulity enter my voice. "Wouldn't it look odd for my bartender husband to be helping me work a case?"

He huffed. "Fuck. I guess so. But I want to know what you find."

"If it relates to your operation, of course I'll share." If it didn't, I wasn't certain I would. So far, he knew more than me in almost every regard. It would be nice not to be the one in the dark for once.

I sensed him glance toward me, but he didn't protest my wording.

"Take me to the apartment. I'll make some calls," he said.

"All right." I stopped at a traffic light. "Tell me about Rodriguez."

His was the name we'd found in the diary, but neither of us had wanted to speak it in public.

"He's Ortez's enforcer. Thanks to a bunch of corrupt officials, he doesn't have a record, but he must have a body count well into the double digits."

"So, he's not a nice guy. First name?"

"Antonio," West replied. "He's in his late thirties. Maybe thirty-seven or thirty-eight. Reports directly to Ortez."

"Hmm." I pressed my lips together, my mind working quickly. "Do you think he could have been the one to kill Sasha? If anyone knew about her coded notes on the organization, she'd have been a liability."

West hummed in thought. "I doubt it. From what I understand, Rodriguez prefers to strangle his victims. It's less bloody, which means less mess to clean up. He's a big guy. Strong. He could easily overpower almost anyone. Besides, if anyone knew about her notes, surely, they would have taken them when they left."

"Or at least searched the apartment," I mused. "It was tidy. Nothing out of place."

We were back to square one. Plenty of people who may have reason to want Sasha Sloane dead, but no evidence tying any of them to the crime scene.

I pulled over outside our apartment building for West to get out. He leaned over, as if to kiss my cheek. I stiffened, and he immediately retreated.

"I'll see you later," I called, and pulled away as soon as he shut the door.

I parked in the underground parking area beneath the station and took the elevator to my floor. Instead of going to my desk, I shut myself in an interview room. I didn't want to talk to Hanson. Not when I still wasn't sure what—if any—role he played in all of this.

I withdrew my notebook and pored over the photocopied diary, recording everything that might be of interest. I paused at the end of each page to take a photograph of it. If I couldn't trust my fellow officers, then the diary might not be safe in the evidence locker and I wanted as many copies of it as I could.

I'd worked out that "bacon" was a general phrase Sasha used to refer to members of the police. Every time she wrote "bacon" in combination with another food, I made a note of it, and then recorded any subsequent mentions of that same combination, certain that she was referring to individual members of the police.

I was nearly two-thirds of the way through when I found mention of the story Portia had recounted about a homicide detective who'd been with one of Ortez's working girls. She labeled him "bacon and potatoes," and described how he went to the strip club and was then invited to the brothel.

According to the prostitute Sasha had spoken to, "bacon and potatoes" had had doubts as soon as he'd arrived, but he'd been liquored up—possibly high—and had gone through with it anyway.

As soon as they were done, he'd started spouting regrets, but one of the brothel's assigned guards had pulled him aside, had a quiet word with him, and he'd left as meek as a lamb.

There was no physical description of the man, and he was never mentioned by name. Could "bacon and potatoes" be Hanson? He doted on his wife, Deborah, so I could imagine him being upset by going behind her back with someone else.

That said, despite his occasional misogynistic tendencies, I had a hard time believing that he'd stray in the first place. He'd never had much patience for cheats.

I sighed. Dwelling on the possibility would get me nowhere. What I needed to do was go through police employment records and find all men who fit the description Portia had given within the city's homicide departments. Then I could work through them methodically.

But how was I supposed to do that without alerting Hanson?

He was my partner. I couldn't just run around doing my own thing all of the time. At some point, he was going to ask what I was hiding from him.

A knock came at the door.

I flinched, and my hand flew to my heart. I tucked both the photocopied diary and my notebook away in my bag, then drew in a slow, even breath, attempting to calm myself so that whoever was on the other side of the door wouldn't notice. I grabbed the handle and turned it.

Hanson stood on the other side, wearing a bemused expression. "What are you doing in there?"

# 15

*WEST*

I passed a glass of whiskey to an off-duty detective and glanced at the pub door as it swung open. Joanna entered, and my heart skipped a beat, but then fell. She was pale—almost pasty—and drawn. Had her case taken a turn? Perhaps she'd discovered something in Sasha's notes that had upset her.

She approached the bar, and I grabbed onto the edge of the wood, determined not to make her uncomfortable by reaching for her the way I wanted to.

"Can I get you a drink?" I asked her.

"Just water." Her eyes were blank, absent any of the emotions I often saw flickering through them.

I filled her glass and handed it to her. "Want to talk? Bartenders are good at listening."

She arched one elegant eyebrow. "Is that so?"

I shrugged. "At least, that's what I've heard."

She didn't smile, but the tension around her mouth eased, so I counted that as a win.

"Can't talk about it here," she murmured.

I looked around. Dean was making drinks, but there was

no line, so he should be all right on his own for a few minutes.

"Out the back," I said softly.

She nodded, gulped down her water, and pushed away from the bar. I met her at the end and led her through the Staff Only door and into Henry's office. She shut the door.

"What's up?" I asked.

She rubbed her temples. She looked so tired. I wished I could rub the knots out of her shoulders and make her feel better, but I wouldn't touch her unless she wanted me to, and she was giving no impression of that at the moment.

"I've gotten through almost all of the diary." She rested her ass on the edge of the desk and crossed her long legs at the ankles. "Including part that talks about the homicide detective, the one Portia mentioned."

"The one you thought could be Hanson?" I whistled. "What did it say?"

She scowled. "That's just it. There was nothing there that Portia hadn't already told us, except that whoever he is, he was drunk when it happened. I'd just finished reading that part when Hanson interrupted. Gave me the fright of my life."

I tensed. "He doesn't know, does he?"

"No." She shot me a look. "But I had to do some fast-talking to avoid answering his questions. I think he realizes that there's more going on here than he knows about. I'm sure he's going to start demanding answers soon."

"Shit. We need to come up with a reasonable explanation for why you'd be keeping things from him." I stuffed my hands into my pockets. Better they be there than where they really wanted to be. "Do you think there's a chance he might be involved? Perhaps it wasn't a coincidence that you guys got this case rather than Neal?"

The fact she didn't react negatively right away made me

wonder if she'd already been considering the possibility herself.

She nibbled on her lower lip, obviously conflicted. "If you'd have asked me a few days ago, I'd have said no. Hanson isn't the most sensitive guy around, but I would never have expected him to be dirty. Now... I'm not sure."

I moved closer to her so we could speak quietly. I doubted anyone was listening, but it was better to be safe than sorry. "If he is the detective Portia and Sasha mentioned, and he was drunk when he went to the brothel, it's possible he did something out of character. But by the time he'd sobered up, it was too late. Ortez would have had all the blackmail material he needed."

She grimaced. "I know, and I can imagine him going to the strip club and thinking it was harmless. He likes people seeing him as a real man's man. But the brothel... He must have known that would be different. Deborah would never forgive that."

"Which could be reason enough for him to work for Ortez," I pointed out, "to avoid her finding out."

She winced, and I felt like an asshole. It's not that I wanted Hanson to be dirty, but we had to seriously consider the possibility that he might be.

"Ugh." Joanna buried her face in her hands. "I don't know. Maybe."

"It's okay." I tried to make my tone soothing. "We can discuss it later, once you've had more time to think it over. Did he give you any reason to worry about going home alone tonight?"

She shook her head. "No. I'm pretty sure I threw him off the scent."

"Good. Then I want you to go home, drink a glass of wine, and read a book. We can talk more after my shift." I couldn't help but wish that I'd be able to arrive home and crawl into bed wrapped around her lean body like I used to, but I was well aware that wasn't an option, and I had no one to blame but myself.

She nodded, and I was a little surprised she didn't protest me giving her directions. Perhaps she had too much on her mind to worry about her traitorous husband bossing her around.

"I'd better get back to work." I held the office door open for her, and she preceded me down the hall and back into the pub.

Captain Thackery glanced up at us from a stool near the end of the bar. "West, will we be seeing you and Joanna at the police fundraising gala this weekend?"

"Fundraising gala?" I echoed, caught off guard.

Thackery snorted. "Of course. Joanna didn't mention it to you, did she?"

"You know that's not my scene, Captain," she complained, narrowing her eyes at me as if daring me to contradict her.

Unfortunately, I might have to. A police fundraising gala would be the perfect opportunity for me to get close to some of the key players in our investigation.

Specifically, I was interested in Detective Neal and his cronies. I hadn't shared my suspicions with Joanna, but I believed one of the names that regularly appeared in Sasha's diary—Ortez's police recruiter—may be none other than her overly territorial colleague.

His possessiveness over the area he considered his would make more sense if he was on Ortez's payroll. The Ortez mansion was positioned on the lakefront and was their suspected base of operations. Neal would be best poised to protect them if everyone knew to steer clear of his "territory."

"If you want a promotion, you'd best revise that opinion.

It's the perfect opportunity to mingle." Thackery smirked. "And for me to show off my best detective."

"We'll be there," I declared, loudly enough that there could be no doubt of Thackery hearing me.

He grinned. "Perfect."

Joanna glared daggers at me. I looked at her meaningfully. Her glare didn't lessen, but nor did she protest out loud. She wanted this investigation wrapped up as quickly as I did, even if our reasons for wanting it over with were completely different.

My heart squeezed at the idea of her leaving me without a backward glance. I couldn't allow that to happen.

"Nice to see you, Captain," Joanna said, tipping her head toward him. "I'm going home before my husband can sign me up for anything else."

She turned, her dark ponytail swishing down her back as she stalked away.

Thackery whistled. "You're in trouble."

"I know." For some reason, that excited me. Joanna's anger was better than her indifference.

I returned behind the bar and got busy serving patrons. Thackery left soon after, and I didn't see any more of Joanna's closer colleagues. As the evening was winding down, a pretty brunette approached.

She rested her forearms on the wood and leaned toward me, a smile quirking her lips. "Hey, handsome."

"Hello. What can I get you?" I didn't return the compliment. Not because she wasn't beautiful but because I refused to flirt with anyone who wasn't Joanna. Especially for a job that was really only a cover.

"How about your number?" she asked quietly, glancing left and right. Ah. Her previous confidence had been feigned.

I flashed my wedding ring at her. Whether or not our marriage was legal, it was real to me.

"Just my luck." She rocked back onto her heels. "I hope I didn't make you uncomfortable."

"Not at all. Can I get you a drink instead?"

She sighed. "I suppose a wine will have to do."

I fixed her drink and by then, another woman was waiting behind her.

The flow of customers slowed ten minutes later, and I closed up soon after. Dean locked the front on his way out, and I exited through the rear, making sure no one could get in before making my way to the car.

Inside, I flicked the locks and called Adam.

"I have some news," I said when he answered. I ran him through everything we'd found out from Portia and Sasha's diary as well as my suspicions about Detective Neal. Then, after a long hesitation, and with a healthy dose of guilt, I mentioned the possible connection to Joanna's partner. I didn't want to throw him under the bus, but if there was a possibility he was on Ortez's payroll, I had to say something.

"Is this Detective Hanson going to the fundraiser?" Adam asked thoughtfully.

"I don't know." I doubted it—Hanson seemed no more the sort to hobnob than Joanna was—but I couldn't rule it out.

"Find out, and if he is, I want you to keep an eye on him while you're there."

"I can do that." Surely, Joanna would know whether Hanson intended to be there.

"He's not the only one I want you keeping close to," Adam continued. "Detective Clancy Neal from Homicide was already on my shortlist of suspects in your district, as are Detectives Ireland and Hernandez from Narcotics, and Officers Greene and Warhol."

"I don't suppose there's a De Luca on your list?" I asked.

"No." Adam sounded confused. "Should there be?"

I sighed. "Probably not." But it would be good for my ego to be able to arrest that flirty fucker. "I doubt I'll be able to cozy up to all your suspects during the gala. I doubt the officers will even be in attendance. Who do you want me to focus on?"

"Neal and Hanson." There was no hesitation. "Neal is the top priority if there's even the slightest chance he's our recruiter, but Hanson's proximity to Joanna makes him a danger to your cover, so keep a close eye on him too."

"Got it."

We ended the call, and I gazed out through the windshield into the dark, lost in thought.

Then I frowned.

I could have sworn I'd seen movement in the shadows by the edge of the building, but no one should be here this late. I grabbed my sidearm, opened the door as quietly as possible, and darted toward the building, keeping low so I'd present a smaller target. Unfortunately, when I reached the wall, whoever had been there was gone.

A shiver rippled down my spine. I was confident they wouldn't have been able to hear my phone call from all the way over here, but the fact someone had been lurking at all made me nervous.

I returned to the car, double checking that the back seat and the trunk were empty before I got in.

I headed to our apartment building, parked, and took the stairs up. I checked the door and was glad to find it locked. I let myself in, then came to an abrupt halt. Joanna lay passed out on the sofa, only the glow of the silent TV screen illuminating her features. Her dark eyelashes cast shadows over her cheeks, and her lips were softly parted.

My gut clenched with an overwhelming sense of rightness. This was what I should find when I got home. I'd walked in on similar scenes many times over the past few months, and I'd always paused to appreciate how lovely she looked in sleep, but now I cherished the moment even more because it might be the last.

I couldn't count on her always being there for me to come home to. Unless I did something about it, she'd be gone soon. Sorrow clawed at my chest. I couldn't allow that to happen.

Joanna stirred in her sleep, her arm moving as if reaching for a blanket, but she didn't open her eyes. I waited for her to still and then slipped off my shoes and padded over to her. I touched the back of my fingers to her forehead. She was warm, but not as much as she ought to be.

I knelt and slid my arms beneath her back and her knees, then lifted her and held her against my chest. I carried her to the spare bedroom, even though my heart screamed at me to tuck her into our bed, where she belonged.

I reached for the door handle, but at that moment, she stiffened in my arms.

"What's going on?" she asked sleepily.

"Shh. I'm just taking you to bed."

But a crease formed between her eyebrows. "Put me down."

Heart sinking, I did as she said, lowering her feet to the floor and supporting her until she was steady. She walked to the bed on her own, crawled beneath the covers and pulled them up to her chin.

My throat constricted. Would she ever let me hold her

again, or was this the last time I'd feel her weight tucked safely against me, where I so badly wanted her to belong?

I turned and left, closing the door behind me. She had every right to stay away from me, and she deserved me respecting her enough to honor her wishes and keep my distance.

I brushed my teeth and dragged myself into the bed we used to share. It felt cold and empty without her. Hell, my whole life would soon be that way if I couldn't change things.

I rolled onto my side and closed my eyes. As I drifted off to sleep, my father's face flashed through my mind. Then, I could have sworn I heard a shot.

## 16



I held my wrist out to West. "Can you do up my bracelet please?"

I hadn't wanted to ask. It felt too intimate. But I'd been fiddling with the latch for several minutes and couldn't quite lock it into place.

"Of course." He shrugged his suit jacket on and moved closer. The spicy scent of his cologne went straight to my head, and I gritted my teeth. Why did he have to be so intoxicating? Couldn't they have sent one of the less tempting undercover operatives to marry me?

West took hold of my bracelet with one hand and used the other to do up the clasp. His fingertips brushed the sensitive skin on the inside of my wrist, and I suppressed a shiver.

He hardly ever touched me anymore. Not unless there was a good reason for it. I appreciated him respecting my boundaries, but it only made me more aware of how badly I craved contact between us.

"You look beautiful," he murmured.

I looked up at him from beneath my lashes. His gaze was

roaming over my body, his eyes the deep shade of green they turned when he liked what he saw. Despite my better judgment, I couldn't help but be pleased that he wasn't completely immune to me.

The body didn't lie. He couldn't fake something like that.

"You look good too," I replied, relieved by the detachment in my tone. I couldn't afford to have mixed feelings about West, and I especially couldn't afford for him to know about them.

I stepped away from him and gathered my jacket from where it lay over the back of the sofa. I probably wouldn't need it once we arrived, but I might want it for the drive over.

"Are you ready to go?" I asked.

West nodded. "You still want to drive rather than book a ride?"

"I think it'll be best that way." I'd drive, which left West free to drink whatever he needed while he made nice with his suspects. Meanwhile, I'd have an excuse not to drink too much—a legitimate one that even Captain Thackery couldn't tease me about.

I donned my jacket and checked that my wallet and phone were in my pocket and my weapon was in place in case I needed it. "Ready to go?"

West patted his pocket and then his hip, no doubt going through the same process I had. "Yeah."

We drove as close as we could to Allan Mansion, where the event was being held. We had to park a couple blocks away and walk the rest of the distance. I clutched my jacket closer around me, grateful I'd brought it because the wind was bitterly cold. At least it wasn't raining or snowing, I supposed.

As we reached the front of the mansion, its gray stone facade towering above us, I spotted Captain Thackery and his wife, Beth, strolling toward us. Thackery's shoulders were hunched against the cold, but Beth didn't seem to feel it. She beamed, her long, tanned legs bare from the knees down. I hated to think about how much cold air must be swirling beneath her skirt.

"Joanna, it's so good to see you," Beth exclaimed, greeting me with a hug. I liked Beth well enough, but I wasn't exactly a "huggy" person. I especially didn't feel comfortable hugging my boss's wife.

"Hi, Beth." I joined the end of the line, creating a few feet of space between us before she could go for a cheek kiss. "You look fantastic."

It was absolutely true. Beth was only a couple of years older than me, which made her a decade younger than Thackery. She took excellent care of herself and had a killer sense of style. Her dress clung to her figure so tightly, it was almost scandalous, yet everything from her neck to her knees was covered.

Beth turned to West as the Captain and I exchanged pleasantries.

"I don't think we've met." She offered him her hand. "I'm Beth Thackery. This stick-in-the-mud is my husband."

"Nice to meet you." West shook her hand. "I'm West Gallo, Joanna's husband."

I eyeballed him, but he didn't look the slightest bit sorry for spreading that lie to yet another person. I got the feeling he'd have "Joanna's Husband" printed on a label and stuck to his suit if he thought I'd allow it. Why did that make me so warm and fuzzy inside?

Thackery nudged my arm, and I realized the line was moving. I hurried to keep up. We reached the entrance, where a dapper man in a tuxedo was checking names against a guest list on his tablet. I gave him ours and waited for him to wave us through.

The ceiling arched high above us as we crossed through the foyer, where I removed my jacket, and went on through to the ballroom. Half of the ballroom was carpeted, and half had a wooden floor. Beautifully carved wooden stands were positioned around the room, with trays of wine and accompanying glasses atop each.

Perhaps thirty or forty people stood in groups, making small talk. Classical music played in the background.

"I'd like to introduce you to one of our donors," Thackery murmured.

I nodded. "Lead the way."

West took my arm and kept pace with me as Thackery and Beth made a beeline for an elegant older gentleman standing with two women on the opposite side of the room. As we drew near, I couldn't help noticing there was something familiar about the man. His thick, gray hair and upright bearing pinged a memory, but I couldn't quite put my finger on it.

"Antony," Thackery called as we drew nearer to the group. "How are you this evening?"

The gentleman, Antony, smiled in welcome. "Very well, thank you, Captain. And yourself?"

Thackery grinned. "Tonight, I'll drink expensive wine and mingle with people I like. What's not to enjoy?"

Antony smirked. I had the feeling he knew that Thackery was talking out of his ass in an attempt to butter him up, and he found the situation amusing.

Antony clasped Beth's hand between both of his. "I hope you won't be too bored while your husband is busy entertaining."

Beth flashed pearly white teeth at him. "Don't you worry, Tony. I don't need him to have a good time."

Antony winked.

Beth gestured toward me. "This is Gordon's colleague,

Detective Joanna Lee. Joanna works in the Homicide department."

He inclined his head. "Charmed. I've heard your name. Ronan King speaks highly of you."

A light bulb went off in my mind.

"You're one of the shareholders of King's Security," I said. "Antony Marcelli. I knew you looked familiar."

He seemed pleased to be recognized. "I'm only a minor shareholder, overall. I have many business interests, and I prefer not to get personally involved with many of them."

"Understandable." I took West's hand, my heart skipping as his strong fingers wrapped around mine. "This is my… husband. West Gallo."

The falsehood tasted sour, and I had to hope no one had noticed my brief hesitation.

West and Marcelli greeted each other politely.

"Have you met Ronan's wife?" Marcelli asked. "If not, I'd love to introduce you."

I grimaced. "I have." I sensed West look at me curiously. I'd never explained my first meeting with Willow to him. "I'm afraid I didn't give her the best first impression, but she seems to have forgiven me."

I'd been more than a little blunt when questioning Willow, but sometimes, we couldn't allow ourselves to be swayed into treating people with kid gloves in my line of work.

"You were just doing your job," Thackery said, waving his hand dismissively.

Now Beth was intrigued too. Her teeth embedded into her lower lip as she glanced back and forth between us.

"Willow is here tonight?" I asked, eager to move the conversation on.

"She is." Marcelli smiled. "She and Ronan came together. I wasn't sure about him at first, but now all it takes is a few seconds in their company to see that he dotes on her."

I cocked my head. "You knew Willow before Ronan?"

"I was close friends with her father." A trace of sadness lingered in his voice.

"I've heard good things about him," I said honestly.

"He was a character. Not perfect, by any means, but he tried." Marcelli's brow furrowed. "Anyway, I haven't introduced you to my companions. How rude of me. These ladies are my protégées, Maeve and Sian MacDougall."

We exchanged another round of greetings and chatted for a few minutes.

"Well, it's been great catching up," Thackery said, his attention focused somewhere over Sian's shoulder. "I'd better circulate though."

"I'm sure we'll talk later." Marcelli turned back to the McDougall sisters, effectively dismissing us.

"Feel free to talk to whoever you like," Thackery said as we moved away from them. "I expect at least another two hours out of you though. No bailing early."

I raised my eyebrows. "I'm under the impression I'm not being paid to be here, so can you really require that?"

He raised his eyebrow in return. "You're a smart woman. Don't play dumb."

He took Beth's hand and led her away. She rolled her eyes behind his back, and I hid a smile.

"What now?" I asked West, glancing around to make sure no one was listening. After all, he was the one who'd wanted to be here. He could take the lead.

He scanned the room. "Why don't you go visit with Ronan and Willow while I try to make inroads with Neal and his crew? Is Hanson here?"

I scoffed. "No. Unless he had strict instructions to be present, there's no way he'd turn up."

"Good. That means I can spend more time with Neal."

"Why can't I come with you?" I asked, sounding more petulant than I'd have liked.

He chuckled. "Because you have a reputation for being a straight arrow. If you're there, he won't speak as freely as he might with only me."

"Fine." I huffed, but I knew he was right. "I'll go chat then."

He kissed my cheek, and I tried to ignore the heat that shot through me in response. "Watch your back."

He headed toward Neal, who we'd spotted earlier, cloistered in a corner with his partner, Detective Sewell, and Detective Liam Ireland from Narcotics. I was surprised Neal hadn't cornered any of the wealthy patrons in the hopes of talking himself up for a promotion, but perhaps he'd already been warned not to.

I scanned the room until my gaze landed on a pair of familiar faces: Ronan stood with a degree of alertness that would have made me think he'd been in the military if I didn't know better.

Willow was tucked against his side, her pale blond hair spilling down her back in loose curls. A braid formed a circlet around her forehead, with jeweled hair pins sparkling in the light. Knowing Ronan, they were probably real diamonds. He wasn't an ostentatious man, but he showered Willow with every material thing she could possibly want—even when she didn't ask for any of it.

Willow noticed Ronan looking toward me and followed his gaze. When her eyes met mine, her mouth formed a small *O* of surprise, and then the side of her mouth curled up.

"Hi." I stopped in front of them. "I didn't realize you two would be here."

I should have, of course. Ronan had done a lot for the

police department. No doubt that was one of the reasons he never got into trouble for stretching a few rules.

Willow sighed. "Fundraisers aren't my favorite, but they kind of go hand-in-hand with marrying the boss."

"I'm pleased you're here," Ronan added, his dark eyes crinkling at the corners. "I didn't expect it either."

I pulled a face. "It wouldn't be my first choice, but Thackery asked, and West has some people he needs to talk to, so..." I trailed off, realizing I probably shouldn't have mentioned West.

"Oh, yeah." Ronan looked thoughtful. "Zeke mentioned that. Don't worry. We won't give him away."

Willow's eyes narrowed. "You deserve better. That's all I'll say, but I hope you know it."

My heart warmed. "Thank you."

Her nose scrunched and her eyes twinkled mischievously. "Should we take a walk around the room? Maybe we can listen in?"

My lips twitched. "We shouldn't."

"But it would be fun," she whispered.

I grinned, a weight lifting off my chest. Willow King had a way of making everything feel better. "It would."

"Behave yourselves," Ronan warned, lifting a glass of wine from a waiter's tray as they walked past.

"We will," Willow assured him as she disentangled herself from his hold and linked her arm with mine. "Let's go."

We circled around a group of people from the police department's upper echelon and slowly made our way toward Neal, Sewell, Ireland, and West.

"I know it probably doesn't help, but West fooled us all," Willow murmured, ducking her head close to mine. "I only met him a couple of times, but I was certain he adored you."

"He's a good actor." I refused to think more of it than that.

Willow hesitated. "Zeke said West's feelings might be real."

I peeked at her out of the corner of my eye. "Zeke can't keep his nose out of anything."

She tilted her head in acknowledgement. "Do you think he might have a point?"

I sighed. I wanted to believe it, although I wouldn't examine my reasons for that too closely.

"I don't know." I met West's eyes as we passed them by. Warmth danced in their depths, and it unsettled something inside me.

We'd barely passed them when Neal made a crack about Willow. I didn't hear everything he said, but the words "rich bitch" were unmistakable. I stiffened, and started to turn around, ready to tear into him, but Willow dragged me away.

"Don't," she hissed.

"But he—"

"I know." She tutted the same way she might at a dog that had crapped in the corner. "But if West needs to get close to them, then you calling them on their poor behavior won't help."

I growled under my breath. "How do you stay so calm when people say things like that right in front of you?"

Willow gave a slight shrug. "Entitled, arrogant men have always been part of my life. My brother mingled with an unpleasant crowd, and if I said anything to them about being inappropriate, he'd have been furious at me, so I suppose I learned to bury my feelings in public."

I frowned. "Ronan doesn't expect you to do that, does he?"

I rolled my eyes. They were being ridiculous. I appreciated Thackery's concern, but a fundraiser really wasn't the place for this conversation.

"Why don't we see what items are up for auction?" I suggested.

The organizer had arranged a silent auction with the proceeds going toward funding for another community liaison officer to work with troubled teens.

"Sounds good." West stretched his hand toward me.

I stared at it for a long moment, then took it. "It was nice talking to you, Thackery. Don't worry about that problem you mentioned. I'm on top of it."

"I hope so," he murmured as we walked away.

"Are you all right?" West asked, placing his palm on my back to guide me to the tables where the silent auction had been set up in the corner. "That looked intense."

I side-eyed him. "Apparently, someone is spreading rumors about you cheating on me."

He grimaced. "Ah."

"Any idea how that might have happened?" I asked.

"I don't suppose Hanson would have...?"

"No." I shook my head. "He's not one to gossip about someone's private life."

"Then I'm not sure. I'm sorry you have to deal with it though." His hand dropped from my back and then he laced his fingers with mine. "I'm sorry. Full stop. I realize this must be difficult for you. Unfortunately, them thinking I'm a cheat is better than them knowing the truth."

"I know." That didn't mean I liked the idea of being some kind of office joke. The naive woman who rushed into marriage with a man who strayed after only a few months. "Did you make any progress with Neal?"

"I did." He brightened. "He runs a weekly poker night, and he's invited me to the next one."

"That's great. Hopefully after a few drinks, he'll relax and say something he shouldn't."

We strolled along the table. I paused to study a painting that had been donated to the cause. It was a silhouette of the city's skyline from a viewpoint somewhere along the lake. Beautiful.

A fuzzy tap came through the speakers, and we all turned to the front of the ballroom. The police commissioner stood on a raised wooden platform, decked out in a black and white suit with a startlingly gold tie.

"Welcome, guests, to our annual Chicago PD Fundraiser Event." He continued to speak, sharing a few details about what the money raised tonight would be used for and then invited one of the larger donors to give a speech.

Almost an hour later, after listening to far too much semipolitical propaganda, the commissioner reclaimed the microphone to announce that a string quartet would be playing for anyone who wanted to dance and that the silent auction was now officially open.

"You'd better get back to your new friends," I murmured to West as the commissioner left the platform.

He smiled down at me. "I think I can spare the time to dance with my wife."

He led me to the uncarpeted portion of the room that was serving as a dance floor. Only two other couples were dancing as the string quartet began to play a waltz. West gathered me close to him and we swayed gracefully to the music.

My chest squeezed. I'd always loved dancing with him. We hadn't done enough of it during our marriage, and now it was too late. No matter how wonderful it felt to spin in his arms, it wasn't real, and I couldn't forget that.

"You're such a lovely dancer." West's breath tickled the shell of my ear as he dipped his head closer.

"So are you."

We moved together, sparks zapping along my nerves everywhere our bodies touched.

"Jo, I—"

Crack!

My eyes flew to his. "Was that a gunshot?"

# 17

*WEST*

I drew my handgun and raised it, pivoting to see where the shot had come from. All around the room, police officers had drawn their weapons and were doing the same. Including Joanna. I blinked at her, wondering where the hell she'd hidden a handgun under such a slinky dress.

That should not be as hot as it was.

A woman screamed. I spun toward the sound. Cops had already surrounded a distraught waitress, who was bent over a prone body on the floor.

Without making a conscious decision to move, I found myself hurrying across the room too. The instant I laid eyes on the body, my heart sank.

Detective Clancy Neal.

He'd been shot through the center of his forehead. His eyes were already glazing over. There was no saving him. He was gone.

I swallowed against my instinctive horror at the brutal display and scanned the room, briefly noting Joanna behind me. No one seemed to know where the shot had come from. Considering how difficult it would be to shoot someone in a crowded event like this without being seen, I had to assume that it had likely been a long-range shooter.

Checking the windows one by one, it didn't take long for me to find the damaged one, set high on the wall facing the street.

This had been a sniper.

A shudder rippled through me. A sniper. Just like the man who'd killed Dad.

What were the odds this was a coincidence? Adam and I were almost completely certain that Neal was involved in Ortez's dirty dealings. If Ortez had ordered the hit on my dad, could he have also gotten one of his men to take out Neal?

Perhaps he knew we were onto him. Neal had been the type to flaunt his ill-gotten gains, and that could have gotten Ortez's hackles up.

I pointed out the hole to Joanna. "Look. The shooter was probably situated on top of a nearby building. We should have a response team lock down all buildings within the perimeter."

She nodded. "Got it." She raised her voice. "Shot fired through the window. Possibly from the roof of another building, or from an apartment inside one of the surrounding buildings. I want the entrances and exits of the mansion sealed, and for at least two officers to report to each building adjoining this one. No one comes in or out. Has anyone called for backup?"

"Yes, ma'am," a younger officer replied. "A tactical unit is on the way, and so is an ambulance."

"Good work, Officer Barrie."

When everyone just stood there, she clapped. "Go."

I grinned and relaxed my stance. God, she was sexy when she took charge.

"You," she muttered to me, "put the gun away before

people start asking why a bartender is carrying a concealed weapon."

I winced and immediately returned the weapon to its holster. She had a point.

"All right, everyone, step back." Captain Thackery appeared beside us. Last I'd seen, he'd been consoling a distressed older woman, but he must have left her in Beth's care. He bent over Neal, his lips in a grim line. "This was a hit."

"Yes, sir," Joanna said. "I would say so, considering this is a perfect kill shot and only one shot was fired. If someone had wanted to cause chaos or ruin the event, surely they'd have taken a different approach."

Thackery's cheeks had a waxy pallor. Surprising, considering how many crime scenes he must have attended in the past—many much bloodier than this.

"It would have been easier to kill him somewhere else." He looked Joanna directly in the eye. "The fact they did it here meant that whoever it was, they were trying to send a message."

My hand twitched, itching to grab my phone. Because Thackery was right. If this was a hit orchestrated by Ortez, it would have made more sense for him to send Rodriguez in to quietly take care of him. Unless he was trying to show the other cops on his payroll what might happen if they got careless.

My assignment may have just become a lot more difficult.

"You're right," Joanna agreed, her gaze quickly flicking to me. "But we can figure that out later, for now we need to secure the scene."

"It's all yours." Thackery raised his voice so everyone still around could hear. "Detective Lee is in charge of the crime scene. No one may leave until she, or one of her officers, has taken your details so we can get in touch for a statement. If you think you saw anything useful, please stay and you'll be interviewed tonight."

A chorus of protests rang out, but they were rapidly silenced as the police commissioner spoke over the microphone, reminding everyone that they were here to support the Chicago Police Department, and right now, that meant being patient and providing whatever information they could.

The ballroom doors opened, and several uniformed officers spilled inside. Joanna jogged up to the police commissioner and held out her hand for the microphone. She ordered the new officers to search the building and to ensure that any doors in or out had been sealed as she'd requested earlier.

"Perhaps you should get a copy of the guest list," I said to Thackery, voice low. "You know, to double check that no one snuck out."

He nodded. "I'll speak to the organizer now."

Joanna passed the microphone back to the police commissioner and jumped down from the stage. I met her at the base.

"What can I do?" I asked. "I want to help."

She pursed her lips, her eyes darting around the room, obviously distracted. "If you want your cover to remain in place, you'll need to lay low. See what information you can get from the other guests."

"All right." I was disappointed not to be able to participate more actively, but she was right; allowing me to join the search or interview others would raise too many questions.

I spotted Detectives Sewell and Ireland lingering a few yards behind the body. Both were pale, although they didn't seem as shell-shocked as the guests who weren't part of law enforcement.

I made my way over to them. "Can you believe this? I was talking to him just a short while ago."

"It's crazy." Sewell sounded numb. "I was standing right beside him."

"Shit, man. That must have been terrifying."

Sewell shook his head. "You'd think so, but it happened so quickly. One minute we were chatting, the next he was on the ground, and it was over. I didn't even have time to be scared."

I shifted closer. "You didn't see it coming?"

"No." He stared blankly at Neal's body, which had yet to be covered. "I didn't even know where the shot came from until Lee mentioned the window."

Damn. No useful eyewitness testimony here.

"How are you doing?" I asked Ireland. "Were you beside him too?"

The detective scowled at me. "How do you think I am? My friend was just shot dead and there was nothing I could do about it."

I nodded. "Sorry. Stupid question. Is there any way I can help?"

Ireland huffed. "Just back off. I know you're trying, but stop."

Double damn.

"Okay. All right. You know where I am if you need me." I backed away, trying and failing to catch Sewell's eyes.

Looking around, I noticed Ronan and Willow King nearby. I joined them, my hands in my pockets.

"Did either of you see anything?" I asked.

"No." Ronan spoke firmly. "I noticed the bullet hole in the window about the same time you did, but I didn't see anyone out there. My guess is that a long-range rifle was used. Considering the accuracy, possibly by a military or law enforcement trained sniper."

"I'd have to agree." Restlessness curled within me. I wanted to be out, hunting this sniper down. If he was the one who'd killed my father, then I needed to punish him.

Willow bit her lip. "Do you think this has anything to do with... you know?"

I narrowed my eyes. "You know."

It was a statement rather than a question, but Ronan nodded anyway.

"Zeke doesn't keep secrets from Kade and I," he said. "But don't worry, no one else knows."

Willow waggled her hand back and forth. "Well, Fiona and Sage do. But beyond that."

"Christ." I dragged my palm down my face. "I'm so compromised."

"We'll protect your secret," Ronan said. "Now, go and talk to people who might actually be helpful."

With a sigh, I left them and joined another group. Then another. But no matter who I approached, it seemed no one had seen anything. Not a soul present had any inkling that anything was wrong until Neal dropped dead.

I even hovered beside a group of the venue's staff, and they seemed as lost as everyone else.

I looked around for Joanna and found her near the entrance, speaking with the venue manager. I strode over, waiting until they'd finished talking before going to her side.

I cupped her elbow and guided her away from the throng. "You should get the ballistics tech to compare the bullet used tonight to the one that killed my father."

Her expression softened. "You think it might be the same shooter?"

"My gut says yes," I admitted.

She hugged me, and I was so taken aback that I stiffened. By the time I'd regained enough self-awareness to return the embrace, she was already releasing me.

"I'll make sure they run the tests," she said. "Do you think you could check on Beth? Thackery has gone into work mode, and I'm not sure he's thought about the fact that she hasn't witnessed anything like this before."

"Sure."

I searched the room. Beth was standing with one of Marcelli's protégées. Sian, perhaps. I cut a line directly for her, grabbing a glass of wine on the way.

As I arrived in front of her, I offered her the glass. "Need this?"

She made a sound that was somewhere between a sob and a laugh. "That's perfect. Thank you." She took the wine and gulped it down so quickly that both Sian and I stared at her, wide-eyed. When she noticed, she flushed. "If witnessing a murder doesn't entitle me to drown my sorrows, then I don't know what does."

"Fair enough," I said.

"Good point." Sian looked around. "I might grab one too."

She hustled away, leaving me and Beth alone.

"How are you holding up?" I asked.

She heaved a sigh. "I've been much, much better, but at least I didn't know the guy. Gordon never introduced me to him. It's just... this whole thing is a lot."

"I get it." I could easily remember how shaken I'd been the first time I'd seen someone killed. The man had taken several people hostage and been shot as he'd tried to escape, using a child as a human shield. Perhaps the shooting was justified, but that didn't stop the moment he'd hit the ground from replaying in my mind on a loop.

Not that I could share my experience with Beth. As far as

she knew, I was just Joanna's husband, not a law enforcement officer in my own right.

"I just..." She shook her head. "This is supposed to be a fundraiser. Drinks, pretty dresses, good music. Not... this. It's so strange how he's just snuffed from existence. Did you know Gordon plays poker with him most weeks? It's part of his regular routine. But now, they won't ever do that again."

My gut clenched. I hadn't realized yet that I'd lost the ground I'd been working on all night. No Neal meant no poker night with his crooked friends.

Not to mention the fact Beth's casual comment had just raised a whole lot more questions. Neal had claimed his poker night was only for his non-cop friends and the guys on the force who "thought like him." If Gordon Thackery attended, did that mean he was dirty too?

## 18

*JOANNA*

"I've got the ballistic comparison you requested."

I glanced up from my computer. Hanson stood in front of me, a printed sheet of paper clasped in his hands. He rocked onto his heels, squinting as if he were trying to use x-ray vision to look inside my head.

"Thanks." I checked the room, but we were the only ones here. Good. I didn't want anyone to overhear this conversation. "Is it a match?"

Hanson didn't answer. Nor did he pass me the paper. When I reached for it, he stepped back.

"Why did you want this comparison carried out?" he asked, still studying me with those narrowed eyes. "What case do you think Neal's death might be related to? You were very vague earlier."

"Just another sniper murder." I forced myself to hold his gaze without flinching. Lying wasn't my forte, but technically, I'd told the truth, so I just had to hope he wouldn't push.

"Really?" He harrumphed. "Because when I tried to access the case file referenced in the paperwork, I was denied. The case is restricted. Only specific personnel know about it, and it would seem even fewer have access to the details. So how did you find out?"

My pulse picked up. "I must have heard about it from someone around the office. It was a similar shooting. A single bullet fired by a long-range sniper, with the shot hitting center forehead. The vic was law enforcement, same as Neal."

Hanson crossed his arms, creasing the paper as he did. "Who?"

I pulled a face. "I can't tell you."

He scowled. "Can't or won't?"

"A bit of both," I offered sheepishly. "I've told you all I'm able to."

"For fuck's sake, Lee." Hanson stomped to his chair and dropped onto it. I was surprised when it didn't give way beneath him. He wasn't exactly a lightweight. "We're supposed to be partners. That means we share information. You're keeping things from me, and it makes it damn hard to trust you."

Funny that he was having difficulty trusting me when the reason I was keeping secrets from him was because I wasn't sure if I could trust him. I gazed over at him, torn. We were partners. We should be sharing information. But until I was one hundred percent certain of his innocence, I couldn't risk him uncovering West's real identity.

"Is it a match?" I asked, repeating my earlier question.

He balled up the paper and tossed it at me. I caught it and smoothed the paper out on my desk.

"It is," I whispered.

The same gun had killed both Detective Neal and West's dad. Most likely, that meant the same shooter had too. But why?

If the shooter had been hired by Ortez, I understood

taking out a cop who was investigating him. But if West was right and Neal had been on his payroll, there would have been no reason to kill him.

Unless he was no longer useful.

Perhaps Neal had had a crisis of conscience. Or, more likely, had run his mouth to the wrong person.

"I need to know what the connection between the cases is." Hanson sounded tired, and I felt a pang of regret at causing him any distress. He might not be the partner I'd have chosen for myself, but he'd always had my back. "You can't keep it to yourself when it's vital to cracking the case."

I sighed. I was going to have to give him something, or this could cause an irreparable rift between us. "I don't know the shooter's identity, but it's likely they're involved in organized crime."

Hanson wheeled his chair around the desks until only a few yards separated us and then stretched his legs out. "Do you think it could be connected to the Sloane murder too?"

I nodded slowly. "It's possible."

"Sasha Sloane was supposedly Carlos Ortez's mistress." Hanson folded his hands on his lap. "Neal should have been the detective assigned to the case. If not for him being sick the day the body was discovered, he would have been. Perhaps this is an attempt to shut down the investigation."

"Worth looking into," I agreed.

It wasn't the worst hypothesis. It's possible the cases were connected, although not necessarily for the reason Hanson suggested. I'd go with it because allowing Hanson to operate under this assumption might allow us to get on with the investigation without too many further questions.

"I'll see if there are any black market mercenaries known to be affiliated with Ortez's operation," Hanson said, looking pleased to have a course of action.

"I need to make a phone call," I told him. "I'll be back in a moment."

"Wait." He reached for me, but then dropped his arm.

I frowned. "What?"

"Before you do, I need to speak to you about something else. Privately."

A cold finger trailed down my spine.

Oh, God. Did he have some kind of confession to make? Because if so, I wasn't sure I wanted to hear it.

But no. Surely if he did, this entire conversation would have gone differently.

Hanson stood, dragged his chair back around behind his desk, and collected another couple of sheets of paper with printed text on them from beneath his screen. "Come with me."

"We're alone in here," I pointed out.

He shook his head. "Trust me. This needs to happen in a private room."

A thread of dread unspooled in my gut as I got to my feet and followed him to an interview room. He didn't sit, so I remained standing too. After a brief hesitation, he handed me the papers. On the top was a printout of West's under-cover driver's license and passport. I flipped to the next page. His name was at the top of the document.

"What's this?" I asked, afraid to know the answer.

Hanson drew in a deep breath and then slumped. "Your husband isn't who you think he is."

Oh, shit.

The bottom dropped out of my stomach.

I struggled to keep a neutral expression. "What do you mean?"

He couldn't know, could he? There's no way he could have figured it out. Not with another agency using all their tools to hide West's trail.

His eyebrows pinched together. "Something about him is off. First, we saw him with that other woman, and then at the fundraiser, he pulled a gun. Don't bother denying it. I saw it myself on the security footage."

"Plenty of people carry concealed." It was weak, but the best I could do.

"Maybe," he allowed. "But most people don't have gaps in their ID."

I clasped my hands together behind my back so he wouldn't see them shake. "Excuse me?"

He nodded. "It's a convincing fake, but it's just that: fake. Westley Gallo isn't real. I don't know who the hell you married, but he's hiding things from you." His expression became even grimmer. "It gets worse."

My head was spinning, and his voice was beginning to sound muffled. I was dissociating. I dug my fingernails into my palms and forced myself to focus on the present. The interview room smelled faintly of cigarettes and antiseptic. The floor was solid beneath my feet, the air cool. A metallic taste filled my mouth. I'd bit the inside of my cheek.

"How can it get worse?" I asked, feeling strangely distant from the situation, even though Hanson was less than two meters from me.

Hanson laid his hand on my arm. Warmth soaked through the fabric of my shirt. "Are you okay?"

"Fine." I shook myself. I was a professional, damn it. I would not fall apart just because West's tower of lies was crumbling. "You were saying?"

He gave my arm a slight squeeze. "West has been in contact with known associates of the Ortez crime syndicate. If you need proof, I have it. Joanna, I need you to consider this carefully. Is there any chance that your husband could be using you to help Ortez stay ahead of the law?"

"No." The denial escaped before I could think through

whether it was the right course of action. Perhaps it was better for Hanson to think West worked for Ortez than for him to know he was investigating the police force itself. "I mean, I don't understand. How could you possibly know that West has been associating with criminals?"

Hanson's cheeks turned splotchy and red, and he scratched the back of his head. "I've, uh, been surveilling him on and off since you said you were working things out. I didn't want him messing around on you."

My heart swelled. I'd never have expected him to care about me so much. "Thank you. That's very sweet."

I just hoped he hadn't seen me and West speaking with Portia.

"Yeah. Well." He cleared his throat. "You're my partner."

"That means a lot, Denny."

The blush deepened. "You don't seem as upset as I thought you'd be."

I stayed quiet for a moment, debating how much to share with him. He'd already put a lot of it together himself, and while I was on the fence about his involvement with Ortez, the fact he'd come to me with this rather than using it against West went a long way toward assuring me of his innocence.

"Damn." Hanson stilled. "Did you know all of this already? Are you in on it with him?"

My breathing stuttered. He thought I was the dirty cop? Incredible.

"No," I told him. "I'm not. But West isn't who you think he is either. Yes, he lied about his identity, and I didn't know that when we met, but I do now. I just can't tell you the details."

He looked confused. "The guy pretended to be someone he's not and you stayed married to him?"

I groaned. Of course he'd question that. My low tolerance for deception was well known. "I left for a couple of nights to get some perspective, but once I had all of the information, things changed."

His jaw jutted out, bulldog-like. "But you won't tell me what's going on?"

"Not won't," I corrected. "Can't. I'm sorry."

His nostrils flared, but he managed to keep his temper in check. Considering how he'd gone out on a limb for me and in return, I was keeping him in the dark, I was impressed by his self-control.

"Just be careful," he warned. "Maybe you think you know what he's up to, but you can't be certain you aren't being played."

I didn't reply to that because honestly, however much I might believe West's claims, Hanson had a point. The only other person I'd dealt with directly who was associated with West's cover was Portia, and she had all sorts of reasons to lie if West asked her to. No matter how much I might want to, I couldn't trust anyone.

***

*WEST*

My phone rang as I stirred the beetroot risotto that was simmering on the stove. The savory aroma of herbs and cheese wafted through the apartment, and my mouth watered. I leaned over the counter to check my phone. My heart lurched at the sight of a familiar number in the center of the screen.

I raised the phone to my ear. "Mamma? How did you get this number?"

"You're not the only one who has law enforcement contacts," she reminded me. "It's been too long since I heard from my son. Is it safe to talk?"

I glanced around. I was alone in the apartment, and it was clear of electronic listening devices. The phone was a burner and I'd swap the number tomorrow. Perhaps Adam would frown on me accepting the call, but Mamma mattered more to me than placating my boss.

"Yes, Mamma. It's so good to hear from you. I missed you."

"I've missed you too," she wailed. "It's been too long. Here I am, never knowing if you're alive or dead, and I'm sure you've been fading away with no one there to feed you properly."

Guilt sank its claws into me.

"I'm sorry, Mamma. I wish there was a better way to keep you up to date, but it's too dangerous to talk regularly or to send messages. My boss would let you know if anything happened to me though, I promise."

"They had better." She huffed. "Tell me. Have you been eating? And I mean real food. Not those awful prepackaged, just-add-water monstrosities."

I laughed. Mamma was an excellent cook, but because of that, she was also quite a food snob. "You know I can cook for myself quite well."

"Well, yes," she agreed reluctantly. "I did teach you."

"And I listened to every word," I promised.

She grudgingly accepted this but moved onto the next topic of questioning. "Aren't you terribly lonely, cucciolo?"

"Actually..." I hesitated, unsure how much to share. But I was in a pickle, romantically speaking, and my parents had enjoyed a long and happy marriage. "There's a woman."

Mamma gasped. "Who is she?"

I stirred the risotto again, noting that the water was evaporating, and it would soon be done. "I can't tell you her name, but I love her."

"You do?" She squealed, but then got a hold of herself. "Does this woman love you too?"

Suddenly, my limbs felt heavy. My heart sank as I realized... I really didn't know.

"She used to." My eyes pricked, and I tried to tell myself it was from the onions in the risotto, but the lie wasn't fooling anyone. "I deceived her. I'm not sure if we'll be able to move past it."

"You did it for your job?" she asked, no judgment in her voice.

"Yeah." I ran my hand through my hair and tugged at the ends as frustration crept over me. "She's well within her rights to be mad."

She scoffed. "I'm sure she is, cucciolo. Tell me more about her. I know, I know, you can't give me her name, but I want to know what kind of person my son fell for."

I grinned despite my heavy heart. "She's amazing. Strong, smart. She seems sharp on the surface, but beneath that, she's so many other things."

"Ah." Her tone was knowing. "She has needed to protect herself before."

"In her line of work, she's something of an outsider. I guess that made her tough."

Fiorella paused. "Is your lady a criminal, Weston? I don't judge. I'd just like to know so I can be prepared."

I snorted, amused by her willingness to accept anyone into her family. "No, Mamma. She isn't a criminal."

Her sigh of relief was audible. "Then you'd best grovel. If this woman deserves you, and you've hurt her, she needs to see you take responsibility for that and do better. Get on your knees if that's what it takes. I want to meet her. I need someone else to spoil. Don't mess it up."

"I'll do my best not to."

Metal scraped on metal. I glanced at the door in time to see the lock turn.

"I've got to go," I whispered. "We'll talk soon, but don't try this number again. I love you."

"Goodbye, darling. Love you."

I ended the call, quickly removed the sim card from the phone and snapped it.

Joanna stepped inside and immediately narrowed her eyes. If she'd been a cat, her tail would have been swishing. "What are you up to?"

"Nothing." I discreetly slid the broken sim card into my pocket. "Cooking dinner."

"Which is it?" she asked, shutting the door. Nothing, or cooking?"

"You'll regret making fun of me if I don't let you eat any risotto," I teased.

She laughed. "Please don't. It smells great."

"I suppose I'll let you have some. It'll be ready in a few minutes. Would you like a glass of wine?"

She considered for a moment, then shook her head. "I'd better not yet."

Something in her tone was off.

"What's wrong?" I asked.

"I'm going to change, and then we can talk." She stalked past me and out of sight.

To distract myself from worry, I sliced crusty bread and placed a slice on each of two plates, then checked the risotto and, satisfied it was done, turned off the stove and scooped the delicious creamy meal alongside the bread.

I carried the plates to the table and poured a glass of water for each of us, then gathered cutlery and waited for her to return. When she did, she came straight to the table and sat.

She inhaled, a smile on her lips. "Mm. I love your beet-root risotto."

My gut heated as my libido mistook her interest in dinner for something else. Determined not to let her notice my reaction, I enjoyed my first mouthful of risotto, silently congratulating myself on getting it just right. Of course, Mamma could do it better, but it was still excellent.

"Hanson suspects you," Joanna said.

The creamy rice turned to ash in my mouth.

"Excuse me?"

She nodded, yet to start eating herself. "He presented me with evidence that you aren't who you say you are and warned me to be wary of you. Obviously, I didn't tell him the truth, but if he mentions his concerns to others, it could be bad for your investigation."

"It could be lethal, if he mentioned something to the wrong person." We still didn't know exactly who was involved. The chances were that Hanson had already alerted someone that he'd been digging into my cover. He wasn't the most subtle guy. "Do you trust him?"

With long fingers, Joanna began shredding her slice of bread, breaking it into smaller and smaller pieces. "I'd like to. He accused me of being in on your activities when I wasn't as surprised as I should have been about your alter ego, and I doubt a dirty cop would do that, but I'm not certain. I wouldn't stake your life on it."

"I'm guessing you have thoughts about what we should do."

She wasn't the type to raise a problem without having at least idly considered potential solutions.

She dunked a piece of bread into the risotto and popped it into her mouth. "Have you thought about reading Thackery into the operation?"

"We can't." The denial burst from my lips automatically.

She frowned, taken aback. "Why not?"

"I don't know." I wished I had a concrete answer for her. "Something about him just doesn't sit right with me."

"Thackery pushes people's boundaries, and he may be more of a politician than I'd like, but he's always been a solid cop," she protested.

I forced myself to eat another spoonful of risotto and mull over my response before speaking. I had to keep in mind the fact that she'd worked under Thackery for years and believed him to be an upright policeman, whereas she'd known me for less than six months and I'd proven myself a liar.

"It's not always the bad cops that turn," I said mildly. "It wouldn't be much use to crime bosses if their pet policemen were useless at their jobs."

She inclined her head. "I take your point. What did Thackery do or say to earn your distrust?"

"According to Beth, he frequented Neal's poker evenings."

"Ah." She ate another piece of bread. "We have no evidence linking the poker games to Ortez's illegal activity, but I can understand your hesitation."

I continued my meal, trying not to let on how much I appreciated the fact that she'd listened to me rather than immediately jumping to Thackery's defense.

She sighed, her palms flat on the table. "So, we don't tell either Hanson or Thackery. We continue to trust only each other."

My heart stuttered. She trusted me?

Her expression grew wary, as if she realized what she'd said, but she didn't take it back. Perhaps she trusted me in a professional capacity but not a personal one. Even if that was the case, I'd accept it. When it came to Joanna, I'd gladly take whatever I could get.

I stood, rounded the table, and held my hands out to her. Hesitantly, she took them. I pulled her to her feet.

"Thank you." My voice was thick with emotion. "It means more than you know that you're allowing me even the slightest bit of trust. I won't let you down."

To my surprise, she didn't snatch her hands back or glower. If anything, her lips curved slightly upward.

"You'd better not."

My smile grew. "I spoke to Mamma earlier tonight. I'm under orders to make things right with you and take you to meet her."

Her lips parted, and she didn't seem to know what to say.

My heart pounded out her name. God, she was so beautiful.

I cupped her cheek. "May I kiss you? I understand if the answer is no, but—"

Her lips pressed to mine, stealing the last of my words.

# 19

JOANNA

I moaned against West's mouth, breathing in his familiar minty scent.

The way he'd been looking at me...

Holy crap, the way he'd been gazing at me as if I'd handed him the world made me believe—finally—that not everything between us was a lie. He really did have feelings for me. He cared. And while I was absolutely the wronged party in this scenario, he'd been hurting too.

I relaxed into his embrace, and when his tongue traced the seam of my lips, I parted them and shivered as he deepened the kiss.

West consumed me. His kiss, his scent, his possessive grip on my hips. He surrounded me. I couldn't breathe without sharing his air. I couldn't move without savoring the delicious friction between our bodies.

However hard I may have tried to keep a distance between us, it was time to admit the truth. My stupid heart belonged to West. Whether his name was Gallo, Conti, or something else.

I was his.

But then, just as I was sinking into the moment, he pulled back.

"Don't," I murmured, tugging him closer. If he gave me time to think, I might decide that this was all too much, too soon after his betrayal. Better not to take the chance. "I want you."

He kept his lips off mine. The inches separating us felt like miles. "Are you sure? There's no hurry. I'll wait as long as it takes."

"I'm sure." I pressed myself against him, urging him to continue.

Please don't make me stop and think this through. For once, I don't want to be sensible.

"What do you want?" he asked quietly.

"For you to take control the way you used to." I couldn't imagine anything better. I had a submissive streak in bed. I wasn't a submissive in terms of enjoying a BDSM lifestyle, but I'd spent so much of my working life fighting for respect that it was nice to be able to stop taking charge and let someone else call the shots for a while.

West's lips curved wickedly. "Then that's what you'll get, sweetheart. How far do you want this to go?"

I huffed in frustration, ready for the conversation to be over. "I want you naked and inside me."

His eyes shone with pleasure, and for a moment, he was the charming bartender I'd met in that train station in Canada, but then any trace of lighthearted emotion vanished, and he became the commanding lover who'd always driven me out of my mind.

The man, I suppose, he truly was.

Dangerous. Thrilling. Competent in the sexiest possible way.

"Wait here for a full minute, then come to the bedroom. Our bedroom." His strong hand wrapped around one side of my throat. "What do you say if you need to stop?"

"Red."

"And if you want to pause?"

"Orange."

"Good, baby." His voice was a low purr that hummed through my core. "What are you right now?"

"Green."

"Perfect." He released me and stalked toward the bedroom. My gaze traveled down his powerful frame, noting the bulge of his erection struggling to break free of his jeans.

Fuck, he was sexy.

And once again, he was mine.

I counted to sixty in my head, then followed him to the bedroom. I gasped, my mouth falling open, and my brain almost short-circuited. The room was dark, except for a glow cast by a lamp on the nightstand. It cast shadows over the gorgeous planes of West's naked form.

He lay in the center of the bed, propped up against the pillows, his legs stretched out and his hard cock resting on the corrugated muscles of his abdomen. My gaze traced the contours of his body, the bulges of his muscles emphasized by the play of dark and light.

"Strip," he rasped. "Make it slow. I want to be teased. It's been too long since I saw you."

My breath caught. He wanted me to put on a strip show for him?

Heat blossomed at the apex of my thighs. Perhaps I should have been put off by the demand, but I couldn't think of anything sexier than showing West everything he'd been missing out on. Maybe then he'd know better than to betray me again.

I unbuttoned my shirt, allowing the two sides to fall

open to reveal my breasts and stomach. West's hands fisted and he slowly opened them and propped them behind his head. I shrugged the shirt off. It landed on the floor with a rustle. West's strong thighs strained, as if it was a struggle for him to remain where he was.

I turned away from him so he could only see my back as I undid the clasp of my bra and allowed it to fall. It was plain black, nothing fancy, but the silken glide of the cups over my skin as they dropped made it feel sexy. I covered my breasts with my hands and turned back to West.

He groaned. "I said tease, not torture."

I smirked at the gravelly roughness of his voice. Yeah, he knew he'd messed up. He was lucky I was allowing him to touch me again.

I released my breasts, relishing the hitch in his breathing as I bared them to him. I bent, angling myself so he could see both my ass and my chest as I pulled my socks off one by one. Not an inherently sexy act, but the way his emerald eyes watched my every movement told me he found it enticing anyway.

I undid the button at the top of my pants and wriggled my hips back and forth as I slid them down.

"That's it," he murmured. "Good girl. Naked except for your panties. Take them off too. I want to see all of you."

I plucked the fabric at the edges of my panties, acting like I was about to remove them before pausing.

"Now," he growled.

The heat at my core turned molten. I did as he said, then ran my hands up and down my body as he feasted on me with his eyes.

I'd never considered myself a seductive person before West entered my life. I wasn't a curvaceous siren like Sasha Sloane, or a classic blonde like Portia. But from the beginning, West had made me feel desirable. Perhaps I'd forgotten that for a while, or questioned it, but I no longer did.

He wanted me.

West rose from the bed and prowled toward me. He grabbed me by the hips and claimed my mouth. Our kiss earlier had been slow and sensual, but this one was ravenous.

"Have you punished me enough, sweetheart?" he asked, pulling back far enough to speak clearly, but his breath tickled my lips. "Can I touch your hot-as-fuck body now?"

"Yes."

Please.

"Good. Get on the bed. Legs spread. Knees up. I'm going to make you feel good, and you're just going to lie there and take it."

I whimpered. "Okay."

I lay down and parted my thighs, lifting my knees a little to tilt my pussy up. His gaze journeyed down my body, leaving a trail of heat everywhere it went. He climbed onto the bed and lowered himself between my thighs, his gaze holding mine. Then he covered me with his mouth and his eyelashes fluttered closed.

He moaned, and the vibrations set me alight. I dropped my head to the pillows and stared up at the ceiling as he licked down the center of my sex and fastened his mouth around me again, his stubble scraping against my tender flesh and sending sparks skittering down my spine.

"You taste so fucking good." He buried his face against me and did things with his lips and tongue that had me arching my hips and squeezing my eyes shut as I struggled not to be overwhelmed by him.

He teased me until I was panting, then sat back on his heels. He studied me for just long enough that I began to blush before scrabbling to find a condom in the nightstand. He slid it on and knelt over me.

"Okay?" he asked.

"Green."

He grinned and positioned himself at my entrance. Then, in one smooth motion, he thrust inside. My head fell back, and I moaned. He filled me so well. As if he was made for me. He leaned over me, grabbed my wrists, and pinned them to the bed.

"Take it." He rolled his hips, seating himself deeper inside me, then withdrew. Green eyes burned down into mine as he repeated the movement, brushing my clit. "You feel so good. So hot and tight for me."

"S'good," I slurred, pleased when he kissed me again.

My mind emptied. All that existed was the man who dominated my senses. His tongue tasted faintly of our abandoned dinner, and whenever I gasped for breath, his minty aroma filled my lungs. He pressed down on me, fucked me, and all I could do was lie there and let it happen.

He was so strong, I couldn't move my hands if I wanted to. He weighed me down, and in doing so, set me free.

"Am I good?" I asked as he broke away from my mouth.

"Perfect." He kissed me. "You're so good for me, sweetheart. So fucking good."

I shifted my hips, rocking into him. He pushed into me again and again, nudging my clit each time, sending me higher. For a moment, I felt almost lazy, but then I reminded myself: this was what West wanted. For me to lie here and take everything he gave me.

A thrill of excitement shot through me. I whimpered. West groaned.

"Fuck, baby, you're killing me. Are you gonna come for me?"

"Yes," I promised, moving sinuously, chasing my release.

"That's it, Jo. That's my woman."

My gaze met his, and I gasped. Adoration gleamed back at me, with a savage edge that only made it more potent. I sobbed his name as I shuddered and came apart beneath him. His lower body jerked as he lost his last thread of control. His hips snapped and he swore as he jerked inside me, emptying into the condom.

We twitched in each other's arms as we came down from the high of orgasm. He kissed my forehead and rolled off me. He tied off the condom and tossed it toward the trash can, then gathered me into his arms.

"That was incredible," he murmured against my hair. "I know it's an honor you've trusted me again, and I won't let you down. Does this... does this mean you're mine?"

"I—" A shrill ringing pierced the sex-drunk fogginess of my mind. I frowned. "What's that?"

"Ugh. My work phone." He looked torn. He clearly wanted to ignore it and finish our conversation, but he knew it could be something important.

"Answer it," I said.

He scowled, but he dug his phone out of his discarded jeans pocket all the same. "This better be fucking important," he growled into the receiver.

A few seconds later, he paled. "What happened to Portia?"

---

*WEST*

"She didn't turn up to dance tonight," the woman repeated. She hadn't given me her name, but considering how I'd answered the phone, I couldn't blame her.

"And that's unusual?" I was pretty sure it was, but it paid to clarify.

"Yes." She sounded impatient, but there was a trace of fear in her voice too. "She always turns up for her shifts. It's how she hooks clients for her other job."

"You're sure she's not just late?"

"She's never late," the woman insisted. "She's not answering her phone either. Look, I can't talk now. I have to go back on stage. Can you meet me out behind the Red Door at eleven?"

I checked the time. That was an hour away.

"I'll be there." I hesitated. "Who am I talking to?"

"Sapphire." She hung up.

I stared at the phone, stunned.

Fuck, I hoped Portia had taken a nap and slept through her alarm or been distracted by an emergency. If someone had gotten wind of her poking her nose into Sasha Sloane's death, I shuddered to think what might happen—and it would be my fault. I was the one who'd recruited her to gather information.

"Portia is missing?" Joanna asked, already clambering off the bed and searching for her clothes. I felt a pang of regret over our moment having ended so quickly—my work interfering, once again—but I couldn't leave Portia if she was in trouble.

"Yeah." I pulled myself together and started dressing too. "She didn't turn up for her shift at the Red Door."

"Which is obviously out of character, or no one would have been concerned," she said.

"Exactly." I paused, my shirt halfway over my head. "I'm, uh, sorry about this."

She huffed. "It's just the way things are until the case is over."

I tugged the shirt down. "I wish it wasn't."

"Me too. So, who made the call?"

"Sapphire. One of the dancers."

Her brow furrowed. "Ah, yes. We met her."

"She says that Portia isn't answering her phone, and considering how much she wanted answers, it's not outside the realm of possibility that she decided to get them for herself."

Joanna winced as she tugged on her pants. "For her sake, I hope she's just sick and forgot to mention it to anyone."

"Me too." But it didn't seem likely.

We were both dressed now—unfortunately—and I took a brief moment to study Joanna's face. I wished I could tell how she was feeling about the fact we'd just had sex. It meant the world to me that she trusted me enough to be vulnerable and let her submissive side show, but she'd quickly become all business.

Did this mean she wouldn't dump my ass as soon as the case was done, or had it been one last romp to remember her by?

"Let me just grab a jacket," she said, smoothing her clothes. "It's cold outside."

"Good idea."

She left the room, and I slung my own jacket over my shoulder, holstered my handgun and double checked that I had everything I needed. I met Joanna in the living room.

"My car?" I asked.

She nodded. "You'll fly under the radar better than me."

She unlocked the door and let herself out of the apartment. I followed, locking it behind us again. We walked together to the car, and I automatically got into the driver's seat and leaned across to open the passenger's door.

"Is the brothel in the same neighborhood as the strip club?" Joanna asked as she got in.

I waited for her to shut the door before backing out and pulling onto the street. "It's a couple of blocks away, where there are a few more residential buildings. My understanding is that it's close by so that escorts can easily take clients from the strip club to the brothel if they need to."

"So, it will be easy to drop by and ask if Portia is around," she said.

"Yeah, but let's save that for a last resort. The fewer people aware of a connection between Portia and me, the better." Introducing myself to her acquaintances would only endanger her more.

I parked behind the Red Door, in the darkest corner of the parking lot, away from prying eyes, and sent a message to the number Sapphire had called from to let her know we were there. She emerged through the back exit a few minutes later, drawing a coat tightly around herself as she hurried across the asphalt on three-inch heels.

She opened the back door and climbed into the car. The scent of her perfume—sweet and floral—wafted through the vehicle.

"Something strange is going on," she said, not bothering with a greeting.

I turned as much as I could to face her. I recognized her immediately, although I hadn't put a face to the name. She was a pretty black woman with long, dark hair that fell around her shoulders and a plump lip caught between her teeth.

"How do you mean?" I asked.

Sapphire glanced at Joanna and frowned. "Hey, you're that detective lady."

"I am," she agreed.

Sapphire narrowed her eyes at me. "Why did you bring her?"

"Because she's my wife, and we were together when you called."

"Oh." She seemed to accept that. "Like I was saying, something is off tonight. Portia has been asking questions about Sasha's death. They were close, so that's not surprising. We all want to know what happened. But then she didn't turn up for work, and now she isn't answering her phone. When I asked the boss whether she'd called in sick, he was really squirrelly about it."

"Squirrely how?" Joanna asked.

Sapphire pulled a face and looked over her shoulder, as if worried Keenan might be able to hear her. "He said she hadn't called in sick but that there was no reason to worry. He was really calm about it though. Usually, if someone isn't here, he loses his shit because everything has to be rearranged last minute."

"So, you think he knew not to expect her ahead of time?" I didn't like the thought of that.

Sapphire shrugged. "Maybe."

"So, how come you called me?" None of Portia's friends should've known who I was, let alone had my phone number.

She looked uncomfortable. "She told me that if she ever went missing, or if something happened to her, then I should contact you. She didn't tell me why. Was I right to call?"

"Yes. Thank you, Sapphire." I supposed I couldn't be annoyed with Portia for sharing my number under those circumstances.

"Are you her boyfriend?" she asked, glancing at Joanna apologetically.

"No, just a friend. Did she have a boyfriend?" Because she never mentioned one to me.

She shrugged. "Not that I know of, but most of the girls here like to keep their personal lives private."

"I can understand that." Mixing my work and home lives hadn't always gone well. Obviously.

"When did you last see Portia?" Joanna asked, picking up the line of questioning. "Was she here yesterday?"

Sapphire shook her head. "She was scheduled to work at her other job. But she was in the night before last."

Joanna pulled out her phone and entered something into it. Perhaps a note to follow up with the brothel. I might need to remind her that if Portia is missing because of Ortez, then alerting his staff that someone is looking into her disappearance isn't necessarily the best idea for her continued wellbeing.

"Did you notice anyone paying particular notice to her that night?" Joanna asked, looking up.

Sapphire started to say no, but then she paused, a furrow forming between her eyebrows. "Actually, yeah. There was a guy. He wasn't one of her clients. He just kind of stood near the back of the club until the end of the night, but I saw him going over to her as I was heading out to change."

The back of my neck prickled. My instincts told me we were onto something here.

"What did he look like?" I asked, trying to keep my tone level.

She squeezed her eyes shut." Uh... maybe in his fifties. Stocky. A bit overweight. Thinning gray hair. Actually, come to think of it, I'm pretty sure he was the other detective with you last time we talked."

Joanna and I exchanged a glance. Detective Hanson. But what did it mean that he'd been here?

"That's helpful. Thank you. Do you have any idea where Portia would go if she needed to lie low?"

"I don't know, sorry." She adjusted her long legs in the cramped back of the car. "Before, I'd have said to Sasha, but now, I have no idea. I could be overreacting though. Maybe she's at her apartment."

"We'll check there," I assured her. "In fact, we'll go there now. Can we give you a ride anywhere first?"

She pursed her lips. "I'm due back on the floor in a few minutes. Good luck though."

"Thanks for calling." Joanna smiled at her. "That was brave."

Sapphire exhaled roughly. "It's the right thing to do. I'd better go."

She pushed the door open and clambered out, then quietly clicked it shut. She shivered as she crossed the parking lot. I didn't blame her. The outside air was bitter, and her legs were almost bare.

"You have Portia's address, I assume?" Joanna asked.

"Yeah. I haven't been there, but I was sure to take note of it in case I ever needed it."

I plugged the address into the GPS, started the engine, and pulled out of the lot.

The drive was longer than I'd expected. I'd assumed Portia lived nearby, but she was a couple of suburbs over, in a solidly middle-class area with tidy apartment buildings and a few standalone houses.

"Do you think there's anything Hanson might have wanted to talk to Portia about?" I asked Joanna as we made our way inside.

Joanna cocked her head in thought. "There would be legitimate reasons to question her about our case, but none of the dancers mentioned her when we visited the Red Door together, and he hasn't said anything about other leads. Of course, there's a good chance he didn't tell me because he doesn't trust me."

"Or that he's up to his neck in this." The words fell between us like bombs. I didn't want to say it, but I had to, and from Joanna's expression, I knew she understood.

"It's a possibility," she allowed as we entered the foyer. "Stairs or elevator?"

"Divide and conquer?"

She grimaced. "I'd prefer not to separate, but we don't want to miss anyone coming the other way. Stay armed at all times. I'll take the stairs."

I grinned. "My legs thank you."

She rolled her eyes. "You think I don't know how fit you are?"

I just laughed and crossed to the elevator. I pushed the button for the fourth floor and waited for the doors to close. The elevator rose slowly, and by the time the doors opened, and I stepped out into a corridor, Joanna was already striding toward me, panting.

"You must have moved quickly," I said.

She smirked. "I've been known to. Which door is hers?"

I glanced at the number on the two doors nearest us, then jerked my thumb to the left. "That way."

Portia's apartment was the second from the end. The door was closed, and when we paused outside, I couldn't hear anything within.

I reached for the handle, and beside me, Joanna raised her gun.

"Chicago Police Department," she called. "Open up."

There was no response.

I turned the handle. To my surprise, it opened. The lock mechanism had been broken, and as I looked inside, my breath caught.

Portia's apartment had been trashed.

**20**

———



"We need to sweep the place." I scanned the apartment's interior, noting the smashed vase, flowers on the floor, and overturned cabinet. "Make sure whoever did this is no longer here."

West stepped closer behind me. "I've got you covered."

I entered the living area, my gun held high, and pivoted, doing a quick visual check of the kitchen where it connected to the living room. I stalked around behind the counter. There were dishes on the floor and the tap was flowing, but there was no sign of anyone present.

I turned off the tap with one hand and strode to one of the two doors attached to the living room. I positioned myself close to the wall and opened the first one. The bathroom was empty, although the contents of the medicine cabinet were strewn on the vanity and floor.

I backed up and tried the next door. It swung open to reveal a bedroom. The bedding had been torn off, the mattress slashed, and the dresser had suffered the same treatment as the medicine cabinet.

A closet stood in the corner. I tilted my head toward it

and West nodded. Together, we crossed the room, picking our way around Portia's belongings. West grabbed the closet door handle, and I stood in front of it, gun raised.

He yanked it open, but there was nothing inside other than a few dresses and an assortment of costumes that must be for Portia's job at the Red Door.

With a sigh, I lowered the gun. I wasn't sure whether to be relieved that we were alone or disappointed not to have discovered someone who could give us answers. I returned to the living room, West on my heels.

"It seems like whoever was here was searching for something," I said, mentally cataloging the damage. The fact every drawer and cabinet had been opened, and all the cushions slashed, suggested this devastation was methodical rather than the result of rage.

I turned to West. His arms hung at his sides; he looked pale and stricken.

"Perhaps Ortez found out that she was helping me, and he wanted to make sure she didn't have any evidence of his criminal activities hidden in her apartment."

I considered this. "It's possible."

His lips pressed into a grim line. I could already tell he was blaming himself.

"This isn't your fault," I told him. "Portia wanted to find Sasha's killer. Maybe she nosed around the wrong person."

He shook his head. "She wouldn't be wrapped up in any of this if not for me. So yeah, I am to blame."

I tucked my gun away and placed my hands on his upper arms, waiting until he looked me in the eye. "Even if Portia had never met you, Sasha would still have been gathering information about Ortez's dealings to further her plans to replace his wife. She would still have been killed, and Portia probably would have tried to find out why."

He pulled away. "We need to see if there's anything here that could lead us to her."

I let him change the subject. After all, he was right. His feelings were important, but they weren't urgent. Ensuring Portia's safety was.

"Do you think whoever did this took her?" I asked, looking around. "Or do you think she came home, found the place like this and ran?"

He tapped his finger against his lower lip, then turned and strode into the bathroom. A moment later, he emerged and ducked into the bedroom.

"If she left of her own accord, she'd have taken toiletries and clothes," he muttered, as much to himself as to me. "It doesn't look like that's happened, unless she has duplicates of all her toiletries."

"Shit." I'd really hoped she was just lying low somewhere, hiding out until we came for her, but West made a good point. "We have to call this in. We need to put together a search team."

"I'll call my handler," West said.

"And I'll call..." Not Thackery. West still harbored concerns over where his allegiance lay. "Deputy Chief Dominguez."

His eyes widened. "Are you comfortable with that?"

My lips twisted. "Not really, but she's our best option if we don't want to involve the captain."

He held my gaze for a moment. "If you're sure."

"I am." I paced to the other end of the living area, giving him space to have a conversation with his handler while I called Dominguez. The phone rang out on the first call, but the deputy chief picked up on the second.

"Lee," she growled, her voice thick with sleep. "Why are you calling in the middle of the goddamn night?"

"I've got a missing woman," I told her. "I tried to contact

Captain Thackery, but he didn't answer. I need approval to put together a search team. There's evidence she may have been kidnapped."

"Fine," Dominguez barked. "Do what you need. Now, I'm going back to sleep. You can update me in the morning."

"Thank you, Deputy Chief."

She'd already hung up.

I made several more phone calls, initiating the procedures to get crime scene technicians to the apartment as soon as possible and officers available to start asking around about Portia's whereabouts. With that done, I hesitated for a few seconds and then tried Hanson's number, but he didn't pick up.

"Hanson isn't answering his phone," I told West, who'd already finished his conversation with his handler.

His expression was grim. "Someone matching Hanson's description was seen with Portia at the club, and now she's missing and he's out of reach. Think it's a coincidence?"

"I don't know," I admitted.

I didn't want to believe Hanson could be embroiled in this. It was possible he was simply sleeping deeply and couldn't hear his phone, but somehow, I doubted it.

"Let's search the apartment," West suggested. "See if we can find anything useful."

We started in the living area and slowly worked our way through the mess. Unfortunately, everything present seemed to belong here. Nothing stood out, and there were no scribbled notes or unidentified substances. Most likely whoever had done this was wearing gloves and had had the freedom to take their time.

"The neighbors?" I asked when our search proved fruitless.

He raised his eyebrows. "They won't be pleased to be woken up."

"If a kidnapping had taken place in my building, I'd want to know," I pointed out. "Besides, maybe they heard something."

"We can't go far. We don't want to risk anyone compromising the crime scene," he warned.

"I know. But we can at least try the neighbors on either side and across the hall."

He sighed. "It's a start."

We left the apartment, closing the door behind us. I walked to the next unit over and knocked. When, after twenty seconds, there was no response, I knocked again, louder.

The floor creaked, and then the door inched open. An eye appeared in the narrow gap.

"Who are you?" a grumpy male voice demanded.

I held up my badge. "Detective Joanna Lee. Chicago PD."

He opened the door wide enough to reveal a skinny, wrinkled face with deep-set eyes and hardly any teeth. "What business do the police have dragging an old man out of bed?"

"We're sorry to have woken you." West stepped up beside me, his charming smile firmly in place. "We just have one or two questions, and then you can head straight back to bed. Is that all right?"

The man grumbled but nodded.

"Do you know the woman who lives next door?" I asked.

He grunted. "Sweet girl. Shows too much skin though. What's this about?"

"She's missing," I informed him.

His jaw dropped, and the haziness vanished from his eyes in an instant. "What?"

"I want you to think hard." I paused to give him a chance

to process. "Have you heard or seen anything unusual tonight?"

He was quiet for a long moment, his bloodshot eyes flicking back and forth. Eventually, his face lit up.

"There was a commotion," he said. "A few hours ago. A bit of bashing and crashing. I didn't think much of it. Assumed someone was moving furniture."

In a way, he was right to assume that.

"What time was this?" I asked.

He pulled a face. "Around ten. Maybe eleven. I was in bed, but I don't sleep well. My memory isn't great either though, so I don't know how much stock you want to put in that."

"Thank you." For now, his guess-timate was all we had. "Anything else?"

"I don't think so," he replied regretfully. "Is there anything I can do to help?"

"Not right now, but someone will be by in the morning to take a statement. Have a nice night."

He grumbled and seemed reluctant to close the door, but he must have realized that there really wasn't much he could do.

"That's something, at least," West said as we passed back in front of Portia's door to try the neighbor on the other side.

I knocked, then knocked again and called out, but it was completely silent within. Perhaps whoever occupied the apartment worked the night shift.

When we tried the door across from Portia's, a young woman opened it, rubbing her eyes. A sleeping baby was tucked against her side.

"What is it?" she asked wearily.

"Did you know the woman who lived opposite you?" I

took the lead again, knowing that West would prefer to remain in the background.

"Portia? Of course. Why?"

"Her apartment has been broken into." I spoke softly, so as not to wake the baby. "We can't find her. Have you seen her today?"

"No." She frowned. "I hardly ever do. She keeps strange hours."

Disappointment sat like lead in my gut.

"Have you heard or seen anything out of the ordinary tonight?"

She shook her head. "Sorry, no. I've been crashed out hard."

"What about earlier today?"

"Hmm... no. Nothing stands out."

I sighed. "Thanks, anyway. Let us know if you remember anything."

The woman cocked her head. "You'll be around?"

I nodded. "Probably on and off until she turns up."

"Okay." She said a quick good-night and shut the door.

"What next?" West asked.

I considered for a moment. "The building manager. I walked past a room labeled 'manager' on the ground floor."

"They're probably not in at this time of night," he pointed out.

"Worth a shot anyway. Do you mind waiting here while I go? I don't want to leave the room unattended."

He smirked. "You'd leave your bartender husband in charge of a crime scene?"

"Better you than no one at all. We can't afford to waste time." Every second we hesitated was another in which Portia was at risk.

His expression sobered. "I know. Go."

I hurried along the corridor and down four flights of

stairs. When I reached the door labeled "building manager," I knocked. To my surprise, the door opened almost immediately. A short woman with long black hair loose around her shoulders, who was wearing a graphic T-shirt, looked up at me curiously.

"It's nearly midnight." She sounded confused. "Is there something I can help you with?"

"Are you the building manager?" I hadn't expected her to be quite so young.

"Yes." Her eyes narrowed. "You're not a tenant though."

"No, I'm not." I showed her my badge. "Detective Joanna Lee. Chicago Police Department. I'd like to look at your security footage from earlier tonight."

She arched an eyebrow. "Do you have a warrant, Detective Lee?"

"No," I admitted. "But one of your tenants has been reported missing by a coworker and her apartment has been trashed."

Her eyebrow inched up even higher. "An apartment you entered unlawfully?"

"No. The lock was broken, and the door opened as soon as we touched it. Besides, we had reason to be concerned for the wellbeing of its occupant."

She opened the door wider to reveal a wall of computers behind her, and a laptop on the center of the desk with a gaming console connected.

"What room?" she asked. "If I can confirm that it doesn't look right, you can watch the security footage. Only the corridors, elevators and stairs."

"I appreciate that," I told her. "I'll get a warrant in the morning to make it official."

I doubted we'd be catching any judges this late, and hopefully we wouldn't need to.

"Good." She offered me her hand. "I'm Kim."

I shook it. "Nice to meet you, Kim."

She released me and hurried away—presumably to check on Portia's apartment. I considered following her but decided to wait instead. West was up there. All would be fine.

When she returned, she was muttering to herself, her face pale.

"Holy shit. I can't believe no one noticed this. Shit. This is bad. This is so bad."

I gritted my teeth. West obviously hadn't calmed her before she came back down. She was spiraling, and I needed her back on task.

"The security feed from earlier tonight," I reminded her. "Start at nine and work forward from there."

"Right. On it." She switched to a different recording, this time of a corridor—presumably the one outside Portia's apartment. She fast-forwarded the footage, and we watched as someone left the apartment beside Portia's and another person farther down the corridor returned home.

Around ten-thirty, a man dressed in dark clothes and a ski mask appeared from the door to the stairwell. He checked the unit numbers and stopped outside Portia's apartment. He knocked, and then knocked again. He waited for several minutes, and when there was no response, he jimmied the lock open.

He wore gloves, and it was impossible to make out many details about him. Based on his height relative to the door-frame, I'd say he was less than six feet. When he glanced toward the camera, I caught a brief glimpse of the skin around his eyes.

"Rewind that and pause," I ordered.

Kim did as I said, whimpering in the back of her throat and muttering under her breath once again about how bad this was.

I leaned closer. "He looks white, right?"

Kim blinked rapidly and tried to focus on the screen properly. "Yeah, I'd say so. He's not black, anyway. Could be Asian or perhaps has some Hispanic heritage. It's difficult to tell from just that tiny bit of skin."

I grimaced. It wasn't a lot, but at least it would allow us to begin narrowing the suspect pool. We were looking for a man, shorter than six feet, possibly Caucasian.

"I need to make a phone call. I'll be just outside." I left the room and closed the door behind me, then scrolled through my contacts and found Zeke's number.

"What did your lying husband do now?" he grumbled after the call connected. "I was sleeping with a sexy redhead, dreaming very nice dreams."

"Sorry for calling at this hour. I hope you left the room, so you didn't wake her too." I was well aware I was stretching the boundaries of our friendship, such as it was.

"Don't worry. Fi is sleeping soundly. What's up?" He sounded more alert by the second.

"I need a favor." I hesitated to ask when I didn't know what he might want in return, but this was an emergency.

"A favor for a favor." The smirk in his voice came through clearly.

"Fine." I explained the situation to him as best I could. "I need to know who took her, or anything that might lead us to her. Do you think you can help?"

"The apartment building has a security system?" he asked.

"Yeah." I didn't ask why he wanted to know, sensing that it would be best if I remained in the dark.

"Then I'll do what I can. I'll get back to you if I find anything."

"Thanks, Zeke." I ended the call and stepped back inside

the office. "I'm going to head up to the apartment. Do you feel safe here on your own?"

She nodded, even though she was more subdued than earlier. "The door has a really good locking mechanism. I'll be fine."

"Okay, but I'll send an officer down as soon as the team arrives." If the men who'd broken into Portia's apartment hadn't tried to take out the security system at the time, they probably weren't interested in it now, but there was always a chance they'd want to destroy any evidence.

"Thanks."

I backed out of the office again, turned, and squeaked, my heart leaping as I raised my gun at the figure immediately in front of me. I relaxed as recognition set in.

"Shit, Sewell. Don't scare me like that. I could have shot you."

He ducked his head sheepishly. "Sorry. Didn't mean to. Thought you'd have heard me arrive."

"I was distracted." Damn, I had to pay better attention to my surroundings. "Did Dominguez send you?"

"Yeah." He cleared his throat. "She tried Hanson but couldn't get an answer, so she asked me to partner with you on this one since... you know, I'm partnerless and all."

Emotion flashed across his face, and I felt a pang for him. I hadn't liked Neal, but he'd still been Sewell's partner. It must be difficult to have lost him.

"I hope Hanson is all right," I murmured, concerned for my own partner. The fact he hadn't answered when the deputy chief called wasn't a good sign. He'd never intentionally ignore her, which meant that he was either dead to the world in bed, in trouble—or he was the trouble.

I prayed he was just sound asleep.

"I'm sure he's snoring as we speak." Sewell flashed me a

comforting smile. "By the way, I talked to Heather from the crime scene team. They'll be here shortly."

"Good. The sooner they get to work, the sooner we'll have a lead to follow. At the moment, we've got next to nothing."

"That's unfortunate." He glanced around, then frowned. "Did you leave her apartment unattended?"

"No." My cheeks heated, and embarrassment coiled in my gut. "West is there."

"West, as in, your husband?" He looked confused. "Why is he here?"

"We were out together when I got the call."

"Uh-huh." He seemed to be processing this. "Who reported her missing?"

"One of her coworkers." I started toward the stairs. "Come on."

He huffed. "Can't we take the elevator?"

"The stairs will be good for you."

He grumbled behind me as we took the stairs back up to the fourth floor. We were both breathing more heavily by the time we arrived, although neither of us were nearly as red-faced as Hanson would have been.

I led Sewell to the apartment, where West was waiting by the door.

"Good to see some backup," West said, greeting Sewell with an up-nod.

"I'd rather be in bed," Sewell replied, from behind me. "You haven't been inside, have you?"

West's lips twisted. "Only while Joanna was with me. I haven't touched anything."

He gave me a look, and I could sense he was frustrated that Sewell's presence would limit his ability to participate and speak freely, but there wasn't much I could do about that.

"Thanks for standing watch." I kissed his cheek and murmured, "A man, less than six feet tall, possibly white," quiet enough that only he could hear.

"No problem. I'll wait out here if you want to show Detective Sewell around."

"Sure."

West stood aside and I opened the door and gestured for Sewell to precede me.

"Holy shit, this is a mess," he exclaimed.

"Someone was looking for something." I gestured for him to look into the bathroom and bedroom.

While he was doing so, a tiny ding sounded from somewhere nearby. I looked around, confused. That had sounded like metal hitting metal.

Nothing within my line of sight moved.

Ding!

I jerked, shocked to realize it was coming from outside. I strode over to the window and opened it. I hadn't thought there was anything out here, but I'd been too hasty in coming to that conclusion. A metal fire escape staircase passed by the window, zigzagging from above, with a small balcony accessible by climbing through the window.

I leaned farther out, squinting in the darkness as I searched for whatever had made that noise.

Ding!

I glanced down, and my jaw dropped. Splayed on the balcony below this one lay the prone and bloody form of Detective Hanson.

# 21



*WEST*

The instant Joanna cried out, I forgot that I wasn't supposed to be inside Portia's apartment. I shoved the door open, spotted her by the window, and raced to her side, grabbing her arm just as she lurched forward.

"Whoa!" I exclaimed. "What's wrong?"

"Did you find something?" Sewell asked, hurrying over from the bedroom.

"It's Hanson," she gasped. "He's injured. On the fire escape. We have to help him."

"Let me see." I nudged her aside and looked out. From here, it was impossible to tell whether Hanson was conscious. "We need to proceed with caution. It's possible he's involved. He could be armed."

Joanna hissed, and when I turned toward her, disbelief was etched into every line of her expression. "He's injured."

I glanced at Sewell, who was watching curiously, and lowered my voice. "We don't know why he's here. Perhaps he was injured while attempting to abduct Portia."

She gritted her teeth together but gave a jerky nod. "You're right."

Sewell was speaking to someone behind us, but I tuned him out and focused on Joanna, who was preparing to—cautiously—run to Hanson's rescue. My wife was an incredible woman. If we got through this, I really hoped she'd take me back.

"You've got this," I murmured. "You go first but keep your weapon on hand. I'll be right behind you."

Sewell cleared his throat. "An ambulance is on its way, and I've requested backup as well. They should be here any minute. Perhaps West could wait outside and show them up?"

I bit down on the inside of my cheek. The last thing I wanted to do right now was leave Joanna, although I understood why he'd make the suggestion. It was logical for the person who supposedly wasn't a law enforcement professional to run the errands.

"I'm staying with Jo," I said firmly.

Sewell made a sound of frustration. "You shouldn't even be here. Letting you remain with her in a dangerous situation is completely against protocol. I should escort you out and—"

"You try that," I interrupted. "And see how it goes."

Sewell glared, but considering his small frame—and my advanced combat training—he didn't scare me.

"Lee, I'm going to have to report this," he said.

"Do what you see fit." Joanna slung her leg over the window and clambered out. She withdrew her gun from its holster, switched on her flashlight, and held the gun in firing position as she started down the stairs.

I climbed out after her and retrieved my own concealed weapon. Sewell swore behind me, muttering about liabilities and amateurs. I followed a few paces behind Joanna, making sure to keep a clear path between myself and

Hanson, in case he was only faking us out and attacked when she reached him.

He didn't move, even as she knelt beside him. I glanced up at the window above. Sewell's silhouette had vanished, so perhaps he'd gone out to meet the paramedics himself.

"He has a bullet wound through his left side," Joanna said, taking off her jacket. She folded it and pressed it to the wound, which was slowly leaking blood.

I skimmed my hands up Hanson's sides, feeling for any weapons. I removed his gun, which lay discarded on the metal beside his body, and then pocketed his Taser.

"Denny." Joanna lowered her ear to his mouth when he didn't respond. "He's breathing."

I squatted beside her and grabbed Hanson's jaw. "Get your shit together, you grumpy old bastard. We need your help."

His lips moved, but he didn't make a sound.

"Come on," I urged. "Wake up. Tell us what the hell you're doing here, because I've got to say, it looks bad."

His eyelashes fluttered but didn't open. Still, it was evidence he was conscious, even if he was barely hanging on.

"How..." He broke off, groaning. "D'you find me?"

"A woman was reported missing by a coworker," Joanna told him, maintaining pressure on the wound. "We came to her apartment, and I heard a noise outside, so I looked down and saw you."

"I... ugh..." His face twisted with pain. "Who's with you?"

"My husband," she said. "Detective Sewell. Others are coming."

He coughed, and blood flecked his chin. "Don't trust him."

"Who? West?"

I gritted my teeth. If Hanson thought I was behind this, there was a good chance we'd get nothing useful from him.

"No," he rasped. "Sewell. Don't—" He broke off coughing, but this time, the hacking grew worse, and bloody red trails spiderwebbed down his chin.

"The paramedics are here," Sewell called from above. "They're coming up."

Hanson's eyes widened, the whites stark against the darkness of the night. "Don't." Cough. "Leave." Cough. "Me." Cough. "Alone... with him."

"We won't," I assured him. "We'll keep him busy here."

A pair of paramedics hustled up the fire escape. I was skeptical as to how they intended to get Hanson down in one piece, but then the light in the apartment beside us came on and the window opened. A uniformed police officer passed a stretcher through, and the paramedics each took an end.

"I'm setting up a table on this side so you can slide him through," the officer said, disappearing from the window. A moment later, he was back, carrying a rectangular dining table, a sleepy middle-aged man helping him. They positioned the table on the other side of the window.

I stepped aside so the paramedics could take my place. West and I backed onto the stairs to give them room to maneuver Hanson onto the stretcher.

"Do you need help lifting him?" I asked.

"No, we're good," the younger paramedic said, grabbing her end of the stretcher while her partner took the other. Together, they hefted him up and slid the stretcher through the window, only stopping when Hanson was lying on the table on the other side.

The officer and the middle-aged man dragged the table back, giving the paramedics room to enter through the window. Seconds later, they were gone, leaving West and I alone on the fire escape.

I took the stairs two at a time, hurrying to make sure that Sewell was still in Portia's apartment. Hanson's warning rang in my ears. At this stage, we didn't know whether we could trust him, but I was still going to proceed with caution where Sewell was concerned.

Fortunately, he was hovering in the apartment while a crime scene technician unloaded their gear bag on the kitchen counter. Another crime scene tech emerged from the bedroom.

"Is there much to see on the fire escape?" he asked.

"Not really," Joanna replied. "A lot of blood—presumably from Hanson. Possibly a bullet. We don't know whether the shot was a through-and-through or if it's lodged inside him."

"Right." He headed for the window. "I'll start there. If we can find the bullet, we can run ballistics to see if it matches anything we have on file."

"Excellent." Joanna turned to Sewell. "Did you order the officers to interview the neighbors?"

He nodded.

"Let them know we already spoke to the one on the left and the one across the hall." She didn't mention the building manager or the video footage, and I couldn't help but wonder if that was an intentional decision. Perhaps she didn't want to put the building manager in danger.

She left the apartment, and I heard voices outside. Sewell and I stood awkwardly in silence while we waited. When she came back, she met my eyes and gave a slight nod. I wished I knew what it meant.

"So, how come Homicide are on this case?" Sewell asked. "There's no body."

I stilled, wondering whether to take charge, but Joanna didn't seem bothered by the question.

"The call came directly to me through a personal connection," she said.

His eyebrows knitted together. "A friend of yours?"

"Something like that."

"And you brought your husband?"

I sighed. "If me being here is a problem, I'll go and wait in the car."

I needed to make a phone call anyway.

Sewell hesitated, then nodded. "That might be best. No hard feelings."

"Sure, buddy." No point in antagonizing him. Not when we might need him later.

I pulled Joanna into an embrace.

"Don't turn your back on him," I murmured against her ear.

"I'm not alone," she whispered back. "I'll be fine."

I released her, my fingers automatically clenching around the air. I wanted to grab her and insist she come with me, but I had to trust that she knew how to take care of herself. She was a kickass detective. She could handle any trouble that came her way.

I left the apartment and took the elevator down. As soon as it opened, I noticed an officer guarding the building manager's door. Good. Perhaps that's what Joanna had been arranging when she'd left the room. That recording had to be protected. Who knew what else we might find if someone combed through the footage?

As I left the building, I scanned the surrounding area, checking to make sure no one was lying in wait. I hurried to the car, unlocked the door and got in, immediately locking it behind myself.

I called Zeke, aware that Joanna had already woken him up.

"What is it with you two?" he grumbled upon answering. "Can't let a guy sleep."

"I've got another favor to ask." God only knew what he was going to ask in return at the end of all this.

"Go on."

"Joanna's partner, Detective Hanson, has been shot. He warned us not to trust another detective in the Homicide unit. Detective Charlie Sewell. I'd really appreciate it if you could go searching for the skeletons in Sewell's closet. He's with Joanna right now, so the sooner I know whether she's in danger, the better."

Zeke sighed. "I'll get on it. But don't leave her alone with him, just in case. If he did something to Hanson and is worried he might talk, he could do something reckless."

---

JOANNA

I knocked on the door of the apartment beneath Portia's and waited. After a few seconds, the man I'd seen through the window earlier opened the door and groaned.

"What now?" he asked. "I'm still trying to clean blood drops off the floor from that guy the paramedics dragged through here."

"I have a few questions," I told him. "Considering a man was shot outside your apartment, surely you can understand that."

"Wait. What?" He blanched. "I didn't realize he'd been shot. I just saw all the blood and thought he must have fallen and cut himself on something."

Clearly, no one had enlightened him.

"Can I come in?" I asked.

"You may as well." He stood aside to let me in, then closed the door behind me. He gestured at a worn gray sofa. "Have a seat."

I sat and he flopped onto an armchair, hanging his head and massaging his temples.

"Perhaps it's best if I give you a quick explanation." This guy obviously wasn't in the mood to waste time, and neither was I. "The woman who lives above you was reported missing. When we arrived, her apartment had been broken into and we found a man with a gunshot wound on the fire escape outside your apartment."

The man frowned. "Was he involved in her disappearance?"

"We're not sure yet." I wasn't about to speculate in front of him. "Did you hear anything unusual before the paramedics arrived?"

He raised his weary eyes. "There were some noises above earlier. Kind of a quiet thumping. I didn't think much of it. I assumed they were having sex or reorganizing the place. It didn't last long, so I let it go."

That must have been when the perp was ransacking Portia's apartment. But had it been Hanson, or someone else?

"Nothing else disturbed you? Or do you recall seeing anyone you didn't recognize in the building?"

He started to shake his head but then stiffened. "Wait. I did hear what I'd thought was a car backfiring. It woke me, but I fell back asleep pretty quickly."

My breath caught. Gunshots could be mistaken for a car backfiring. "Do you have any idea what time that was?"

"I'm not sure." He scrunched his face up, thinking hard. "Maybe an hour before the paramedics showed up at my door."

Shit. We'd been at the apartment a good while before

the paramedics had arrived, so if he was right, then Hanson must have been shot shortly before we got there.

"Am I safe?" he asked, catching his lower lip between his teeth. "Should I leave?"

"If you lock your door and shut the window, I don't see any reason for you to be concerned. We'll have a police presence in the building to keep an eye on things, so you should be able to get another few hours of sleep in safety."

Assuming he could calm his mind for long enough to fall asleep. There was every chance that would be asking too much of him, given what had happened.

He deflated. "Okay, thanks. Is there anything else you want to know?"

I rose to my feet. "Not right now, but someone will be by to take your statement when it's light out."

He followed me to the door and waited while I left. I paused in the corridor and the lock clicked into place. I walked over to the next door, debating whether to knock. They might have heard something useful, but it felt like a waste of time canvassing the building when I should be out searching for Portia—and hunting down the bastard that shot my partner.

My phone rang, saving me from deciding. I accepted the call and raised the phone to my ear.

"Jo?" It was West.

"I'm here," I told him.

"Zeke got back to me with something interesting. Are you alone?"

I looked both ways down the corridor, a bad feeling creeping up my spine. "Yes. Why?"

"According to Zeke's intel, Sewell isn't on duty."

I frowned. "Okay, so maybe he got called in on his time off."

"If he did, Dominguez wasn't the one to make the call.

She's been trying to organize a pair of detectives from the Missing Persons unit to take over the case."

My stomach hardened. "But we haven't seen anyone from Missing Persons."

"Because she hasn't managed to assign a team yet," he replied, as if he'd expected that response. "She's having difficulty getting anyone to answer the phone. There's something else."

I rested my back against the wall and lowered my spare hand to my holster. The hairs on my arms were standing up. Something felt very wrong. "What?"

"Detective Sewell's older brother, Dirk, is a former Marine Corps sniper."

I sucked in a breath. "Shit. He's been discharged?"

"Dishonorably, after a female colleague accused him of sexual assault."

My mind raced. I ran through the facts. Sewell was here under false pretenses. His brother was a military-trained sniper. West's father and Detective Neal had both been killed by a skilled sniper.

"Is he in Chicago?" I asked, even though I suspected I knew the answer.

"His last known address is an apartment near Sherman Park, which he shares with his brother."

"Holy shit." This couldn't be a coincidence. The Sewells had to be involved. Another possibility struck me. "Sewell might have been the one going through Portia's apartment. That could be how he arrived on the scene without being called. If he was inside and we scared him off, he could have returned pretending to be on official police business."

West hummed thoughtfully. "That would also give him a valid excuse if any of his fingerprints or DNA were to turn up at the scene."

I straightened. "I need to get eyes on him."

At the moment, Sewell was the most senior officer present at the crime scene. That didn't sit right with me if he was also a suspect. I still had a difficult time getting my head around the idea he could be involved. He was just so innocuous.

"Wait for me," West said. "You need backup in case he realizes we're onto him. Stay on the line and meet me in the fourth floor stairwell."

A slam came through the line and then muffled noises as West crossed the parking lot.

"Perhaps he's being blackmailed," I said as I made my way back to the stairs and started to climb. "If his brother is in trouble, he might just be trying to help him."

"Hmm." A door shut and his footsteps sounded against a hard surface. "We can untangle his motives once we've confirmed his involvement and have him in custody. Until then, they don't matter. We have to consider him a potential threat. I'm not risking your safety just because you want to think the best of him."

"Fair enough." I reached the fourth floor, and listened through the phone as West drew closer.

When he was in sight, he ended the call. "Are you ready for this?"

I grabbed the handle of my gun, feeling its weight against my palm. "As much as I'll ever be."

We needed answers. Portia's life was on the line. West jerked his head toward the stairwell door, gesturing for me to go first. I cracked it open and peered out. The only person visible in the corridor was the uniformed officer, so I shoved the door farther open and stepped through. West followed close behind.

I strode to the apartment and the officer moved aside with a respectful nod. I pushed the door gently, and it opened with no resistance. A crime scene technician was crouched in the living room, in front of the sofa. The window was ajar, so presumably the other technician was still outside.

There was no sign of Sewell.

"Where's Detective Sewell?" I asked, my gun at my side, my nerves primed, ready to fight at any moment.

The tech looked up. "He was called away."

Considering he wasn't on duty, that seemed unlikely. Unless it was a personal matter.

"Where to?"

She shrugged. "He didn't say."

Fuck. "Did he mention who called?"

"No." She didn't seem concerned by this, but then, why would she be? As far as she knew, Sewell was a respected detective and a legitimate part of this investigation.

"He's definitely not here?" West asked, scanning the area warily.

The technician huffed. "You guys have got to work on your communication. No. He's not here. He left maybe five minutes after Detective Lee went to speak to the guy who lives downstairs."

"Thanks." I forced myself not to let my frustration show. "Did he say anything before he went?"

She cocked her head, quiet for a few seconds. "No. I don't think so. Is everything okay?"

"I don't know," I admitted, turning to West. "We need to know where he is. I should call Dominguez and update her too."

"I agree with you about finding his location." He spoke quietly, his gaze darting to the technician, who seemed to have returned to work but could very well be listening in. "We should hold off on informing the police though. We still don't know who's involved."

I gritted my teeth. "Dominguez is a good cop. I'd stake

my career on it." She'd had to fight a biased system to get to where she was. There was no way she'd roll over and play dead for a mob boss wannabe.

West's expression became imploring. "All I ask is that you wait for a couple of hours. See if we can track him down first."

"Fine." I didn't like this.

"Thank you." He kissed my cheek. "I'm going to call my handler. Why don't you ask Zeke to help with Sewell? That's right up his alley."

I nodded. "I'll do that now."

"Good. Let's check in with each other in five minutes."

I left the apartment and strode to the far end of the corridor, where I could be sure that no one would be able to overhear my phone call. I hit the redial symbol and waited.

"You two want to swing with us, don't you?" Zeke asked, cheerier than earlier. "That's what all of this is about. You just want to get closer to me and Fi."

"Zeke..." I laced my tone with warning.

He sighed. "You're no fun. How can I help?"

"Sewell did a runner while West and I were distracted. If I give you his phone number, can you trace him?"

"I'll sure as hell try." Rhythmic tapping signaled that he was on his computer.

I read him the number. "Should I call back?"

"Just let me try something first." More tapping. Some muttering. Then a laugh. "The stupid asshole didn't even bother to turn off his phone. I'm sending you his coordinates now."

# 22

*JOANNA*

I rushed back to the apartment, a wide-eyed officer who'd recently arrived to guard the door getting out of my way as I breezed through.

"I have an address," I called to West.

He pocketed his phone. "Let's go."

"Wait." I held my hands up. "We should call for backup."

"We can do that on the way." He strode over to me and took my hand. "If Portia is in danger and there's a chance that Sewell abducted her, then we need to save her."

"We will," I assured him. "But we don't know what we're walking into. We can't do it alone."

He nodded. "Come on."

We left, passing the still-ruffled officer on our way.

"No one comes in or out," I told him. "That includes Detective Sewell. Do you understand?"

His brow crinkled. "Ma'am?"

"This scene is now locked down. If anyone else tries to enter, call me. No one gets in without approval, even if they have a badge."

The furrow between his eyebrows deepened. "What's going on?"

"I'll explain later. Do I have your word?"

"Yes, ma'am. If anyone tries to get in, I'll call you."

I smiled. "Thank you."

West and I walked until we were out of sight, and then we flew down the stairs and across the parking lot. He pushed a button on his key fob to unlock the car doors and we both got in. I added the coordinates Zeke sent me to the GPS while West started the engine.

He backed out and then paused to hand me his phone. "Get in touch with Adam. Put it on speaker."

I scrolled through his short contacts list and hit the 'Call' button when it appeared beside Adam's name.

"Update?" a male voice asked through the speaker.

"You're on speaker with me and Joanna," West said. "We're tracking Sewell. He might lead us to Portia. We need backup to help get her out."

Adam didn't reply.

"Sir?" West asked.

The silence lingered. Dread curled in my gut. I had a bad feeling about this.

"Conti," Adam said slowly. "This is a massive operation. If we bust Sewell now, then there's a good chance Ortez will find out. I'm not sure that we can justify risking the entire operation for the sake of one confidential informant."

"What?" West sounded outraged.

I grimaced, but somehow, I wasn't surprised by his words. Someone who masterminded the duping of an innocent detective surely didn't mind a little collateral damage.

"Hold off for an hour or so," Adam said. "Let me think it over."

"Hang up," West growled.

I ended the call. "That's your boss?"

"Yeah." A muscle in his jaw ticked. "There's a reason he's in his current role. He's a good actor, but I'm pretty sure he doesn't give a shit about anyone besides himself."

"You're not waiting an hour, are you?" I asked quietly.

"No." He white-knuckled the steering wheel and turned onto a main road out of the residential area, into a more industrialized one.

"It's dangerous without backup." Him and I against who knows how many thugs? It wasn't just dangerous; it was practically suicidal.

He glanced at me, his green eyes burning with intensity. "I trust you, Jo. You and no one else. If we call in a police taskforce, we can't guarantee they'll be fighting for our side. We could be arming the opposition—and letting them know we're coming."

I squeezed the bridge of my nose, a headache forming behind my temples. "Then I guess we're going in alone."

I couldn't believe it. A month ago, I'd been happily married and oblivious to the poison infecting our ranks.

Only a short time ago, I'd hated my fake husband and would have been glad to never see his face again.

Now, I was gearing up to walk into battle with him.

How the hell did that happen?

I turned toward the window and rolled my eyes at my reflection. I knew exactly how it had happened. I'd gone and fallen back in love with my goddamn husband. Or maybe I'd never fallen out of love with him in the first place, and I'd just been fooling myself.

I turned back to him. "Tell me you have weapons hidden in here."

A slow grin spread across his face, although it didn't reach his eyes. "That, I can do. This girl is hiding all of my favorites."

At least that was something.

He slowed and took another corner, then another, moving deeper into the industrial district. Finally, we turned onto a street lined with warehouses. He parked on the side of the street, killed the engine and switched off the headlights.

The sun was beginning to rise, and we could see enough of our surroundings not to need flashlights. We got out of the car as silently as possible, and I cringed as the cold air whipped around us.

West lifted a panel on the floor in front of the driver's seat and withdrew a gun. I noticed a similar tab hidden on the passenger side, so I copied him and revealed a large compartment with a semi-automatic pistol inside. I clicked it together and checked the magazine. It was loaded. I pocketed more ammo.

"Got a knife?" West asked. "We might need to cut her free."

When I shook my head, he reached beneath the driver's seat and carefully slid out a box. He unlatched the box and offered me a large hunting knife inside a sheath, handle first. I connected it to my holster, and he tucked a second, smaller knife into his jacket pocket.

"Do you have bulletproof gear?" I murmured.

"Unfortunately not."

"Damn." A bulletproof vest and a helmet wouldn't go astray right now. I should have packed mine before I left home but I'd been preoccupied by the missing escort and hadn't considered that we might end up in a firefight before dawn.

"Ready?" he asked.

"Not really." I doubted either of us was truly prepared for whatever we were about to face.

We snuck around the side of the warehouse nearest us and picked our way around the buildings, approaching the warehouse Zeke had indicated, moving toward the rear rather than the front. If it had guards, they were more likely to be keeping an eye on the street than the surrounding properties.

I scanned the area as we approached our target. Perhaps we'd been wrong to suspect we were walking into a bad situation. No one moved on the perimeter. Not even a shadow flickered. Something about that gave me the creeps, but I didn't pause to wonder about it, instead darting across the open space to the side entrance.

I tried the handle. "It's locked."

"Here. Let me." West moved alongside me, holding a set of lock picks and a small electronic box.

"Drop it," a voice barked behind us. "Get on your knees and put your hands up."

I spun. A uniformed officer stood behind us, his gun leveled at my chest.

"I'm a homicide detective," I explained. "My badge is in my pocket."

I started to reach for it, but the officer just laughed. "I know you are."

Figures moved out of the darkness to join him, and within seconds, we were surrounded on all sides—only our backs protected by the warehouse.

The officer's finger tightened on the trigger. "Get on your knees, put down your weapons, and push them over here."

My heart sank. This man—whoever he was—wasn't the only uniformed policeman here. I recognized several around the precinct. Narcotics. Major Crimes. And there, front and center, was Detective Sewell.

Sewell put his hands on his hips and laughed. "Did you really think I'd be dumb enough to let you track me?"

His mouth was twisted in a cocky smirk, his back straight, and his attitude was all insolence. He no longer looked weary or beaten down by life. Despite his small stature, he was obviously in charge.

"I could tell you were suspicious of me," he continued, not waiting for us to reply. "I don't know what Denny said to you, but it was clear he'd been spilling his guts about something. I couldn't risk word getting out. One of our buddies who isn't on the force is on his way to visit Denny now. He won't be talking to anyone else."

A bolt of fear ran through me.

"No," I whispered.

We'd been wrong to suspect Hanson. He was just an innocent bystander caught up in this horrible mess.

I was tempted to ask what Sewell wanted with us, and why he'd allow us to see the faces of so many people involved, but I knew the answer to that last part: He didn't expect us to have a chance to tell anyone what we knew.

"Where's Portia?" I asked, trying to remain as calm as possible.

He scoffed. "That whore? She's long gone."

West stiffened, and I grabbed his arm before he could make a dangerous mistake. Attacking Sewell wouldn't get us anywhere when we were so outgunned and outnumbered. We didn't have a hope of escaping with brute strength. If we wanted to get out of here, we'd have to be smart about it.

"Cuff them," Sewell barked to the men nearest to us.

We allowed ourselves to be restrained and led around the warehouse and in through the main entrance. Only a few of our captors joined us. One frisked us both and removed our weapons.

Someone shoved me, and I dropped to my knees, wincing as the impact jarred my kneecaps. West stumbled beside me, landing on his ass. Sewell marched around and stood in front of us.

"So," he said, his hands on his hips. "What is it that you

think you know?"

Neither of us answered.

I'd never been in a situation like this before and I wasn't sure if West had either, but I knew that Sewell intended to dispose of us. The only reason he hadn't yet was because he didn't know how much knowledge we had of their operation —or whether we'd told anyone else.

If we gave him answers, he'd have no reason to keep us alive. Even if we were tortured, it would allow time for someone to notice we were missing and come looking. Better to be injured and alive than have a painless death.

Sewell sighed. "I really wish you'd make this easy. It would be nicer for all of us that way. Believe it or not, I don't actually want to hurt you."

We both remained silent.

He huffed. "Okay, next question. What was it that gave me away? Was it just Hanson, or did I do or say something to make you suspicious?"

No response.

He paced back and forth in front of us. "See, I don't think you've been onto me for long, but I do believe that someone has cottoned onto our operation, and it seems awfully suspicious to me that a famously straitlaced detective just happened to meet the man of her dreams at exactly the same time things started to go wrong for us."

I raised my chin. "It sounds like you're reaching."

His laugh had a manic edge. "Does it? Because I happen to think it stinks of a setup. I wasn't sure before tonight, but it's obvious to me now that you were in on this from the beginning. You helped the feds get close to your fellow officers. Where's your loyalty?"

I cocked an eyebrow, intrigued by the assumptions he'd made. I actually preferred his version of events to the real one, so I wasn't going to correct him. If I'd been in on the operation from the start, then it made me an active player. Infinitely preferable to being a pawn.

"I'm loyal to people who deserve it," I told him, refusing to let him cow me.

He chuckled. "You are, aren't you? Unfortunately for you, that makes you the weak link right now."

He picked up the discarded hunting knife and scraped it along the underside of West's chin, digging the point hard enough into his skin to draw blood. A single droplet rolled down his throat and soaked into the fabric of his jacket.

"See?" he continued, stepping back. "I can tell you care for your phony husband. It's sweet, in a way, and I'm grateful for it, because it means I can do this."

He made a quick hand gesture and a man dressed in black kicked West in the gut, just below his rib cage. I gritted my teeth as the air gusted between his lips and he groaned. His green eyes caught mine, wide with surprise.

The man kicked him again.

"Start talking," Sewell ordered me.

West's gaze implored me not to, so I pressed my lips together. If he was willing to endure pain to keep his operation on track, I respected that. These men were responsible for killing his father, after all. I could understand him wanting to give them the metaphorical middle finger.

Sewell made a sound of disgust. "Get me a bucket of water."

The man in black jogged deeper into the warehouse, between the containers that rose over two meters high. I wondered what was inside them. He'd said Portia was gone, but perhaps he'd lied. Could she have been stashed in one of these containers?

When he returned, he set the bucket in front of West. With no ceremony, Sewell grabbed him by the head and forced his face into the water.

I jerked, lurching toward them, determined to help as West struggled, his cuffed hands opening and closing around nothing. The man in black planted his foot on my diaphragm and shoved me backward. I landed hard on my tailbone and bit my lip until I tasted blood, determined not to give him the pleasure of hearing me scream.

Sewell yanked West out of the water. He sputtered, spitting out water and dragging in a lungful of air.

"Who knows about us?" Sewell demanded.

"Fuck you," West gasped.

Sewell shoved him face-first back into the bucket and held him there for so long that I stumbled toward them again, dodging the man in black's attempt to sweep my legs out from under me. Unfortunately, before I reached them, he grabbed my shoulders and held me back.

West surfaced again, panting heavily as water streamed down his face and dripped off his chin.

"West," I whispered.

I wasn't sure I could watch them do this again, even if it was what he wanted. What if they left it too long and he passed out?

What if he drowned? Could I live with that?

Sure, I didn't know as many of the details of the operation as West did, but I knew some. Possibly enough to make them stop.

Sewell pushed him backward, and West only just caught himself before his head cracked against the concrete floor.

The dirty detective's mouth twisted. "Do you know how I confirmed that you're not really a bartender?" he asked West, rounding on him. "I just showed a photo of you to my brother, and lo-and-behold, it turns out you were with the cop he took out last year. A little more digging, and I realized he's your dear departed dad."

"Don't talk about my father," West hissed, his eyes gleaming with fury.

Sewell cocked his head. "Don't you want to know who pulled the trigger?"

"Your brother," West ground out.

"Yes." Sewell's lips quirked. "Clever. Dirk?"

The man in black stepped forward. My heart dropped.

He had killed West's dad.

Now that Sewell brought my attention to him, his military bearing was undeniable.

West's eyes shot fire at Dirk Sewell but he didn't say a word.

Detective Sewell huffed. "I was really hoping you'd be one of those people who run their mouths when they're angry. I guess I'll have to try another tactic." He turned to me. "Lee, apologies for assuming you were the weak link in this arrangement. I shouldn't have said that just because you're a woman. Let's try this all again, shall we?"

He closed the distance between us in three steps, grabbed me by the arm and jammed the knife into the fleshy part of my left shoulder. Searing pain tore through me.

I bit through the soft interior of my lower lip and swallowed a scream. I stared at the blade, embedded in my shoulder, and resisted the urge to try to yank it out after he let go. Doing so would only worsen the bleeding and possibly cause more damage.

"Jo!" West shouted, drawing my attention. His face was pale, his eyes full of horror. "I'm sorry. I'm so sorry I got you into this."

I didn't respond because, really, what was there to say? I wished we weren't in this situation too, but wishing and praying wouldn't do us any good right now.

**23**

———

*JOANNA*

Sewell smiled. "How sweet. He cares. Let's aim for something more important next."

My mind blacked out for a millisecond as he ripped the knife out of my shoulder. He scanned me from head to toe, as if deciding what part of a prime cut of meat he wanted for himself.

"Or, we could go old-fashioned," he mused to Dirk.

"A finger?" Dirk asked.

Sewell nodded. "It sends a message without killing her."

Fuck. My heart sped up.

I didn't want to lose a finger, even though they were right that it wouldn't be fatal. I'd seen enough torture victims to know how painful it was.

"Put your hand on the ground," Sewell ordered. "Fingers wide."

Shaking, I lowered myself down and splayed my left hand on the concrete, the other tucked behind it. I gritted my teeth through the pain. Putting my right hand forward would have hurt less, but I'd rather lose a finger on my left hand than my right one.

"Hold her," Sewell ordered his brother.

Dirk grabbed my uninjured shoulder and pushed down firmly enough that I couldn't get up if I tried. Sewell rested the bloody blade of the knife on the base of my pinky finger and used his other hand to add pressure until the bite of the steel became painful.

"Stop!"

Sewell stilled, and the pressure eased up.

"Stop," West repeated raggedly. "I'll talk."

My throat constricted. "Don't," I choked out, unable to look at him in case he saw my fear. "I can take it."

"Maybe you can." His voice was strained. "But you're stronger than me. I can't watch you suffer. Especially not when it's my fault."

Now, I did risk a glance at him. His head hung low, his shoulders slumped. He looked defeated.

"You'll regret it," I said, knowing it to be true.

West raised his eyes and looked straight at Sewell, ignoring me. "You're right. I'm a federal agent. We have a small team investigating corruption in your precinct."

My breath stuttered as Sewell released my hand.

What was West doing?

Sure, it wasn't the whole truth, but it was more than he should have admitted.

"How many on this team?" Sewell asked, still holding the knife as if he might use it on me at any moment.

"Four. My handler, a tech guy, and another undercover agent. It's top secret because we're not sure who we're able to trust."

"Good." Sewell looked pleased. "I want names."

"No names."

I exhaled sharply, relieved that West at least had the sense not to rat anyone out. Of course, from what he'd said, there were many more than four people involved, but it would make Sewell less jumpy if he believed the knowledge was localized to a handful of federal employees.

Sewell nodded to Dirk. He pivoted toward me, and I barely had time to brace myself before his knee drove into my gut. I gasped, my lungs struggling to drag in air. I keeled forward, catching my weight on my forearms.

"I swear, I don't know their names," West cried.

Sewell gestured for Dirk to hit me again. This time, he stood on my hand. I whimpered as something crunched and a dizzying wave of pain swept through me. Had he broken one of my bones? The ones in the hand were notoriously delicate.

"Fuck." West started crawling toward me but was quickly stopped. "Adam. My handler's name is Adam Teller. I only know the others through their code names: Firewall and Delta."

A slow smile spread across Sewell's face. "Excellent."

"What are you doing?" I hissed at West, horrified by what he'd just admitted. "You can't tell them that."

He looked at me helplessly, as if he didn't know himself why he'd caved. My gut churned, and I swallowed, doing my best to pretend I couldn't feel the throbbing of my shoulder or the sticky wetness of my shirt, which was soaked with blood.

Sewell chuckled. "Poor Joanna. Wants to think everyone is as strong and righteous as her. Sometimes, men are foolish and weak."

I searched West's gaze, ignoring Sewell. There had to be more to it than that, but he looked so pathetic and down-trodden that I didn't know what to believe.

Sewell scoffed. "Dirk. Let's take your team on a hunting mission."

"Wait," West protested. "Joanna needs medical attention."

Sewell glanced at me dismissively. "She'll survive. Or at least, she'll survive long enough for me to verify the information you provided. If it doesn't check out, I'll be back and I doubt you'll like the outcome."

"But—"

"Sullivan, you stand watch," Sewell said, cutting him off. "Call for backup from outside if you need, but I doubt they'll give you much trouble. They've got their own problems."

He and his brother strode past us, taking most of the remaining men with them. The man I assumed was Sullivan, a broad-shouldered guy of indeterminate age and built like a linebacker, remained with us, his hand hovering over his sidearm.

"What were you thinking?" I asked West quietly.

He scooted closer to me. Sullivan twitched but didn't seem inclined to move from his position leaning against one of the containers.

"If they look up that name, all they'll find is the address of an abandoned former safe house," he murmured, shifting closer until his breath ruffled my hair. "Adam isn't my handler's real name. It's an alias, set up for this purpose. The instant they show up at the address, my team will know one of us has been compromised. Considering my conversation with Adam earlier, I'm betting he'll be able to guess who."

Relief trickled through me, quickly followed by another splash of fear.

"They'll be furious when they realize no one lives at the safe house." I angled my face toward his so it would look like we were nuzzling each other rather than speaking.

"Then we'd better get out of here before then," he replied.

"Stop whispering," Sullivan snapped. "And do something about that arm. I don't want anyone dying on my watch or the boss will have my head."

"What do you suggest we do when we're handcuffed?" West asked.

The guy narrowed his eyes and opened his mouth to respond, but before he could, there was a crash outside. With a sigh, he drew his gun from its holster and waved it at us.

"Don't try anything while I'm gone." He circled around us, keeping a wide berth, and opened the door. He peered out, then apparently not seeing what he wanted, took a few steps outside.

"I'm really sorry for all of this," West said, carefully getting to his feet and shuffling toward me. "You'd never be here if not for me."

I shrugged, then winced as the cut on my shoulder protested the movement. "You were just doing your job."

"Yeah," he agreed, taking hold of my sleeve and ripping open the hole where the knife slashed the fabric. "But I let it get personal. Involving you the way we did was wrong, even if it was for a good cause. I just... I never thought you'd get hurt."

I snorted, then swore as he pressed chilled fingers to my torn skin. He was deluded if he'd never expected me to get hurt. Yeah, perhaps he meant physically, but I was always going to be emotionally destroyed by his deception. I didn't see how he could think anything different.

Footsteps slapped the pavement outside, the door flew open, and Sullivan sprinted toward us, shoving the door behind him but not pausing to lock it. He grabbed me by the waist and yanked me away from West, who stumbled and came after me, but with his hands cuffed—and shaking from being doused in cold water—there was little he could do.

Sullivan spun me around and lifted me until my toes were hardly brushing the ground. His gun touched my temple.

"Don't move," he muttered near my ear.

I stared at the door, a strange combination of emotions rioting through me. He was using me as a human shield, which meant someone must have arrived who he viewed as a threat. Perhaps Adam had changed his mind about backup and sent them after us. Damn I hoped they didn't come in firing.

But it wasn't federal agents who rushed through the entrance.

It wasn't the police either.

A tightly grouped cluster of people in dark tactical gear with the King's Security logo on their breast pockets moved into the warehouse as a unit.

My jaw dropped. What the hell were they doing here?

I recognized the man in front as David, one of the unit leaders in Kade Campbell's personal security division. By his side was a short, feminine figure with a badass gun.

Hallie.

"Stand down," David said, his tone even. From what I could recall, he had a background in hostage negotiation. Helpful at times like this.

"Don't move or I'll shoot," Sullivan replied, his voice shaking.

I grimaced. We were in a standoff. If nothing changed, we could easily get stuck here with neither side making any progress.

Clang!

A metallic sound outside distracted Sullivan for a couple of seconds.

That time was all I needed.

I ducked forward, then snapped my head back, ramming

the back of my skull into his nose. The cartilage crumpled and hot blood showered my hair as I forced myself to become a deadweight.

Sullivan didn't have the presence of mind to hold me in place. He let me drop to the floor, and in doing so, made himself vulnerable.

West lashed out at him, kicking the side of his ankle. It rolled beneath him, and he stumbled. I swept my legs in an arc, knocking him off balance.

He tripped forward, landing heavily on his palms.

In an instant, Hallie stood over him, her gun aimed at the back of his head. David unclipped a set of handcuffs from his belt and fastened Sullivan's wrists together behind his back.

Hallie holstered her weapon and scanned me, her eyes widening as she noticed the blood drenching the side of my body.

"Boss. Cuff keys," she said.

While David searched Sullivan's pockets and emerged with a pair of keys, Hallie called for an ambulance. I held my wrists out to David, and he unlocked the cuffs before sliding them off. I turned my wrists in circles, trying to get the feeling back. David unlocked West's cuffs as well, and then West was wrapping his arms around me and cradling me against his strong chest.

"Thank fuck," he murmured against my hair. "You're all right."

"We're all right." I buried my face in his jacket, wishing it was his bare skin.

I pulled away enough to address the others.

"How come you're here?" I asked Hallie.

Through the visor in her helmet, I saw her smirk.

"Zeke's spidey senses were tingling," she explained. "Apparently, it was easier to track down your perp than he thought it should have been, and that made him nervous. He did a sweep of the cameras in the area and realized you were in trouble."

"Thank God for that." If they hadn't come, there was no way to be sure whether West's team would have intercepted Sewell before he returned to us. I shook my head. "Zeke will be constantly calling in favors after this."

West kissed my forehead. "As far as I'm concerned, he deserves them."

With his free hand, he took his phone from his pocket. "I'd better call Adam."

I started to move away, but his grip tightened.

"Stay," he murmured.

"Okay."

Hallie raised her eyebrow at me, and I shrugged my good shoulder. Yeah, it must be pretty obvious that I wasn't mad at West anymore. In fact, I was just as crazy about him as ever.

West dialed the number and waited for the call to connect. He briefly outlined the situation to Adam. I listened, able to hear both sides of the conversation if I concentrated hard.

"We've already got a team en route to the safe house." Adam's voice was tinny and distant. "Do you want to meet us there and be the one to slap the cuffs on Dirk Sewell?"

My breath caught. Obviously, West would want to do that. He'd been searching for his father's killer for months. But as he held my gaze, his expression warmed, and he blew me a silent kiss.

"No thanks," he told Adam. "You do it. I'm needed elsewhere."

# 24



"Make sure to keep the stitches dry for at least the first forty-eight hours," the doctor said as they finished the dressing on Joanna's shoulder. "You should be on light duties for the rest of the week. And stay out of the gym."

She nodded. "I will, thanks."

"And you." The doctor turned toward me, his expression stern. "Come back immediately if you experience any difficulty breathing. I'm not worried about the swelling and bruising. That will heal. But secondary drowning is still a possibility if you inhaled water."

"I'll keep that in mind," I told him.

Joanna's eyes narrowed. "If anything is off, I promise to bring him back."

"Good." The doctor straightened. "I'll send a nurse in with your discharge paperwork, and then you can leave whenever you're ready."

Ten minutes later, we were making our way slowly along the corridor toward a hospital room with a uniformed police officer stationed outside. I ached, but thanks to a strong dose of painkillers, it was a nuisance rather than anything more severe.

Joanna was fortunately uninjured except for the cut on her shoulder and some swelling in her hand. I felt terrible that they'd hurt her to get to me. She'd suffered enough because of me. She shouldn't have had to endure further pain.

I was also worried that the second I turned my back, she might disappear. There was no way my undercover role was still viable, which meant she no longer had to keep me around. If she asked me to get out of her life now, all I could do was say yes, no matter how much it pained me. There was no reason for the pretense to continue.

"Matthews," Jo said as we approached the officer, "how is he?"

Matthews scanned us both, her eyes widening. "Safe. They put me here to make sure it stays that way. What happened to you two?"

Joanna waved her hand. "I'll explain later."

"Okay." Matthews seemed disappointed but didn't push the matter. "He's awake and cranky as ever. Go on in."

She stepped aside and I opened the door and held it for Joanna to enter first. I closed it behind her, breathing in the familiar hospital scents of antiseptic, blood, and body odor.

Hanson lay on a narrow hospital bed, propped up on pillows, his eyes half open. With visible effort, he opened them fully and scowled at us.

"You look like shit," he rasped.

Joanna laughed. "I think this is a case of the pot and the kettle, Denny."

One corner of Hanson's mouth hitched up. "Maybe so."

I remained standing while Joanna took the seat beside the bed.

"What's the prognosis?" she asked.

He rolled his eyes. "Women. Always fussing over me. The doc says I'll survive. Should recover fully, although I'm thinking about riding a desk until retirement. I don't fancy getting shot again."

"You could do the paperwork and research while I'm in the field," Joanna said. "I'm glad to hear you'll be all right. Has anyone called Deborah?"

"Yeah." He closed his eyes and then forced them open again. "She's getting herself a coffee and a salad in the cafeteria. She'll be back soon."

"Denny." Joanna's good hand twitched, as if she'd almost reached for his and then decided against it. "What were you doing at that apartment building?"

I moved to stand behind her and rested my hands on her shoulders. Hanson's eyes followed the movement.

"I'll tell you that when you tell me what he's doing here," he grumbled.

"Soon," Joanna assured him.

He harrumphed. "Fine. I went back to the Red Door. Had some more questions. I saw Portia and recognized her as the woman your husband was having coffee with. She wouldn't answer my questions, but I got the feeling she was the key to everything. I'd been trying to catch her after one of her shifts to try again, but I wasn't having any luck, so I persuaded the manager to give me her address. Real scumbag, that one."

"You didn't think that asking about her could put her in danger?" Joanna asked, chastening.

Hanson cringed. "I pretended to be a fan of her dancing."

"And he bought it?" She sounded dubious.

"Well, I thought so, but who the hell knows?"

"So, you went to her apartment, looking for her," I prompted, eager to hear the rest.

He tilted his head toward me. "The lock was broken, and when I pushed the door open, who should I see inside but fucking Detective Sewell. He ran out the fire escape. I followed, but someone shot me before I could catch him."

I doubted he'd have been able to catch the younger, fitter man anyway, but I kept that thought to myself.

Joanna frowned. "It wasn't Sewell who shot you?"

"No." He sighed. "I didn't see who the fucker was that pulled the trigger."

Joanna glanced up at me, a question in her eyes. Could it have been Dirk Sewell?

If Detective Sewell had been there to search Portia's apartment for something, it made sense that he'd have taken someone for backup. His brother, Dirk, was a crack shot and should have killed Hanson.

That said, the older detective had been a moving target in the dark. Perhaps because of that, Dirk had only managed to hit his chest rather than his head. If he'd seen Hanson go down, he might not have even realized his mistake.

"What's going on, Lee?" Hanson asked tiredly. "What's all this about?"

This time, she did take his hand. I checked the door to make sure it was firmly shut and nodded for her to share as much information as she thought he needed to know. He'd nearly bled out on a freezing cold fire escape because of this case. He deserved the truth.

"This is confidential," she said quietly. "You can't even tell Deborah. Understand?"

He snorted. "Wouldn't be the first thing I haven't told my wife."

Joanna's nostrils flared, but she didn't reprimand him for the remark. "West is an undercover federal agent working on a task force to identify dirty cops in the employ of the Ortez crime syndicate."

Realization dawned on Hanson's face. "That's why you didn't kick him out after seeing him with the dancer. She's an informant, isn't she?"

"I can't comment on the status of anyone who may or may not be a federal intelligence asset," I said.

"Right." He clearly saw the ass-covering statement for what it was. "So, Sewell is getting paid off by Ortez."

"We believe so," Joanna confirmed. "As are a number of others, most likely including Detective Ireland. The operation is massive. Not restricted to our district. Unfortunately, this whole thing has botched it a bit."

"I'll bet."

"Denny..." She dragged his name out as if unsure how to go on.

He grunted. "What?"

"No one ever tried to recruit you to work for Ortez, did they?"

His expression didn't change. "If they did, they were sneaky about it. No one ever came right out and asked me if I was willing to accept bribes to betray everything we stand for."

She released his hand and tucked her hair behind her ear. "Detective Neal didn't ever invite you to the Red Door?"

His forehead furrowed. "What's that got to do with anything?"

"Humor me."

"Yeah. Clancy invited me to a strip club, although he never said what it was called. I turned him down." He scrunched his nose. "What do I need with barely legal strippers when I have Deborah at home?"

The tension slipped out of Joanna's shoulders. I knew it had been weighing heavily on her, wondering whether

Hanson was involved. Especially after reading Sasha's diary. But Chicago was a big city, and there were plenty of older male detectives with wives. It could have been any of them.

Hanson turned to me. "So, what happens with your operation now?"

A throat cleared in the doorway. We all snapped around. Whoever was there had approached so silently, none of us had noticed.

Adam stood with his hands in his pockets, one eyebrow raised. "I'm going to pretend I didn't hear that question. After all, I'm sure that no federal agent would ever communicate the details of a secret operation to anyone not cleared to know about it. Right, West?"

I stared at him flatly. Once, his tone might have made me nervous, but after the way he'd left us without support when we needed it, I wasn't inclined to care what he thought.

Adam's thin lips twisted into a smirk. "In fact, we'll consider me forgetting this conversation to be the first part of my apology for not having your back, shall we?"

I blinked, startled. It was eerie how he seemed to know what was going on inside my head. "I didn't hear an actual apology."

He nodded. "Good point. I'm sorry, West. I hesitated, and as a result, you and Detective Lee were endangered."

No apology would make up for the terror I'd experienced when Sewell had plunged the knife into Joanna's shoulder, but I knew it was the best I'd get from Adam. I just had to hope he wouldn't pursue disciplinary action after how much had gone wrong in the past couple of weeks.

"Would you like to know what the second part of the apology is?" he asked, striding farther into the room.

"What?" Honestly, I just wanted him to get to the point.

"An update." He shifted his weight from one foot to the other. "Not to be repeated outside this room."

Joanna pivoted her chair to face him, and I circled around so I remained at her back. "Tell us."

Adam eyeballed her, but I couldn't tell from his blank expression what he was thinking. "Over a dozen arrests have been made this morning, including those of Charles and Dirk Sewell, who were found in possession of a rifle with the same type of ammunition used to shoot Detectives Conti, Neal, and Hanson. I expect ballistics to confirm the connection. He will likely serve a life sentence."

The air vacated my lungs. My vision swam as tears filled my eyes.

The man who'd killed my father had been arrested. He was going to prison.

Thank God.

I'd finally be able to look Mamma in the eye and tell her we'd found the man responsible and that he would pay for his crimes.

Joanna laid her hand over mine. "You okay?"

I nodded, my throat too tight to speak.

"Charlie Sewell isn't talking," Adam continued. "But your friend there is willing to testify that he was inside Portia Lowry's apartment prior to any missing persons report being made."

"Good riddance," Hanson muttered.

"We also suspect that Sewell told Ortez that Neal was becoming a liability, and that's why he was killed in such a public manner—to send a message to others to be more careful. Not that he'll likely admit as much," Adam added.

"Do you think the scare tactic would have worked if everything else hadn't gone off the rails?" Joanna asked.

Adam's smirk deepened. "I don't know. But given that one of the arrested policemen—a homicide detective named

Hamilton—is singing like a canary, it clearly isn't working now. Hamilton claims to have been pressured into bedding a prostitute and subsequently blackmailed with the threat of losing his job and his marriage if he didn't help."

Joanna's dark eyes met mine and a silent understanding passed between us. We'd have to check a photo of the detective to see if he matched the description, but it seemed likely he was the one we'd mistakenly believed might be Hanson.

"Personally, I think he was as tempted by the payoff as he was driven by the blackmail." Adam's upper lip curled scornfully. "But that's for a jury to decide. The point is, he's naming as many names as he possibly can, and he's provided a written statement that he overheard Ortez admit to killing Sasha Sloane when he discovered that she was keeping a written record of his confidences in her."

Joanna exhaled sharply. "I guess that's that then. Did he know about the baby?"

Adam shrugged. "Hamilton didn't mention it. With how early the pregnancy was, it's possible even Sasha herself didn't know. Nevertheless, we're hoping we can put pressure on Ortez now and get him to cough up the names of any bad seeds remaining within our ranks."

"Looks like you've got your collar," I murmured to Joanna.

Deal or no deal, Ortez wouldn't walk free when faced with a homicide charge. Although I wasn't as confident as Adam seemed to be that he'd give up his police assets to protect himself. Men like him did well in prison. He probably wanted them in place so he could continue running things from behind bars.

"Is Ortez ours?" Joanna asked Adam. "Or have the feds taken him?"

He grinned. "We'll let you lead the charge with the homicide conviction while we put together a case."

She nodded, obviously pleased. The pieces were coming together nicely. All except...

Shit.

"Portia," I gasped. "Has there been any sign of her?"

Joanna's eyes widened, and I could tell that with all the excitement of the past hours, the confidential informant had somehow slipped off her radar too.

But Adam just laughed. "Miss Lowry is safe and sound. She went to ground after one of Ortez's men tried to abduct her off the street. She lost her phone during the altercation and was afraid to return to any of her usual haunts in case they were waiting for her there, so she slept rough in a homeless encampment and then, when the sun rose, returned to her apartment to find it overrun with police."

"She's okay?" I may not know Portia well as a person, but she'd gone above and beyond as an informant, and she'd been a loyal friend to Sasha. That said a lot about her character.

"Fine," Adam assured me. "Smudged makeup, a bit tired, but unharmed. It seems she can run like a gazelle when she has to."

I chuckled, my heart lightening. "Of course she can."

No doubt she'd had to run many times in her life— although probably usually *from* the police rather than *to* them.

Adam's expression sobered as his gaze landed on Joanna. "Detectives Lee and Hanson, I'm sorry to be the one to break the news, but Captain Gordon Thackery is one of the names that have come up during the course of our interviews. Captain Thackery has been suspended from the force pending a full investigation..."

"Oh." Joanna's face fell. "We knew it was a possibility, but I'd hoped we were being paranoid. Poor Beth. She'll be distraught."

I turned my hand over to lace my fingers with hers. "She'll need a friend."

She nodded. "I suppose she will. Provided she didn't know about it."

Adam laughed heartily. "You don't have to worry about that. I listened in when they broke the news. She was irate. God, I wouldn't want that woman on my bad side." He glanced between us, apparently done dropping bombshells, at least for now. "I'll leave you to it. But... uh... if you two want to have any personal conversations, you'd better do it soon. You won't get a moment of rest after this."

He spun on the heel of his expensive Italian leather boot and sauntered out.

"I hope I never meet that man again," Joanna said distastefully. "There's just something about him I don't like."

I had to agree with her there. Adam had his moments, but they were few and far between.

"Damn fed," Hanson cursed. "But Thackery? Really?"

Before anyone could respond, there was a light knock on the door behind us, and then Deborah entered. Her bright blue eyes lit as she broke into a smile.

"Joanna," she said warmly, rushing toward us and bending to scoop Joanna into a motherly hug.

I got out of the way.

"I can't thank you enough for saving my Denny," Deborah said.

Joanna awkwardly patted her back. "He's tough. He'd have been fine without me."

Both Hansons scoffed.

Deborah drew back, her hands on Joanna's shoulders. "Let me cook you dinner later this week so I can thank you properly."

Joanna softened. "That would be lovely. Thank you."

"Let the girl go, Debs," Hanson grumbled. "She and her

man need to have a conversation before they're swamped with paperwork." The sly old dog winked at me. "Better make it a good chat."

Joanna rose to her feet, and immediately, nerves riddled my gut, and I recalled how anxious I'd been when we'd arrived. Speaking with Adam and Hanson had distracted me, but there was still every possibility that Joanna could leave me in her dust now that my role in our operation was over.

"Take care of him," Joanna told Deborah. She waved and headed out of the room.

I followed behind, feeling remarkably as if I was marching to my doom. I needed to get ahead of this. I couldn't take a back seat. There was an unmarked door to our left, so I tried the handle. It opened onto a small storage closet. I grabbed Joanna's hand and pulled her inside.

I took her other hand, so I was holding both, and gazed into her eyes. "I'm so sorry for everything." I wished I could kiss her, but I didn't dare cross that line right now. "You've been through a lot and it's all my fault. You're officially free of me now, if you want to be, but I hope you'll let me prove to you that I really do love you. I never lied about that, and my feelings for you haven't wavered."

My instincts were screaming at me to keep talking because as long as she stayed silent, she couldn't actively reject me, but I forced myself to be quiet and give her a chance to speak, even as my heart hammered against my ribs threatening to break free.

To my surprise, she smiled and returned the pressure of my grip. "Whatever the personal consequences, we did something good. That's what my job is about. Maybe I'd have preferred our relationship not start the way it did—"

I snorted. That was an understatement. But I shut up when she arched her eyebrows.

"But I know in my heart that you're a good man and you were trying to do what was right in a difficult situation," she continued. Her tongue darted out to moisten her lips, and my muscles tightened in response. "The thing is, I never stopped loving you, even when I felt like I didn't know you. Even when I wanted to hate you. That's why your betrayal hurt so much."

"Jo, I—"

She disentangled her hand from mine and pressed her finger to my lips. "Shh. Let me get this out." She drew in a deep breath then released it. "I want to try being with you for real, but we're not keeping up the facade of being married. Let's date again."

My heart swelled. "You mean it?"

She nodded, her lip caught between her teeth. "Don't lie to me or I'll end you."

"I won't." I cupped her face between my hands and kissed her. She tasted of everything I loved. If I could bottle this moment up and make it last forever, I would. But then I'd miss out on a lifetime with her, and that seemed like a terrible loss.

Her lips curved against mine.

"What are you smiling about?" I asked.

Her smile widened. "Just wondering how I'm going to explain all this to my māma."

I groaned. "She's going to gut me."

Māma Lee may be tiny, but she was scary as hell when she was mad.

"Could we just... not mention it?" I pleaded.

Joanna's eyes gleamed evilly. "Where's the fun in that?"

"Fine." I slumped my shoulders. "I guess you deserve to have your fun."

"Damn right I do." Her smile changed into something

softer, and she kissed me again. "But at the end of the day, we'll make it work, right?"

I kissed her beautiful face, silently thanking whatever fates had brought us together. "Absolutely."

"Then that's all that matters." With one hand still linked to mine, she pushed open the closet door and we stepped out, startling an orderly who was scurrying past. "Shall we sneak home and take a nap before Dominguez calls me?"

"Only if I can hold you."

She rolled her eyes. "You don't have to be so cheesy."

I flashed her my teeth. "You love it."

She didn't reply, but her secret smile told me more than words.

We took the elevator to the ground floor, but as we were passing reception, a familiar figure came into view. Short, slightly plump, and with a voice they could probably hear the next ward over.

"Mamma!" I exclaimed.

Joanna's eyes widened. "Mamma?" she echoed.

Mamma swung toward us. "Weston! There you are." Tears shimmered in her eyes, and my gut dropped. "All I've been trying to do is see my son and these ridiculous people wouldn't tell me where you were."

I opened my arms, and she threw herself into them. I caught her and she squeezed me so tightly I winced, my battered body instinctively recoiling.

"Ow, Mamma. Careful."

She pulled away, horrified. "My poor baby. You're hurt." But before she could fuss over me, she finally noticed Joanna, and her worried frown vanished. "Is this my new daughter?"

I bent to kiss her cheek. "Yes, Mamma. This is Joanna. She's a detective in the Chicago PD. Jo, this is my mamma, Fiorella Conti."

Mamma reached for Joanna, but then stopped. "You're hurt too. Santa cielo, what on earth happened?" She didn't give either of us time to explain. "No, don't tell me yet. I'm taking both of you home. I was married to a detective. I know what you need. Rest and a good meal."

"It's nice to meet you, Mrs. Conti," Joanna said.

Mamma waved her hand dismissively. "None of that. You can call me Fio or Mamma. Now, come along."

She bustled toward the exit.

Joanna looked at me. "What just happened?"

I stifled a laugh. "My mother adopted you. Come on. Let her fuss over you a little."

A slow smile spread across her face. "I like her."

"Don't worry," I whispered. "She likes you too."

"Yes," Mamma called over her shoulder. "I do."

We both laughed, and warmth unfurled in my chest as I took Joanna's hand again. For the first time, I didn't have to yearn for a future with her that I'd never get to have. She may not be my wife in truth, but one day soon, she would be.

# EPILOGUE – 4 MONTHS LATER

*JOANNA*

I gazed out the window, watching people bustle around the train station outside as the train I was on gently rolled into motion. Snow was falling despite the fact it was spring, creating a sense of isolation that would only be compounded once we left civilization behind.

"Excuse me. Is this seat taken?"

I looked up, and my heart leapt. The most handsome man I'd ever seen stood before me, his green eyes twinkling and a mischievous smile on his lips.

"No." I instinctively smiled back. "It's not. Would you like to join me?"

"I'd love to." He sat and beamed, his eyes crinkling at the corners. "It's nice to meet you. I'm Weston Conti."

I accepted his proffered hand, playing along with him. "Joanna Lee."

He raised my hand and kissed the inside of my wrist. "Charmed."

Butterflies swooped in my stomach.

"What is it you do, Weston?" I asked.

He released my hand and reclined in the seat, making

himself comfortable as we picked up speed. "I used to be an undercover federal agent. Now I work as a private investigator at a company called King's Security."

"That sounds like an interesting job."

"It is." He cocked his head. "My father was a detective, but I lost him in a horrible tragedy. I have a wonderful mother who loves cooking and who keeps me in line."

I laughed. "She sounds great. I also have a mother with plenty of opinions, and a father who lets her get her way because he absolutely adores her."

His lips twitched. "As he should."

I glanced out the window. We were on the outskirts of town now, and if I leaned at just the right angle, I could see the outline of the mountains we were heading toward.

When I turned back to West, my breath caught. He was no longer seated opposite. Instead, he'd dropped to one knee on the carpet in front of me. I opened my mouth to ask what he was doing but closed it again when I noticed the ring box clasped in his hand.

"Joanna." He drew in a deep breath. "My smart, beautiful, courageous Joanna. I love you more than I ever dreamed was possible, and I want to marry you for real. With both of our families present, all of our friends, and a brand new ring. I want to be with you forever. What do you say?"

I blinked at him, emotion swelling in my chest. Sincerity was etched into every line of his beloved face.

Perhaps the start of our love story hadn't been what I would have chosen for myself, but we were stronger because of everything we'd been through, and our happily-ever-after could still be fairy-tale perfect.

"Yes," I whispered. "I will marry you again."

He took my hand and slid the single white gold engagement band onto my finger, alongside the wedding ring I'd never taken off. Then he cupped my face and kissed me as we hurtled into the countryside, snow falling softly outside.

I wrapped my arms around him and blinked back tears. "I love you."

When he kissed my forehead, everything inside me settled.

No matter how we'd started, West and I had the rest of our lives together, and it all began now.

## THE END

# EXCERPT FROM FIGHTER'S HEART

*Lena*

Eight words. That's all it takes to ruin my day.

"LaFontaine, I have a special assignment for you."

I recognize the voice without looking up from my desk. It's my prick of a boss, Adrian, and anything he's terming a "special assignment" will inevitably be a nightmare. That's all I get these days. The unfixable cases. The spoiled, self-entitled sports stars who screw up so badly, no one else wants them.

God, one massive win and I become the go-to public relations girl for the biggest jerks-with-abs in Vegas. Why can't I, just once, get a client who's a marginalized feminist with a cause? Sighing, I raise my head and meet Adrian's beady little eyes. This douchebag has my career in his hands, and he knows it.

"What's the case?"

His thin lips curl in a self-satisfied smile. It doesn't escape my notice that he's yet to close the door, which makes me wonder if he's keeping it open as an escape route.

"Jase Rawlins."

*Oh. Hell. No.*

"Nuh-uh," I say. "No freaking way."

Jase "The Wrangler" Rawlins is one of the bad boys of MMA. I don't even have to ask why he needs our services. Anyone who pays attention to the sports industry knows his ex-girlfriend has come forward with allegations of domestic abuse. I've seen photos of her bruised cheek and read the story in popular magazines. The guy is violent. But I suppose I shouldn't expect any different from a cage fighter.

I know the type. I've *dated* the type.

"There's no way I'm working with that asshole. Absolutely not. Find someone else. I'm not aiding and abetting a jackass who thinks he can get away with hitting women."

The door opens wider, and Jase Rawlins himself steps into my small, airy office, his gaze immediately drawn to the view out the window, which looks over the business district. I know him on sight, and I'm not even sorry he overheard my comment. He deserves all the condemnation he gets, and more. Fuck him.

Adrian's brows draw together, as if he didn't expect me to argue. "Everything is organized, Lena. The papers are signed. It's a done deal."

My teeth scrape together loud enough I'm surprised no one else hears them. I meet Jase's eyes, and a jolt runs through me. They're a strange color. Dark gray, or maybe green, it's hard to tell, and fringed with the thickest lashes I've ever seen. Pretty eyes. Out of place on a man known for choking his opponents into submission. He has high, arrogant cheekbones and plush lips, although the upper one is marred by a thin scar.

This is a face a woman could study forever—if she wasn't too caught up in his body. Because holy shit, he has a *body*. Broad shoulders, tapered hips, and strong legs with muscled calves showing beneath his shorts. Unfortunately, however panty-meltingly hot he is, he's also a brute, and I'm done with men like him. If I have anything to say about it, I'm not touching another MMA superstar—not with a ten-foot pole.

Time to shut this shit down.

"I'm *not* working with you," I tell him, and watch for a change in his expression, but his only reaction is a quick flick of his eyes to the right, where a man in an expensive suit has followed him into my office. "This is *not* a happening thing." I aim this comment at the suit, and he glowers. I don't care. There are some jobs even I won't take, and Adrian wants me to cross a moral line I'm not prepared to.

"Lena," Adrian says in a cautioning tone. "Hold on a moment."

Crossing my arms over my chest, I stare at him, wondering how far he's prepared to push. Considering Jase Rawlins is worth seven or eight figures, I'd hazard a guess that dollar signs are flashing in Adrian's eyes. Too bad. I don't operate that way. Money isn't my driver, and he knows it. So what approach will he take?

---

*Jase*

Sometimes, I wish it was legal to put someone in a chokehold outside of the cage. Like this uppity image specialist, for instance. Yeah, she may look like a schoolboy's wet dream in an ass-hugging pencil skirt and V-necked blouse, but it's obvious from the second she opens her mouth that she's already judged me and found me wanting. Nothing I'm not used to, but it still stings.

Maybe it's the fact my dick has some really great ideas about what he'd like to do with those gorgeous red lips, which are currently set in a sulky pout, or maybe it's her instant dismissal, but I want to rile her. To ruffle up her silky feathers and find out just how mouthy she can get.

I step forward before her boss can intervene, and raise a hand. As expected, everyone falls silent, which only seems to piss the redhead off more. Fuck, we haven't even gotten as far as exchanging names before she's mentally convicted me. That's the shitty part of being in the public spotlight. Everyone thinks they know me. They believe every stupid lie anyone tells.

Well, guess what? This girl doesn't know a goddamn thing.

"Calm down, cutie pie." I love it when her eyes chill to an icy blue, silently threatening to cut my balls off. Yeah, I knew she'd hate the pet name. Considering what she thinks of me, I don't give a crap. "Turns out, I don't want to work with you either." I raise a brow at Nick, my manager, and ask, "Is this really the best you could do?"

The redhead gasps, and I want to check whether she's crossed her arms tighter over her chest, plumping her little tits up, but I resist the urge to look.

"We can go somewhere else," Nick says. "I was told these guys are the best for miracles, but I'm sure we can find someone else just as good."

"Now, wait a minute," the stuffed shirt interjects. I wasn't listening when he introduced himself so I didn't catch his name. "Lena is the best there is. You won't find anyone else."

Finally, I succumb to the desire to glance at her and see how she's taking this. I catch the tail end of an eye-roll, and it makes me soften toward her a little. She's not drinking up the flattery the way some might.

*Lena.* I try her name out. It suits her. Pretty, bordering on pretentious but not overstepping the mark.

"Whatever puppy dog stunts *Lena*"—I emphasize her

name now that I know it—"wants to pull, they aren't going to do jack." I address Nick. "I still don't get why we're here. Give it a couple of days; Erin will decide she doesn't want to act on her threats, and the hubbub will die down."

Lena's face twists into a sneer. "Die down?" she demands. "The only way this shit-nado is dying down is if someone gets proactive about putting out your fires, and fast. Also, have a little respect for your girlfriend."

"*Ex*-girlfriend."

"Whatever." She says it like the "ex" part doesn't matter. As if Erin and I didn't break up more than two months ago now. "She's not some problem that will disappear if you ignore her. Domestic violence is a serious crime, and you can't just hand-wave it away." Her nose crinkles like she smells something bad. "It disgusts me that you're callous enough to think otherwise."

Callous? Me?

I count to five in my head and remind myself she doesn't know me. Her perception of me is based on what she's seen in the news, and I have to admit, it's damning. It also isn't true, but I don't bother saying that because this woman isn't going to believe me. Stuffing my hands in my pockets, I decide the best way to deal with her is to call her bluff.

"Okay, so you say the problem isn't going away on its own. What did you have in mind to fix it?"

"I... I..." She flounders, and I can't stop the smile that tugs at my lips. She's all bluster and no bite.

"That's what I thought." I turn to leave, but her smarmy boss lays a hand on my arm. When I stare at it, he snaps it back like he's been stung, his cheeks going pale. This guy is even worse than Lena. At least she has the balls to say what she thinks to my face. He's the type who'll pretend to be on my side, but all the while he's secretly fucking terrified of me.

"Wait, wait, wait," he says. "Give me two minutes to speak to Lena in private and talk her around. I promise you won't regret it."

Lena looks like she wants to bash him over the head with a paperweight, and I don't blame her. He's a condescending little shit. "Adrian—" she says.

"My office." He snaps his fingers, like he's ordering a dog to heel. "Now."

They leave, her trailing behind, practically dragging her feet, and Nick gives a low laugh. "Good old Jase. Always charming the ladies."

I jerk a thumb at the door. "Can we go? I've had enough of this."

He sighs, his expression regretful. "I wish we could, but what she said is true. Whether you want to believe it or not, this situation has the potential to derail your career."

"How can it, when I have the championship bout so soon? I'll blow Karson out of the water, and everything will be fine."

Nick ums and ahs. "That's if you don't get arrested before the fight."

"Pfft." I shake my head. "Not gonna happen. Erin is full of hot air."

"She also has a taste for the spotlight, and she'll keep spouting this bullshit as long as the cameras are rolling." Damn, he's right, and he must sense he has the winning hand because he powers on. "Not to mention, you promised Seth you'd take this seriously and do whatever you could not to tarnish the reputation of Crown MMA gym."

*Ouch. Low blow.* Nick knows I'd go to war for Seth if he asked. My trainer gave me everything. He had faith in me, took a chance on me, and he had no way of knowing I'd pan out to be a good investment. I was just a kid from a poor neighborhood with a mother of a chip on my shoulder and a willingness to shed blood to escape.

"Fine," I concede, not surprising either of us. "I'll hear them out."

But I have a bad feeling about this, and my gut doesn't often lie to me.

# ALSO BY A. RIVERS

***King's Security***

*The King*

*The Veteran*

*The Spy*

*The Liar*

***Crown MMA Romance***

*Fighter's Heart*

*Fighter's Best Friend*

*Fighter's Secret*

*Fighter's Second Chance*

***Crown MMA Romance: The Outsiders***

*Fighter's Frenemy*

*Fighter's Fake Out*

*Fighter's Mercy*

*Fighter's Forever*

***Standalones***

*All Your Pucking Secrets*

# ACKNOWLEDGMENTS

Writing a book is a solitary endeavor, but turning it into something that can be published takes a village. Many thanks to my village for your invaluable help and support in getting The Liar out into the world.

To Kate, Dinah, and Anne, thank you for providing suggestions and tidying the story until it was ready for the world to see.

To Maria, thank you for once again creating a spectacular cover.

To my review team, you make every release exciting as I get to experience the book all over again with you. Thank you for your ongoing support, and for being such a positive community.

Thank you to my husband, my friends and family, and my colleagues taking this author journey with me. Much love,

Alexa XO

# ABOUT THE AUTHOR

A. Rivers writes steamy romance books with take-charge heroes and strong heroines who aren't afraid to fight the odds for love. On the rare occasions when she ventures out of the writing cave, you can probably find her face down in a book, cuddling her pets, or planning her next overseas adventure with her husband.